Published by Thomas & Mercer
P.O. Box 400818
Las Vegas, NV 89140

ISBN-13: 9781612182087
ISBN-10: 1612182089

Chronic Fear

SCOTT NICHOLSON

THOMAS & MERCER

CHAPTER ONE

"Surely you didn't think we could let you live, after what happened."

Dr. Alexis Morgan's lungs froze in shock at the words. She didn't recognize the male voice on the phone, and the caller ID had been blocked. She'd answered out of habit, because she'd become a reliable source not just for academic types, but among the pop-culture journalists as well. Answering the phone was the price of becoming the Carl Sagan of the mind's vast cosmos.

Alexis made herself take a breath, glancing around her office in the University of North Carolina neurosciences department, seeking reassurance in the fat books lining the shelves, the research notes pinned to the bulletin board, and the cold eye of the computer screen.

Yes, everything was normal, or at least typically abnormal.

"Who is this?" she finally managed to whisper.

The voice chuckled on the other end of the line. "You could call me a 'watchdog,' but that wouldn't narrow it down much, would it?"

"If you're threatening me, I'll report you to the university police."

"That would be wonderful, Dr. Morgan. Then they'd open up that whole barrel of monkeys and my work would be done."

"I'm a neurobiologist, not a kindergarten teacher. I'm afraid you have the wrong—"

"You didn't like playing second banana, did you? You want it all to yourself."

She should have thumbed the phone dead. But people tended to let things slip that revealed secrets they'd hidden even from themselves. No matter how carefully the psychological vault was built, it always had a crack. Maybe she could bait him out.

"Is Burchfield behind this?"

"We gave you a chance to forget," the voice said. "But, no, you just had to keep digging."

Because the neurosciences department dealt with sensitive information as well as private health records, the technical security was high. But the best hacks were employed by the people with the most power, and right now, Senator Daniel Burchfield was in the running for the most powerful position on the planet.

"Halcyon is dead," Alexis said.

"See, you didn't forget," the voice answered. "But you never wanted to forget, did you?"

She couldn't really place the age of the caller. She flipped through a mental file as she might go through a series of brain scans, trying to summon a face, but she was pretty sure she'd never heard the voice before.

Of course, she could have heard it and had her mind wiped clean. One of the lasting effects of the Monkey House trials was that stretches of the past were garbled or blank, like a cassette tape with Coke spilled on it.

"If you were just going to kill me, I'd be dead," she said. "So I must have something you want."

"Maybe lots of somethings."

"And maybe you can save us both some time by telling me what it is."

"What fun would that be?"

"You can tell your boss that Halcyon is buried, and so is the past."

And a lot of people along with it.

After a pause, the caller continued. "We know you've been playing around in your lab. Here's what you need to—"

Alexis killed the signal. That was the only thing she needed to do: make him shut up.

Her main research lab was three floors below. For some reason, even in its modern science buildings, UNC still confined much of its research to the basement. It was a tradition dating back to Memorial Hospital's founding, when the dead were wheeled away in the middle of the night and kept out of view of the living patients. Mortality was bad for business.

Unless you were in the business of murder.

Alexis thought about calling Mark, but he always turned off his cell when he was at the shooting range, and he'd be wearing ear protection, anyway. Besides, she didn't want to scare him until she knew what the caller wanted. Mark was scared enough already, considering what was happening inside his skull.

She hurried from the office to the elevator. She hit the button twice but the light was stuck on floor seven. That was the out-patient floor, the one on which Anita Molkesky had undergone intensive therapy for her bipolar disorder and suicidal ideations.

We were so close to getting away with it, Anita. But you know that there's really only one escape.

Alexis gave up on the elevator and made for the stairs, jogging down the three flights with her heels clacking on the concrete. She passed an intern she recognized, mumbling an impersonal greeting. Only three people had keys to her lab, except for the master key held by housekeeping. But the cleaning staff was under orders not to enter any labs without direction, since most of the research was proprietary, classified, or potentially hazardous to human health.

She reached the basement, wondering whether the mysterious caller had been from a legitimate federal agency, a drug company, or that special class of mercenary operating slightly beyond the influence of either. Burchfield trolled in all three of those murky pools.

Alexis had projects going in three labs, but two of the labs were shared. The private one was a perk, containing functional MRI, PET, and CT scanners for her neural research. The department head had granted it as an unspoken reward for her work on the president's bioethics council. She'd resigned from the council three months before, citing personal reasons, although the council's shift in focus from mind-changing drugs to synthetic biology had made her a bit of a dinosaur anyway.

But this was one dinosaur that didn't plan on going extinct. Not until she'd saved her husband, the world, and possibly herself, in that order.

Her imaging lab was in the farthest corner of the basement floor, which was underground on three sides with a main entrance to the rear, a rectangular hallway connecting the labs. Although the hallway was brightly lit, she could feel the weight of the earth and the darkness that waited beyond the waterproof concrete walls. It was early evening and much of the research section was empty, but a few doors were open. She didn't glance in, lest someone call out to her in greeting.

She had a feeling she didn't have much time.

She rounded the corner and saw two men outside the imaging lab. They were dressed like hospital interns in green scrubs, with cotton masks fitted over their mouths. The lab door was open.

"Hey!" she shouted.

The two men glanced at her, then each other. The taller one bolted to the left, where the hallway led back to the main entrance. He carried a white canvas bag in one gloved hand, and its bulk and sagging weight made her think it held machinery or books.

Alexis started after him but the second man stepped forward, blocking her path. She was so enraged by the invasion she didn't consider that he might be armed.

"You're not allowed access," she shouted at the fleeing man, but he was already around the corner.

The remaining man spread his arms as if to tackle her if she tried to run past. Most of his body was covered, but his dark eyes and brown skin suggested someone of Indian or Middle Eastern descent. There was a large Indian and Pakistani population in the medical department, but she had a feeling this wasn't an inside job.

"I've called the police," Alexis said, hoping she sounded more commanding than she felt.

"We are the police," the man said. She detected a Middle Eastern accent, but his voice was muffled enough that she couldn't tell whether he was the same man who'd called. Had the caller wanted to tip her off, or send her into danger?

The sounds of conversation and shoes squeaking on hard tiles came from around the bend, in the direction opposite the one in which the man with the canvas bag had fled. Alexis considered calling out to the approaching people, but she didn't want anyone else involved. Involvement meant complications, which would lead to questions.

And the man knew it. Because he stood his ground. She wondered if he was smiling behind the mask.

Alexis lowered her voice. "You have what you wanted. Now get out of here."

"I don't think so, Dr. Morgan. Not even half of it."

"Are you going to start making threats again? Because I can't take you seriously while you're dressed as House."

His black eyebrows lifted as if he'd never heard of the misanthropic TV doctor. The people around the corner were moving closer, and Alexis recognized one of the speakers as Franz Huber, a visiting neurobiologist from the Planck Institute in Heidelberg. Huber was typically Teutonic, blond and broad-shouldered, and would have been just as suited for fur and a stone ax as a lab coat. If trouble erupted, she'd bet on him over the slim man who was blocking her way.

Assuming he wasn't hiding a gun in his scrubs.

"We'll talk later, Dr. Morgan," he said, pulling his mask up a little higher on his face. Huber and his companion, a female in a pants suit whom Alexis didn't recognize, rounded the corner, and Huber hailed Alexis. The man in the scrubs walked away with a forced ease, as if he preferred to run but was holding back.

"Dr. Morgan, you're working late," Huber said in his deep voice, barely glancing at the man in scrubs.

Elitism. I'd have reacted the same way. If that guy hadn't been raiding my lab, I wouldn't have given him a second look. Just another nurse handling specimens.

"Hi, Franz," Alexis said, straining a grin and hiding her impatience. They went through the formalities of introductions while Alexis kept glancing behind her into her lab to see if anything had been disturbed. It wasn't until Alexis said her husband was waiting that the pair continued on their way.

Alexis went inside the lab and shut the door. At first, everything seemed as she had left it. The scanning machines were intact behind the lead-lined glass window, the computers were on, and the support vector machines were busy analyzing hundreds of brain images collected from student volunteers. Sabotage obviously wasn't a motive, or the creeps could have caused millions of dollars in damages and wiped out months of work.

No, they were after something that was inside the lab, a tangible, portable item. Intellectual property could be stolen in a dozen ways. Her experience with the Monkey House trials had proven that crimes of the mind left no fingerprints. She wouldn't go to the extremes of her deranged former mentor, Dr. Sebastian Briggs, who kept critical notes only on paper, but she'd also learned to run double sets of data, in much the same way a crooked business owner ran two sets of accounting books.

There was only one thing she could think of that anyone would want here. And she was smart enough to keep it off-site. Except for the secrets stored in her mind, the ones she couldn't trust to even a computer or a piece of paper, because that might make them real.

But the first goon in scrubs had definitely been carrying something in the canvas bag. The array of thick technical manuals and books on the shelves appeared untouched. The vector machines that housed most of her records were bolted to the floor and too heavy to move without machinery. Although some of the imaging equipment was expensive, the specialized technology was pretty worthless to somebody looking for her secret research.

Whether or not one of the fake nurses was the man who'd called her, the incidents were clearly connected. It was too much of a coincidence. Her life had been relatively calm for the past year, and the Monkey House incident had been covered up just the way Mark had predicted, including the loss of his vice-presidency of CRO Pharmaceuticals.

After all, you couldn't keep paying a man who'd just cost you billions in profits and lost you a critical ally in Washington, DC.

But the caller had threatened to kill her, and the two thieves in scrubs hadn't so much as barked at her.

Which meant they didn't have what they wanted yet, so they needed her alive.

For now.

CHAPTER TWO

"Are you sure Burchfield's behind it?" Mark asked.

They were having dinner at their wooded ranch house just outside Chapel Hill, which provided convenient access to the university, Raleigh-Durham International, and CRO's headquarters in the Research Triangle Park. But since Mark had been axed and Alexis had resigned from the ethics council, they had traveled little, although Alexis still made occasional speaking appearances to support her new book on personality-altering drugs.

"Who else would it be?" Alexis responded.

"The deal was that everyone forgets the Monkey House. All the Seethe and Halcyon was destroyed, and the facility was leveled. A minor chemical leak contaminated the property, the health department condemned it, and CRO leveled the facility and took the tax write-off. It all looked good on paper."

"Even the four deaths."

"Only three, remember?"

Alexis frowned. She and Mark had discussed the events of that night many times, but they could never quite put all the pieces together. The Seethe exposure had induced bouts of fear and rage, and Halcyon had punched holes in their memories. Alexis would have happily believed the whole thing never happened except both of them still bore scar tissue from fighting to stay alive in the Monkey House.

While Mark's scars were on the outside, including the jagged purple line on his cheek, hers mostly remained hidden.

"That doesn't matter now," Alexis said, pushing at the mashed potatoes and salmon on her plate. "We trusted Burchfield to keep it quiet. He has more to lose than any of us."

"He wasn't running for president then. Now the stakes are higher. The first task of any campaign is to run a minesweeper and see if any explosives are waiting to detonate. Maybe he's decided it won't stay quiet on its own."

Daniel Burchfield chaired the Senate health committee, and Mark had been one of his Washington allies. As a CRO executive, Mark's job was to encourage the senator to back legislation favorable to the pharmaceutical giant. Not that Burchfield needed much prompting. Generous campaign contributions would have been enough, but Burchfield also saw the potential to exploit personality-altering drugs for political gain.

Alexis understood the stakes were higher now. Since Burchfield was running for the Republican presidential nomination, maybe he'd decided he couldn't risk a potential bombshell from his past. As long as the bomb wasn't ticking, everyone was happy. But if someone had started the countdown, wouldn't Burchfield seek to defuse it completely? If he couldn't wipe it away from their memories, the only response left was to wipe their existence from the face of the Earth.

"Yeah, I understand he might want us out of the way," Alexis said. "But what would he want with my research?"

"Maybe he thinks you're still pursuing Halcyon." He said it with the cruel sarcasm he'd developed since the Monkey House.

The sneer and the scar worked together to arouse in her a mixture of guilt, sorrow, and anger.

I'm doing it for YOU, Mark.

But, as always, she failed to completely convince herself. She pursued Halcyon for many reasons, and some of them scared her more than Mark's frightening decay had.

Because you want to be its mother. You want to own it and be responsible for it. You want to be first banana.

Alexis glanced at the front door, wondering if Mark had locked it. She'd never felt this vulnerable, even in the immediate aftermath of the Monkey House trials, and their home's relative isolation now was a worry instead of an asset.

"You destroyed all the Seethe and Halcyon," she said, trying to hide the big lie behind her bitterness.

"You saw what that stuff turned us into."

She dared him with her eyes. Her memories of the Monkey House tangled in oscillating bands of terror and violence, but she was incapable of such terrible acts. His accusations were even more proof that his condition was deteriorating.

"I saw a drug that had a potential to help ease people's suffering," Alexis said. "But you had to play God and take it out of the hands of science. You had no right to make that decision."

"Making people's lives better by helping them forget? It hasn't helped *ours* very much, has it?"

"Two months of law-enforcement training, and suddenly you're the world's morality cop."

"If it wasn't for you and your Frankenstein complex, I would still have a career. But at least you have *your* career, right?"

"Mark, you know why I stayed on in the neurosciences department. It was our best chance to find a treatment for—"

Mark slammed his fist down on the table, causing his glass to jump. Mark and Alexis watched the white wine quiver a moment before settling down. Then he looked at her.

"Sorry," he said, lifting his palms in supplication. "I'm not angry. Not anymore."

At least this time he noticed his outburst. I don't know if that's an improvement or not.

"We'd better stop fighting each other," Alexis said. "Soon we might be fighting to save our lives."

They fell into silence at the thought. They both lifted their heads as if expecting to hear something in the woods outside. A truck rumbled down a distant street and a jet swept over on its way to RDI.

"If it was Burchfield, what could he possibly want in your lab?" Mark asked, taking a half-hearted bite of salmon. "Halcyon's dead. Seethe's dead. Briggs is dead. There's nothing left."

"That's what has me stumped. We're working on fear response, sure, but nothing like what Sebastian Briggs was doing. All those brain scans I've been looking at, all that mapping? That's just tracking basic emotional and motor responses, grunt work."

"I don't see what Burchfield would want with that, unless he plans on clubbing his Republican challengers over the head with a budget ax."

"Exactly." Alexis wondered if she should tell him the rest. But his rages had become more sudden and uncontrollable over time, and she was increasingly reluctant to risk riling him.

If he found out I'd been lying to him for the past year, there's no telling what he might do.

"Okay, maybe there's another possibility," Mark said. "I just can't see Burchfield adding a couple of corpses to his resume. At least not until the primary's over."

"Very funny. You do gallows humor so well."

"I've had lots of practice tying my own noose. So, is there anyone else from your closet of horrors that might be popping up now?"

"You know about the other Monkey House subjects. Anita is struggling..." Alexis twisted her napkin in distress.

"Is David Underwood still in Central Regional?" Mark asked, not allowing her to wallow.

"Yeah." The state's largest hospital for the mentally ill was in nearby Butner, where Alexis had conducted some post-grad research. "He's probably being blasted with psychosocial modalities, and they're still doing pharmacological clinical trials for schizophrenia. Sort of like what Briggs was doing, except this is sanctioned and funded by the state."

"You think his shrinks found out about the Monkey House?"

"Even if David remembered anything, I doubt if he could communicate it clearly. If they asked a question that hit too close to home, he'd probably start singing 'Home on the Range.'"

Mark shuddered, no doubt recalling the man's incessant broken warbling after enduring years of Briggs's sadistic research.

"Okay, so Anita and David haven't spilled the beans—or the pills. That leaves Wendy and Roland. Are they still together?"

"Unless they lied, they headed for some peace and quiet in the Blue Ridge Mountains."

"I thought you and Wendy stayed in touch."

"We did for a while. I haven't seen her since we had them over for dinner last year. But she quit calling a few months ago. Unfriended me on Facebook and everything. She even took down the website where she was selling her art."

"Not surprised. I figured Roland would turn into one of those survivalist nut jobs and head for the back country."

"You barely even know him."

"When you kill people together, you kind of learn a thing or two about each other."

"Nobody killed anybody. I don't know why you hang onto that particular delusion when there are so many others to choose from."

"Because it makes me feel better about being a heavily armed lunatic," Mark said.

They'd had this argument so often that she might as well have read straight from the script. "Briggs and the others were killed by Burchfield's bodyguard."

Mark pushed his plate away and stood, going to the window. "You remember it different every time, so there's no point in talking about it now."

She studied his reflection in the glass as he looked out. The scar zigzagged from his mouth where he'd injured his face during their escape, later explaining that the pain from the self-inflicted wound had helped him focus. He was still handsome, maybe even more so than before, because his cuteness had taken on a hard, bad-boy edge. However, his eyes were dark and troubled, and occasionally they flared as if some black magic potion was bubbling away inside his skull.

"You think they're watching the house?" she asked.

"Depends on who 'they' are. I don't think Burchfield's people would, but the CIA and FBI were watching him. That was a year ago, though. I don't know what the hell's going on now. I'm so far out of the loop I might as well start believing the Internet."

"There's one other possibility. One of my research assistants was doing some work on frontal-lobe activity. She was measuring response to various stimuli, showing violent, erotic, romantic, or pastoral photographs and then noting the electromagnetic activity resulting from each."

"Let me guess. The neurons got busy when they saw the dirty pictures. Always works for me." Apparently satisfied no one was approaching the house, Mark turned away from the window and went to the closet to check his firearms. It was a nervous compulsion he engaged in with increasing frequency. Alexis wondered if his decision to become a cop had merely been an excuse to pursue a higher grade of weaponry.

"It wasn't controversial, but if somebody got wind of it, they might have thought I was trying to revive Halcyon," she said.

"They can't be that dumb. They know you know they're watching. Therefore, they should be looking for the things they don't see."

"Wow, you *did* spend too much time in Washington."

"In a way, we'd be lucky if these guys are federal," Mark said. "At least then, they'd be reporting to someone, which would mean accountability up and down the chain."

"But what if it's rogue? A terrorist group or a tech company? Maybe even CRO?"

"Fuck CRO." Mark pulled his Glock from the top shelf and checked the clip. "And terrorists aren't that patient, whether they're domestic or foreign. Part of their gig is to make a big splash. 'Subtle' doesn't appear anywhere in the training manual."

"So they're teaching homeland security at community college now?" She knew she was provoking him, but she was on edge, and in a sick way, mutual uneasiness had become a comfort zone. Once they fell into the routine, they both relaxed a little. Fear had become safe.

Their marriage had remained solid through the crazy travel schedules and their hectic careers, but the past year had taken its toll. Alexis missed her romantic, goofy, ambitious husband, who had been replaced by this tight-jawed, nervous gun freak. The man she'd married had somehow become a stranger.

One more casualty of the Monkey House.

"Here's all the homeland security you need." He took a weapon from the closet that looked like a machine gun from a war movie and spoke in an instructional tone, as if she might actually have to use it one day. "This AR-Fifteen is the perfect weapon for home defense. Flip this little knob here—that's the safety—and then just press the trigger as fast as you can. You have thirty bullets. This little baby can really clear a room."

The gun repulsed her, or maybe it was Mark's sudden glee as he cradled it. "They wouldn't be that brazen, would they? To break in here?"

"They broke into your lab, right? And they didn't find what they were looking for, because you aren't hiding anything, right?"

Alexis glanced away from his intense stare. "Right."

"So they're not going to believe you have nothing to hide. That means they'll keep looking."

"Why won't they just leave us alone?"

"Because Burchfield tried to buy me off," Mark said. "Wanted me to join his security team or take an advisory role. 'Keep your friends close and your enemies closer,' and all that."

"Yeah. And I'm sure my job offer from the CDC was just a coincidence, too. Maybe I should have taken it. Then I could be teaching teens about the dangers of mood-enhancing drugs."

"You know the problem with that? The word *enhancing*. There's no way to talk about drugs without making them sound good."

Alexis knew about enhancements. Mark didn't. She'd hoped her refinement of the original Halcyon formula would allow

Mark to be able to turn his anger off and on. That was one of the big flaws in Briggs's synthesis of Halcyon that had resulted in Seethe—Seethe turned the tap all the way open and every nightmare in Pandora's box would bust free at once. And then only Halcyon could close the tap by suppressing memory and emotional response.

She hadn't mentioned the other possible source of the surveillance, because Mark didn't know about Darrell Silver, the underground chemist she'd hired to develop her version of Halcyon. Silver had delivered the one batch in liquid form, saying he needed more time and more money, but he'd been arrested for dealing drugs two months ago. From the outside, it looked like just another dopehead getting busted, and Silver didn't know anything about the drug's provenance.

But she didn't know what records or chemicals he'd left lying around, or whether he was clever enough to use her as a bargaining chip if someone pressed. Some of his charges had been federal because he'd been trafficking across state lines. But despite his obvious genius, his basic personality was childlike and innocent, failing to comprehend why The Man would frown upon the act of spreading joy and escape from the square world.

While Silver would never question her motives, he also might be tempted to brag about the fine craft of drug manufacturing. Brilliance rarely kept its illumination cloaked.

But Silver's loss meant she was alone. Despite her frantic research, and the measured doses of Halcyon she'd been slipping Mark, he was disintegrating, and she was afraid she'd lose him to Seethe forever.

But Mark wasn't just the test pool, he was her husband. She had to keep reminding herself of that fact.

"It could be much worse," she said. "I hate to think where we'd all be if Briggs had turned Burchfield loose with Seethe."

"Why haven't you been honest with me?" he asked. He still held the AR-15, although he'd lowered it to his hip. She couldn't read his expression. When he was Seething, his lip or eyelid would tremble, but at the moment he seemed utterly calm.

And that was scarier than his blind rages.

"What are you talking about?"

"You must be doing something, or nobody would bother raiding your lab."

"Mark, I told you I was done with that."

"And you got rid of all the Seethe and Halcyon? Not holding any back?"

Why did he still blame her for sneaking some of the Halcyon pills from the Monkey House? She was sure the molecular compounds had beneficial uses. The chemicals themselves had done nothing wrong, because compounds didn't possess morality. It was Briggs's twisted use of them that was evil.

Mark had forced her to flush the pills down the toilet after he'd discovered them hidden in her jewelry box, but he didn't know about the single pill she'd given to Silver for analysis.

"The doses you found were the last ones," she said. "I promise."

The lie had mutated for so long that it now felt like the truth, and she wondered if a similar evolution had justified Sebastian Briggs in his sick research. But Mark wouldn't understand her work, and he would never accept her help voluntarily. Especially if that help came in the form of Halcyon.

But he also wouldn't accept that he'd changed since the Monkey House. The Mark that had gone in had not come out.

And his only hope—*their* only hope—rested in Alexis's race to synthesize a better form of Halcyon, one that wouldn't wipe his mind of all he'd been.

But the race had been interrupted.

Somebody knew.

CHAPTER THREE

God, grant me the serenity to accept the things I cannot change, the courage to change the things I can, and the wisdom to know the difference.

Roland opened his eyes and, for the hundredth time since his last drink three years ago, wondered why God didn't grant exemptions for control freaks, the cowardly, and the foolish. At times he'd been all three, and he still wasn't sure he understood the Serenity Prayer and which things he could actually change without fucking them up. All he knew was that he was grateful to be here and to be sober enough to struggle with it.

He was sitting in his rocker, laboring over a laptop, but the beauty of the Blue Ridge Mountain evening stole his concentration. And his gaze kept roaming over to the painting Wendy was working on.

Well, it roamed over Wendy a lot, too.

She was wearing a thin cotton blouse, off-white and splotched with multi-colored stains, and Capri pants that accented her petite Asian shape. Her black hair was pulled back in a ponytail and she looked more like a teenager than a woman soon to enter middle age.

"That's pretty cool, sweetie," Roland Doyle said.

Wendy frowned and stepped back from the canvas, brush in hand. "Anything looks good in this light."

Which was true. It was the kind of sunset that cast the world in perfect pink, the ultimate rose-colored glasses. Flaming clouds billowed over the forest in the west while the coming bruise of night claimed its turf to the east. The wet, loamy aroma of the forest added to the magical dusk, and a more fanciful person might have imagined faeries and sprites would come spilling out at any moment.

But Roland didn't care for games of the mind. He'd played enough of them.

"Personally, I'd go in for some cadmium yellow," Roland said. "It's getting a little bleak."

What he really meant was maybe she should try some new subject matter. For the past year, she'd been indulging in surreal and claustrophobic imagery, jagged and dark shapes full of menace. It was how she chose to deal with the Monkey House experience, but he hoped she would shut that door for good and paint over it with the thickest layer of black.

He had, as best he could.

But then he was the only one who seemed to remember much about it. For Wendy, it was bottled up and stored in a sick wine cellar of the soul, its fermented pulp turning to slow poison.

"I've never had much use for critics," Wendy said, a slight resentment riding under the humor. "I've got something to say. I just don't know what it is yet."

Artists. God help 'em, because nobody else can.

When you loved somebody, you had to put up with a few idiosyncrasies. And Wendy certainly had to endure her share. After all, she was married to a murderer.

"You'd better clean up," Roland said. "It's getting dark. Sleep on it and I'll bet you feel better."

She gave him a sly look with her almond-shaped onyx eyes. "I'd planned to sleep on *you*."

"That can be arranged."

He glanced at his laptop screen. He'd had to leave his job selling display advertising, but many of the same skills translated to the Internet. The only difference was he had to think smaller. Which was a relief, actually.

Wendy wiped her brush and dipped it in a jar of soapy water to soak. She was in an acrylics phase, which put her in a better mood. Watercolors were too delicate and oils tended to go to mud when she vented her frustration and painted too rapidly.

She crossed the porch and stood over him. "Husband. Did you ever think we'd get back together again?"

He took her hands, although they still had flecks and smears of paint on them. "I knew it all along. We were meant to be together."

"That's what men say just before they kill their spouses in a jealous rage."

He studied her face. Was she joking? Was she starting to remember? "No, sweetie. That's 'If I can't have you, nobody can.'"

She leaned forward and kissed him. "Okay, you're the expert in obsession."

He stroked her hip and ran his fingers behind her. "If you were married to this, you'd be obsessive, too."

"Dinner, and then we can play OCD in bed."

"Tell you what. Let me fire off this e-mail and I'll be right in."

"Sure. And two more e-mails arrive before you shut down, and then you get to deal with those. The ever-expanding inbox of client obligation."

"I promise. Really."

She swatted him playfully with her rag. "So much for moving to the mountains to get away from it all."

He tracked Wendy's alluring rear as she crossed the covered porch and entered the screen door. Even after twelve years, he still liked the way she moved. *My Tibetan tiger*, he liked to call her. The tiger was also her sign of the Chinese zodiac, while her Western zodiac sign was Cancer. Both had claws.

He was eager to polish off the last e-mail. As a freelance graphic designer, he'd found a niche in e-book design and intuitively grasped the differences in marketing on a computer instead of a bookshelf. He'd also taught himself formatting, and although he wasn't sure where the technology was headed, he'd been able to carve out a sustainable small business. Which was fortunate, because he considered himself pretty unemployable now.

Roland sent the sample file and was just about to close down when a new e-mail popped in. He winced and didn't allow himself to read the subject line.

You promised her.

But it's only one more little broken promise. What does it really matter on the scorecard of a marriage?

The subject line said: "Every four hrs or else."

"What the fuck?" He didn't even realize he'd spoken aloud.

Spam. It had to be spam, a solicitation promising a Nigerian erection the size of a dictator's bank account.

The sender was "No-reply@ncs.cia.us.gov."

He knew he should log out immediately. Clicking could trigger a virus. Or exhume a past he'd nailed shut and painted black.

"Hon?" Wendy called from inside. He'd already used up the window of good grace, and as a committed mate, he didn't like forcing kitchen chores on her.

Holding his breath, he opened the e-mail.

It said simply: "We have a job for you, David Underwood."

"David Underwood" was the fake identity Briggs had foisted on Roland while tricking him back to Wendy and the Monkey House. It had turned out the real David was alive, although hopelessly traumatized, and Roland had burned the identification cards after their escape.

The e-mail looked contrived. Why would the CIA send out e-mails? He doubted they even used e-mail.

"Roland, these cucumbers don't peel themselves," Wendy said, with an edge of impatience.

"Just a sec." He Googled the CIA site, wondering if the agency tracked the ISP of every citizen who browsed it. A quick scan revealed that NCS stood for "National Clandestine Service," which engaged in a murky mission called "human intelligence." Especially surreal was the description, "We are accountable to the U.S. president, Congress, and the American taxpayer."

Yeah, sure you are. Except those three are on different sides in your little ideological war. And to think I helped fund your cheesy little website.

Hell, it's getting so that cheating on taxes is the last pure act of patriotism.

But what would the CIA have to do with Seethe and Halcyon? The drugs were all stamped out. Mark and Alexis had made sure of that, despite Burchfield's blubbering about "government property." And Roland had personally put a bullet in Briggs's hard drive, as well as his chest.

A browsing of the CIA site revealed no e-mail addresses. Any public contact had to issue through Cold War means like postal mail and telephone, aside from a handy form page where freedom-loving citizens could rat on their suspicious neighbors. Or just the neighbors they didn't like.

"What are you looking at?"

It was Wendy. He'd been so engrossed that he hadn't heard her come out on the porch. She stood behind him, and now he could smell her—paint, chamomile, and faint, sexy sweat.

Roland caught himself before he snapped the laptop closed. "Uh, researching for a client. She's got a thriller thing going on, and I wanted to make sure this logo was right for her book cover."

"Ro, your hand is shaking."

He forced a chuckle. "Yeah. Blood sugar must be low. How about them cucumbers?"

He logged out of the program and shut down as Wendy nuzzled the back of his neck. She reached one arm around and slid it between his legs. "There's the cool kind of cucumber, and then there's the *other* kind."

He stood abruptly, and the rocker knocked back against Wendy.

"Ow," she said. "Boy, you sure know how to respond to foreplay."

"Sorry, sweetie," he said, squeezing the folded laptop as if it were a box of venomous snakes. "I'm a little wired right now."

She knew that drill. His alcoholism had led to a painful separation, and if not for the divine intervention of the insane Dr. Briggs, they would likely still be apart. Of all the consequences stemming from the Monkey House, their reunion was the only positive outcome that Roland could see.

"Too much peace and serenity," she said, glancing at her current work in progress sitting on the easel. "It can drive anybody nutty."

"Let's eat," he said, taking her hand and giving her an apologetic kiss on the cheek. Before entering the cabin, he studied the woods.

Every four hours. We played that game already.
Now what?

CHAPTER FOUR

Dominic Scagnelli had been watching her for days, but his favorite part was at sundown.

That was when Anita Molkesky took her long, luxuriant bubble baths, surrounded by candles. Since she'd given up porn stardom masquerading as "Anita Mann," her cash flow had been a little tight, as evidenced by the financial records he'd cracked. She'd downgraded her cable package, pushed her two credit cards to the max, and traded her Corvette for a Jetta. She was overpaying for the little cottage, $1,200 a month, but it was located on the edge of a university town where the entire market was inflated.

Despite the hardships, Anita allowed herself two indulgences: an evening soak, and multiple classes of barbiturates, painkillers, and the occasional bottle of wine that corralled the dulling effects of the other drugs.

As Scagnelli looked through his binoculars, he wondered how much his boss was keeping from him. After stints in two national security agencies before becoming a "consultant," he'd learned that you could count on getting half the truth. The trouble was they gave you the half that didn't matter and withheld the half that would have helped you do your job.

And that's what it was all about. Doing your job.

Some of his fellow agents had wasted their time banging against the Puzzle Palace in DC, trying to make sense of the decisions made by higher-ups. Scagnelli tried that his first couple of years, but then he figured out that nobody knew the whole story anywhere. Nobody knew the motives, nobody owned the agenda.

While some agents grabbed their crotches and saluted the flag, and others were sucked down the drain by the political intrigue, Scagnelli made peace with the idea that there was a job, somebody had to do that job, and he might as well be the one doing it.

He'd become a free agent because the proliferation of security agencies in the wake of 9/11 had created a lot of cracks. For the entrepreneurial types, the rampant intergovernmental mistrust had fueled opportunities. Some agents hated to serve as wingmen for politicians, but an election year was coming, and there were jobs to do. And he doubted if any of his fellow consultants were sitting in the bushes looking at a marvelous pair of boobs topped with sparkly white froth.

The book on Anita Molkesky was that she was an exhibitionist, fragile, and constantly on the verge of a psychotic breakdown. At least, that was half the story. Scagnelli had filled his idle hours between baths by speculating on the other half.

I wonder if porn actresses have agents like regular movie actresses do. If so, I'd say she got screwed as hard by them as she did by her costars.

He twisted the focus on the binoculars as she lifted herself from a leaning position and reached out of his field of vision. Not that he really cared what she was reaching for, because those amazing globes dangled like skinned papayas. They looked smaller now than they had in the dossier photos, and he wondered what kind of idiot in LA had taken them down a size. Probably some fetishist who thought normal-sized boobs were the next big thing.

Still, he could not complain a bit. What they lacked in volume was more than offset by their undulating sway and dark, swollen nipples. Some boobs were greater than the sum of their parts, radiating charisma in the same way that some normal-looking women somehow became beautiful when they were splashed across a movie screen.

Tits with charisma. Did Oprah ever do a show on that?

Despite the exhibitionist streak, Anita wasn't going out of her way to flaunt it. Her curtains were open, sure, but the window was six feet above ground level. Scagnelli had found the only spot that afforded a clear view, and as he crouched in the suburban shrubbery, he glanced around to check the lights of the surrounding houses. It appeared everyone was safely occupied by their televisions or computers.

He was close enough to her to hear a mellow twang and gentle backbeat spill from the half-open window. She settled back amid the mounds of bubbles. She'd turned on some tunes, Fleetwood Mac, mood music for the mellowing druggie.

Speaking of which.

Scagnelli lowered the binoculars and pulled the mint tin from his pocket. One of the fringe benefits of being a free agent was he didn't have to wait for a monthly paycheck. Compensation came in many forms, and a stack of unmarked bills was only one of them. His boss apparently had far-reaching connections, which wasn't surprising given his background.

The surprising part was the moral ambiguity. Somebody with his boss's reputation should be a prude who made sure every penny was reported to the Eternal Fucking Revenue Service and with no hanky-panky on the side.

Just went to show what Washington did to people. It was a place where you could only afford to show half the truth at any one time, but you also had to be able to change the truth at a moment's notice.

Scagnelli's fingers trembled only a little as he opened the tin. As a frontline observer of the War on Drugs, he'd come to see the "war" part as the public half of the story. The more important half of the story featured all the tidal forces of big industry, political expediency, and good old departmental pissing matches that fed the pipeline on the front end. The United States had the muscle to stamp out any drug supply in the world, but regulation was selective. The U.S. could easily cut the balls off the Taliban by whacking down all the opium poppies in Afghanistan, but billionaires were turning into trillionaires through the use of military force and cartoon diplomacy. And the trillionaires had purchased Congress decades ago.

But such thinking was for the idiots who gave a crap about democracy, freedom, and those other words that had people eating shit and smiling like it was cake. Scagnelli's job was to keep his eyes on charismatic tits. And Scagnelli's game was that he was always just doing his job and nothing more.

Anita was listlessly soaking as he slid a tablet into his mouth. Some nights, she lazily stroked herself, nothing serious, and he figured she was one of those frigid types who only put out for the cameras.

His cell vibrated inside his pocket. He'd silenced it for the surveillance mission, but being reachable was part of the job.

He pulled out the prepaid phone and, shielding it with one hand, flipped it open to check the text message.

He recognized the number. The message contained a single word: *Tonight.*

The next text buzzed in right after that: *Then to Morgans.*

He closed the phone, gave a last wistful glance through the binoculars, and shrugged. A job was a job.

Scagnelli tucked his binoculars into his leather tool belt and slid his arms into an orange mesh safety vest. The time for subterfuge was over. Now he needed to be conspicuously ordinary. The white hardhat and clipboard were his tickets to the working class.

Scagnelli had spent the past couple of days monkeying with the telephone switch box around the corner, the central feed for numerous land lines in the area. Everybody had a cell phone these days, but people still needed wires for a number of important services. The phone company trucks had been visible around the neighborhood, although the technicians were probably scratching their heads over the random problems.

So Scagnelli would be just another soldier in the faceless army of service workers, meeting the needs of the customers they cared so much about.

Scagnelli emerged from the bushes and crossed the small lawn. He would be visible from the two houses across the street, but with the brim of the hardhat pulled low, no one would be able to make an ID. A car went past, doing well over the 35 mph speed limit, and Scagnelli didn't even look. After all, he carried a clipboard and had a job to do.

He slipped on a leather work glove when he reached the small stone patio. The door was unlocked, so there was no need for the burglar tools hidden in pouches along his belt. He stepped inside, checking the neighborhood again before closing the door.

Thank you, American Idol, *for keeping the sheep drowsy.*

The layout was as he'd mapped it during his down time. A kitchenette, a combined dining and living room with a breakfast nook, and a short hallway that split the bedroom and bath.

Scagnelli glanced into the open bedroom as he passed. It was neat, tidy, and boring, with none of the mirrors on the ceiling or leather restraints on the bedposts one might have expected of a porn star. The most controversial object visible in the room was the folded-open paperback on the nightstand.

He'd give it a better search after he finished his job.

Unlike the front door, the bathroom door was locked for some weird reason, just the kind of harebrained shit a woman would do for a false sense of security. But it was a cheap privacy catch, and with the backbeat of Fleetwood Mac providing cover, he slipped a metal slim jim into the catch and bumped the door with his hip.

She didn't notice him at first. She raised handfuls of bubbles above her head and let them fall. She was low in the water, submerged from the neck down. Scagnelli was relieved in a way, because he couldn't afford to be distracted by her charisma.

"Evening, Miss Molkesky," he said, over the vocal harmonies of Christine McVie and Stevie Nicks.

An odd expression crossed her face, a mixture of alarm and anticipation, as if she'd been expecting a special delivery of flowers instead.

Or maybe a boyfriend?

The report said she was not dating anyone, and although her on-screen activities suggested few boundaries, in her personal life Anita appeared reclusive to the point of celibacy. Scagnelli wondered how much that had to do with what happened a year ago. He wished he'd been wearing one of his sharp suits instead of this Johnny-Bob working getup. It never hurt to impress a pretty woman, even if she wasn't your type.

"You're late," she said thickly.

Scagnelli glanced at the open door behind him as if she were talking to someone else.

"You work for them, don't you?" she said.

"I work for myself." If she screamed, someone might hear, but the music might disguise it, too

"That's what they all say," she said.

The CD player rested on the lid of the closed toilet, the cord snaking up beside the sink. He stepped forward and turned the music up a couple of notches, but not enough to disturb the neighbors. He was careful to use his gloved hand, although it limited his dexterity.

"Fleetwood Mac," he said. "Crazy band. Probably sets the all-time record for different lineups."

"Stevie Nicks drags me down," Anita said. She was still submerged to her neck, and now her arms were beneath the water, too. The bubbles framed her pretty face, making her look angelic. The plastic surgeons had left that part alone.

"You shouldn't put an electrical appliance so close to the bathtub," he said. "If it fell in, you'd get electrocuted."

That's when he noticed the two razor blades laying flat and clean and silvery on the edge of the tub.

"And the window open this time of year," he said. "You might catch your death of pneumonia."

Scagnelli leaned over the toilet and slid the window closed with his gloved hand. The water sloshed, and some of it spilled onto the floor. When he turned back around, she was sitting up and there were those tits in all their charisma. Up close, they weren't all that special.

Or maybe he was just emotionally distancing himself. In his former life, he'd seen agents get too personally involved in their work and make a mess of things. He had to remind himself he was just doing his job.

He pointed to the razor blades. "That would be real messy," he said. "And probably hurt, too."

"I read that if you make the bath real hot, you don't feel a thing."

She lifted one lovely calf from the water and wiggled her toes at him. The skin was slick and light brown, and clumps of white bubbles took a sensual rollercoaster ride down the curves.

He sat on the toilet lid and took her foot in his gloved hand, then stroked the instep with his naked hand, careful to use the backs of his fingers. The whiz kids in the forensics lab could do wonders with DNA evidence. Not that a manic-depressive porn star's suicide would get much scrutiny.

"Can I ask you something?" he said, wondering if she was sizing him up the way she might a costar.

She stifled a giggle. That was good. She was probably halfway to an overdose already.

"What?"

"In those movies, when you're…" He glanced away.

"When I'm what? I did a lot of things." She sounded a little impatient now, as if he were breaking the mood.

"Like, when you're doing it with those guys, how come you never kiss them?"

Now she *did* giggle, and it rolled up into a laugh, and Scagnelli felt like he had when the high school cheerleading captain shot him down for a date. Why did the pretty ones always turn out to be bitches?

Scagnelli let go of her leg and it surprised her. The limb slapped back into the water. A few drops darkened the legs of his trousers.

"Okay, if you're going to play rough," she said. "Here's why you don't kiss the guys. It's too romantic. It's too personal. When you fuck for money, you're just doing a job."

Scagnelli nodded thoughtfully. That was something he could understand. He was about to ask how come it was okay to kiss during the lesbian scenes, but she'd reminded him why he was here.

"Like I said on the phone, they couldn't let you live, after what happened," he said.

She nodded, her eyes moist, and she slid back down to her neckline, and Scagnelli didn't even miss the view. "I'm tired," she said. "I wish they'd killed us last time. That whole Monkey House thing messed with me. And that other guy, Kleingarten? Were you friends with him?"

Scagnelli had heard the rumors. Kleingarten was a free agent, too, but a low-level thug who was totally out of his league at the government level. The death certificate had him down for a heart attack, but he'd been tied up with Burchfield last year. Scagnelli wanted to make sure he himself didn't become Burchfield's latest heart-attack victim.

"What's this about the Monkey House?" Scagnelli would bet a porterhouse steak she knew the half of the story that wasn't in the dossier.

"I don't remember," she said. "But ever since then, I've been a wreck. The lithium made me get fat, and then they switched me to valpro, and—"

"They don't understand," Scagnelli said, adjusting his hard-hat. "They always think drugs are the answer, but it's something inside, isn't it?"

The song ended and the next began, this one featuring a male singer and a cowbell, jarringly upbeat.

"Do you have any Halcyon?" she asked.

"Of course," he said, noting it was the same word Alexis Morgan had used. He was edging into the other half of the truth, and maybe he could keep her talking with more than just his smile. A hooker had once told him he looked like the actor Steve Buscemi, only with better teeth. He probably could have been a movie star if he wanted. Hell, he'd been acting for years. "That's what you were expecting, right?"

"I think they should legalize it. Imagine a world where everyone forgets."

"Yeah, some world that would be, huh? This Monkey House. What happened there?"

She shook her head, glittering drops of water rolling from her cheeks. "All I remember is Kleingarten trying to kill us. But Lex and Roland and Mark saved us."

"Do you remember a guy named Burchfield?" He didn't want to spend too much time here, but he hid his impatience so she didn't spook.

Her pretty lips pursed in distaste. "I think we did it, him and me. You know how it is, when you suddenly come around and you got somebody's slime all over you, and you don't know how it got there?"

Scagnelli was tired of her now. She was no longer attractive and sexy and mysterious, no longer special in any way. She was just another job, just like she'd been the job for a lot of guys and gals during her career. "Yeah, I know how it is. I don't blame you a bit."

"The last time, they gave us pills every four hours." A tuft of bubbles dangled from the tip of her nose. "I want so much to forget." She glanced at the razor blades. "Forget *everything*."

"The prescription's changed since then," he said, fishing the vial from one of the pouches on his belt. "What have you taken tonight?"

"Nothing much," she said, and her words were slurring now. "Six Valium and a couple of oxies. Couple glasses of wine."

"We'll fix you right up," Scagnelli said.

"Will I forget everything again?"

"You betcha." He twisted the lid from the vial and knelt beside the tub.

"Good, because I was starting to remember more stuff. That senator, the one who wants to run for president—"

"Burchfield." She'd already forgotten. These Monkey House people were a mess.

Her glazed eyes were staring at the window, where a moth was thumping against the steamy glass. "I don't know. Maybe I was in a movie with him or something."

Bedtime for Bonzo. Every Republican president needs a monkey as a sidekick. It's a wonder Clint Eastwood hasn't run for the Oval Office yet. With a fucking orange monkey as VP.

"I'll bet you two made a cute couple," he said, shaking some pills into his hand. "A real Brangelina."

"They said we'd forget everything," Anita Molkesky said. "That it would all go away."

"These will help," he said, pushing a couple of the pills against her lips. She opened automatically and he shoved the rough leather finger of the glove in her mouth, forcing the pills against the back of her throat. Her eyes widened, and she had no choice but to swallow.

She raised a lethargic arm, smearing soap bubbles against his cheek. He fished a couple more tablets from the vial. The barbiturates contained a gram each, and one could be fatal. Even with the toxins already swirling in her bloodstream, she probably had built up quite a tolerance over the years. But someone of her weight, which he judged to be around 110, would never metabolize four grams.

She coughed and he was afraid she'd vomit, which would definitely taint her charisma. He pushed the pills against her mouth and this time she took them willingly, although her tongue acted numb and uncoordinated.

"Halcyon," he said, squirreling the name away in his memory. *Sounds like something I should know more about, if I want to do my job right.*

She was already on the ropes, sliding lower into the water, her head lolling. He was doing her a favor. The blade would have been messy and probably hurt a lot, even with all the painkillers coursing through her bloodstream. This way, she'd just drift off to a land where it was okay to kiss the guys.

He sat through two more songs by Fleetwood Mac, and he decided he didn't like the band. Anita was right. Stevie Nicks was depressing as hell. Made you want to slash your wrists.

Anita snorted, and her breathing was uneven and shallow. Scagnelli carefully placed his gloved hand on top of her head and lowered her into the water. A few bubbles rose, creating more froth that veiled her angelic body. She gave a couple of spasms but didn't splash him this time.

When they were done with one another, Scagnelli stood and picked up his clipboard. "We'll have your phone working by tomorrow, Miss Molkesky," he said. "You have yourself a good evening, and don't hesitate to call if we can ever be of service."

A quick search of the cottage revealed nothing significant, and her bedroom was disappointingly clean, without even a dildo under the bed. He'd been instructed to look for any strange pills or medications, but all she had were plenty of prescription meds. He took her cell phone just in case she'd stored any numbers or messages, but otherwise he left the place as he'd found it.

He let himself out and retraced his trek across the lawn. The moon was up, a curved scythe of white against the endless night. It looked sharp enough to slice a hole in the never-ending darkness and reveal whatever lay behind.

The other half of the story.

Scagnelli headed for his rental sedan and the next assignment. Unfortunately, the boss wanted Dr. Alexis Morgan alive. But a job was a job.

CHAPTER FIVE

Alexis fired up her home computer and scrolled through the data she'd compiled on her husband.

She'd induced Mark into intermittent brain scans to "test her equipment," joking that she couldn't have found a cuter guinea pig, and then buried the files in a different research project.

Of course, the vector machines had multiple backups of all images, logging time and subject as well as the operator of record. She'd carefully constructed fake records so that, on the books, Mark was listed as "Donnie Davis," a student volunteer who was one of hundreds being examined for a benign analysis of brain-wave patterns before and after exposure to certain kinds of images.

The theory was that the stimulation would trigger heavier frontal-lobe activity than usual, although Alexis was pretty sure the effects of recreational drugs, collegiate hanky-panky, and the latest trending Twitter topic offered far more stimulation. But the experiment was the perfect smokescreen for her analysis of her husband's head.

The only question now was whether someone *else* had cracked into his head.

The MRI revealed hundreds of slices, a series of images that tracked across the entire brain. In "Donnie's" images, tiny lesions were identifiable as deposits of iron left by leaking blood. Such lesions were fairly common in older people and were associated with stroke, Alzheimer's, or certain types of risk factors like high blood pressure and smoking. His anterior cingulate cortex, an area that processed rewards and punishments, displayed minimal activity, while his amygdala, the primal emotional center of the brain, appeared overstimulated.

Scans of her own brain, conducted by her graduate assistant Haleema, revealed no such damage. However, Alexis was convinced the lesions were caused by Mark's exposure to Seethe, the designer rage drug developed by Sebastian Briggs. The brain was such a highly individualized and unknown organ that reactions would vary widely, and until she could compare images from David, Anita, Wendy, and Roland, the other Monkey House survivors, she was shooting in the dark.

The irony was that Mark had the least exposure of all of them, yet he'd suffered the most intense long-term effects. She suspected he'd built up no tolerance, the way the original subjects had. Which made him ripe territory for unlocking both Seethe and Halcyon and finally using them for good instead of evil.

Damn, Lex. There you go with that "evil" thing. Briggs wasn't Satan. He was just another mad scientist trying to save the world.

Might be a cautionary tale in there for you. Maybe the world doesn't need saving.

The real records and notes wouldn't be safe in the lab. Burchfield would never let it go. And his holy-roller sidekick Wallace Forsyth, her old nemesis from the president's bioethics council, wouldn't abandon a divine mission once he'd heard the trumpet sound.

Her home office didn't have fancy equipment, but it was relatively easy to keep secure. Unlike the neurosciences labs, no one else had access. Mark didn't even have a key, though she let him nose around in it every once in a while to avoid arousing suspicion. Ever since he'd caught her hiding the Halcyon she'd stolen from the Monkey House, she'd made an effort to stay transparent.

Not that his mistrust had eased.

Outwardly, the room had all the trappings of the after-hours home office: a desk, computer, bookshelves, filing cabinet, and a bulletin board feathered with notes. It would withstand a search by Mark, the police, and possibly even national intelligence agencies. The biggest lesson she'd learned from Briggs was you stored as much of your information in your head as you could.

That was the one place into which, as far as she knew, no one would be able to hack.

She'd devised a code for her written research records, and while it could be cracked, she used a cross-referencing system that would yield only the pieces but not how to put them together, like a Rubik's Cube of chemical compounds.

The powerful computer, which mirrored many of the records from the lab, held nothing that would give away her search for a new Halcyon formula.

If Darrell Silver hadn't been arrested, she would have cracked the puzzle by now. But failure and difficulty only made her more determined. Maybe even obsessed.

"I'll save you, Mark," she whispered, tracing through her notes once more.

A sudden knock caused her to bolt upright in her chair. She glanced at the clock. It was nearly midnight. Mark had begun going to bed early since the headaches had started.

"Who is it?" she asked.

"Who do you think? Why did you lock the door?"

She minimized the computer images and opened the door a crack. "I thought you'd be asleep."

"What's going on in here?" He wore a tattered Carolina Tar Heels T-shirt and striped pajama pants, and his Glock was in his hand. He barely seemed aware of it as he scratched his thigh with the barrel.

"I'm working on that study I told you about," she said, gauging his mood. "You know, the brain activity of college students."

"Got any dirty pictures I can look at?" He chuckled, but there was no humor in it.

"How are you feeling?"

"Took four aspirin."

"It's not getting any better, is it?"

His eyes looked haunted, wrinkles of fatigue around them. "Sometimes I feel it like a pulse. Like a glowing wire up my spine."

"Maybe we should see a specialist." Alexis hated to even make the suggestion, because then Mark Morgan would be a public case and she'd lose control of his treatment. But Mark had even more reason than she to stay away from the machineries of modern health care.

"I worked for a drug company, remember? A shady, powerful company. For all I know, they want me comatose or dead. I wouldn't take a prescription medicine if my life depended on it."

Paranoia was one of the many special gifts of Seethe. In Alexis, it had manifested as an apparent primal rage, although she had little memory of the events in the Monkey House. Mark was deteriorating into delusion, and if his escalating violence blended with his suspicion, he'd be a danger not just to himself and Alexis but to everyone.

Especially Senator Daniel Burchfield, one of the frontrunners for the Republican presidential nomination, who'd also been exposed to Seethe.

"I'm done in here," she said. "Let's get ready for bed. Why don't you put away your gun?"

He nodded vacantly, as if already forgetting their conversation had taken place. "I know what they took from the lab."

"What's that, honey?"

"My brain."

His expression was so innocent that she almost got teary-eyed. With his tousled brown hair and bed clothes, he was like a child who'd been awakened by a disturbing dream. Except this nightmare kept on rolling around the clock.

She went to him and gave him a hug, careful not to confine his gun hand. "Your brain is right where it's always been," she said, though she suspected he might be right. "Behind that gorgeous face."

She kissed his forehead. "I'll get you a glass of water and see you in the bedroom, okay?"

He nodded again and shuffled down the hall. She locked the office door and went into the kitchen, feeling its stark stillness in her bones. The smell of fish lingered, and dishes were piled in the sink. On impulse, she drew the curtains closed and checked the door lock. Then she went to the refrigerator.

On the back of the middle shelf were four plastic bottles of water, still tethered by a six-pack ring. She removed the one that had been opened and drained a few ounces of it into a glass.

Darrell Silver had welcomed the challenge of working with a clandestine drug. He'd been her graduate assistant, clearly brilliant and clearly too unorthodox to last in the rigid discipline of biochemistry. He'd been expelled for manufacturing a potent contraband version of OxyContin, making a good living on the side selling the powerful painkiller made popular by the likes of Rush Limbaugh.

When she approached Silver, Alexis had stressed secrecy while also downplaying the drug's intended efficacy. Silver had suspected it was a new class of recreational drug, and he'd probably even sampled some himself. But a casual thrill-seeker would never notice the subtle effects. Only repeated treatment made the memory loss evident, and Silver had plenty of easier ways to kill brain cells.

Seethe was a different story, but she'd never trust someone like Darrell Silver with it. She wouldn't trust anyone but herself.

She carried the glass to the bedroom after watering it down. She didn't know how long the sixty ounces of Halcyon formula would last, so she dispensed it sparingly. She didn't know if Silver's version was even in the ballpark, because she couldn't risk sampling it herself.

Because if I started forgetting, all my work would be lost, and so would Mark.

She only hoped it wasn't making his condition worse. But she had no other options.

Mark was half-asleep when she entered. The pistol was on the nightstand.

"Here, honey," she said, sitting on the bed and stroking his cheek.

He took the glass and raised his head with effort, eyes shot through with red streaks. "When I get to be a cop, you know who I'm going to take down first?"

"That's still a year or two away, honey."

"The drug dealers, that's who. These legal drugs are bad enough, but that stuff on the streets…kids killing kids, that's what it is. Kids killing kids."

"What's sad is society's need for escape, as if this world is a horrible place to spend your waking life," she said.

"There's only one escape."

Alexis left that one alone, undressing as he took his illicit drug. Halcyon wasn't technically illegal—the FDA review had quietly disappeared, as had any connection between CRO Pharmaceuticals and Burchfield, so it wasn't even on the DEA's radar, much less listed in the Physician's Desk Reference.

She was glad to be rid of the crisp work clothes, and as she unfastened her bra, shyness overcame her. They hadn't made love in several weeks, and she felt unattractive and awkward in the nude. She left her panties on as she slid into bed beside Mark, who'd downed the "water."

"Maybe we need a vacation," she said, snuggling against him. Despite his sluggishness of late, he was still in good shape and she was comforted by his strength.

"Camping," he said. "Somewhere without computers. Where not even the goddamned cell phones can reach us. Much less a bunch of spy-movie rejects."

"That sounds wonderful," she said.

She wrapped an arm around him, pulling him close to kiss his cheek. She liked the roughness of his fresh stubble. She rubbed her nose against his earlobe.

He turned to her, smiling. "I'm feeling better. *Much* better." He guided her hand along his chest down to his swelling erection. "*This* much better."

"Somebody wants to play," she murmured, trying to relax. However, uneasiness held her back, even as he stroked the underside of her breast.

"Do you mind putting the gun away?" she said. "At least hide it in the drawer."

"What if I need it?"

"The doors are locked."

"But they have my brain."

Alexis wondered if the lesions could lead to schizophrenia, or whether this was just another lingering symptom of Seethe. "We're out of the Monkey House, honey."

"We just escaped into a bigger Monkey House."

The ember went out in her belly before it could be fanned into a flame. She released his erection and gave it a friendly pat. "We're both exhausted," she said. "Let's save this for later."

He didn't argue as she turned out the light. They lay there in silence, and it felt like hours to Alexis before she drifted into a restless sleep as Mark twitched beside her.

CHAPTER SIX

"What's wrong, honey?" Wendy asked, propped up on pillows and flipping through a book of Gauguin prints.

Roland dropped the curtain. "It's quiet outside."

"We're half a mile from the nearest neighbors and twenty miles from town," she said. "We wanted quiet on purpose, remember?"

"Yeah, but it's April. Where are all the crickets and night birds and critters? It's like the pope's funeral out there."

"Everybody needs a break once in a while. Maybe God is taking the night off."

"I don't like it," he said.

"You've been antsy since dinner. What's wrong?"

He unbuttoned his shirt and stroked his belly. After he'd quit drinking, he'd lost about fifteen pounds, but lately a little fat had crept back. His dad had been chubby, a truck driver whose sedentary lifestyle led to a fatal heart attack on US-70 while hauling a trailer-load of culvert pipes. He'd steered to his right with his last breath, running off the road and avoiding a likely pileup that might have kept the coroner busy for weeks.

Or the last turn could have been a little of that infamous Doyle luck. Roland preferred the hero story, because it would have been the only positive act of Denny Doyle's fear-ridden life. And fear was a chronic disease that people happily spread to others, especially their loved ones. For Roland, the infection had taken liquid form, a handy excuse to destroy himself and those around him. Especially Wendy.

But this new fear was a little unsettling, because it was one he didn't think he could just pour down the sink or turn over to a higher power.

"Where do you go when it's already as good as it gets?" he said. "You're the hillbilly Bohemian and I'm the creative entrepreneur, and we're here in the oldest pocket of dirt in the universe. But what's the next level?"

"Maybe there's no next level," she said. "Maybe when you get to heaven, it's okay to stay there."

He finished undressing and climbed into bed. He didn't think heaven could exist on the same planet that once contained the Monkey House, and where now the hellish past refused to leave them alone. But Wendy's memory of those events was mercifully erased, and Roland had to carry that cross alone.

Well, with the help of his higher power. But the higher power was the one that had built the cross in the first place.

"Do you miss teaching at the university?" he asked.

She closed the art book and set it aside. "That was a different life, honey. I like this one better."

He couldn't help probing a little, though he didn't really see any upside to jogging her memory. "Heard from Alexis lately?"

"She IMed me a few months back," Wendy said. "Mark's having some physical ailments but nothing serious."

Yeah, I'll bet. Getting your brains scrambled in a blender and then shoved back inside your skull is no big deal.

"Maybe we ought to invite them up for a few days," he said. "I'm sure they'd love to get away from the big city for a while."

"Chapel Hill isn't that big. Besides, where would we put them? You got a one-bedroom cabin on purpose, to make sure children weren't an option anytime soon."

"A small cabin is something we can pay off in five years," he said. "In this economy, I don't want to be tied down to a redneck Taj Mahal."

"So quit complaining about the silence," she said, turning to him and shoving the pillows until their faces were inches apart.

"Yeah," he said. "So shut up and kiss me."

Their lips brushed, and the electricity went through Roland's body. As much as the notion repulsed him, he'd come to accept that the Seethe had charged his libido. Wendy could send him from zero to sixty faster than a Maserati.

And he had a handy excuse whenever a new paranoia arose. When somebody else was in control, that made the consequences somebody else's fault.

Every four hours or else. Sounds like a good prescription for a happy marriage.

Her breath teased across his cheek and she licked his neck, then blew on it, sending shivers down his spine. He reached for the hem of her T-shirt and peeled it up, brushing her belly with the back of his hand until he came to the valley between her small, pert breasts. He ran one thumb over to tease a nipple, pleased to feel it stiffen and push back.

"I love you, Roland," she whispered.

Damn. I fall for that line every single time. But who doesn't?

"So shut up and turn off the light," he whispered back.

He didn't mind doing it with the lights on, but he felt the need to hide a little. Honesty was not only the foundation of his sobriety, it was the foundation of a good relationship. But sometimes honesty just meant shutting up, especially when a mysterious e-mail hinted at a best-forgotten past.

Roland had her shirt off by the time she reached the lamp, and he curled behind her to pin his erection between her buns. He stroked there a moment, running his hands over her front, his face buried in her thick, luxuriant hair. He didn't know whether her Tibetan genetics gave it that faintly musky aroma, but it always evoked strong memories of past pleasure.

Right now, all he cared about was the present, and pleasure yet to come.

He nuzzled the back of her neck in that special spot, then gave a playful nip to her earlobe. She pushed gently back against him, undulating so her vagina moved against his rigid length. He swept his hands underneath her breasts, gently, rubbing up to the nipples and circling in a soft rhythm.

Her body was like a warm instrument beneath his hands, and he worked his fingers in harmony, teasing her nipples. When he could stand it no longer, he rose and maneuvered over her until he could apply his tongue. She moaned and gave him her breast, and he sucked like he was drawing juice from a peach.

He resisted the urge to bite, as the sickness rode in with his lust. Their sex had darkened in the past year, becoming uncertain, explosive, and fraught with veiled violence. And part of him loved it. Loved it very goddamned much.

As she pinched his nipple, he went to full hardness, and in response he bit her nipple, careful to tuck his lip under his upper teeth. She grunted and pulled away, planting her tongue deep in his mouth, and they parried for a moment in a swap of hot saliva.

Wendy came up for air first, turning so that she was under him, then sucked hard on his nipple until it swelled to a painful point. When he could stand it no longer, she gave him teeth and he gasped, then she gave him more than he could stand.

His hand played down her hips and stroked the smooth insides of her thighs, moving into her downy thatch of hair, which was already moist. He cupped his palm over her heat, kneading gently for a moment before sliding a fingertip to her clitoris. He brought the juice to his lips and smeared, then she licked away the remnants, sharing her taste with him.

She rubbed the head of his penis, where a jewel of dew had already formed, and they repeated the fluid game on her lips before sharing a tender kiss, the calm before the storm.

"I love you," he said, sliding his tongue down her neck and chest as his hands cupped her behind. He probed his tongue into her belly button and gave a few playful pokes before heading further down, where her scent was already consuming his senses. His nose rode the length of her cleft, and he marveled at the soft texture that was so much like a flower's swollen and honeyed petals.

She purred and pressed his head forward, and he fought her for only a moment before yielding and letting his lips tug the soft folds into his mouth, where he alternately nibbled and licked until his chin was soaked with her juice. Her clitoris was swollen and he ran his tongue underneath it, lifting up hard before easing the pressure and taunting the tiny bud of sensitive flesh with delicate nudges.

Again he felt a compulsion to hurt her, to squeeze the tender flesh and hear her squeal in pain. But he recognized the urge and was able to beat it, backing off enough to vary his motion, silently cursing the contamination in his brain that had screwed up his thoughts until he barely knew love from hate. And he loved her. Loved her.

He repeated until she came, the fluids gushing in the sudden deluge that always caught him by surprise, though her trembling had heralded it. She moaned as the second release came, and he realized he'd have to change the sheets. But he'd promised her that he'd gladly change the sheets every day if he had to and never complain about such a wondrous gift as female ejaculation, even if it had only entered their sex lives after the Monkey House.

Seethe had opened something inside of her as well, an untapped reservoir, and he tried not to think about it. It was bad for his ego, and made him wonder what else she had bottled up.

Every four hours or else.

The e-mail swam before him and he fought off the memory, wanting nothing to distract him from one of his favorite moments, the feel of his wife's powerless and uninhibited pulsing.

Fuck you, whoever you are. You're not allowed in here. This is private.

Taking advantage of her spread legs, he wiggled up and ran his erection along her leg, annoyed that he'd softened a little at the memory of the message. He wasn't David Underwood. He was Roland Doyle, and he was married to Wendy Leng, the woman he was about to penetrate or die trying.

Wendy had other ideas, though, and she shoved him hard on the shoulder, pushing until he rolled and she had him pinned on his back. She leaned over and gave him a breast and he took it as she rubbed her slick bottom against him. With the weak moon coming through the curtains, he could only see her dim outline, but her face was as clear to him as anything in this life.

And her dark eyes were full of love, sacrifice, vulnerability, exposure, surrender, and conquest as she reached down with one hand and guided him inside.

"Ah, yesssss," she said as he hit home, and she slid along the turgid length until he was almost buried inside. She pulled up agonizingly slowly and then repeated the descent, squeezing her vaginal muscles to massage him as she made the mad ride back down. When she was close to bottoming out, she wriggled and quivered until she took the last inch, releasing another gush that wet his testicles.

I'm going to have to wash the comforter, too. Awesome.

He was momentarily distracted by the image of blood gushing out of her, binding them where their flesh met, the ultimate proof of love. He pushed the vision away. Because he still loved her.

Don't I?

She worked up and down, then swayed side to side to make sure he touched every secret part of her, the tips of her hair feathering against his face. He grabbed her hips as the need took him, and he thrust as he shoved down on her waist. A wet slapping filled the bedroom—

Sebastian Briggs fucking her in the Monkey House—

His jealousy and rage made a perverse transition into sexual energy, and he felt himself swell even more.

"Yes," she urged. "Drill me hard."

Which was odd, since she was the one driving the train, but who was he to argue with such a command? He assisted her frantic pummeling, the friction increasing. And then the change occurred, the one recurring hiccup to his innocent desire.

The lust merged into fear and rage and he clutched her hair, not hard enough to hurt, not yet—he still loved her—though he wanted badly to yank until her neck snapped back.

The madness came back as strongly as it had in the Monkey House, when he'd killed Sebastian Briggs. He'd told himself it was self-defense, an involuntary reaction, but honesty was a hard, hot edge of a knife that pressed against the thin fabric of every deception.

He'd killed Briggs because Briggs had seduced Wendy.

Even though she had no recollection of her surrender—however involuntary—he couldn't bury it, and the only way he could defeat it each time was to become a little like the monster Briggs had wanted him to be.

As he plunged upward, his hips slapping against her moist bottom, he curled his hand into a claw and grabbed the back of her neck, forcing her shoulders down.

And she responded with her own inner sickness, exploding yet again, and this time he joined her, the fervid volcano of his demented passion driving deep into her soft and hidden self.

As they relaxed, grinding together to squeeze out the last drops of joy and shame, Roland couldn't help but feel that Briggs was getting the last laugh from the safe comfort of the grave.

CHAPTER SEVEN

"I thought we'd buried them," Senator Daniel Burchfield said. He adjusted his tie in the mirror, brushing some of the powder from his cheek. "Goddamned makeup. I want to look smooth, not like the corpse of a French mime."

Wallace Forsyth looked around the small dressing room. He didn't trust these cable news outlets. They were in the business of catching people with their pants down, looking for the gaffes that would feed the cycle until the next natural disaster, shooting spree, or Lindsay Lohan arrest.

"Is the room clean?" Forsyth asked.

"Abernethy went over it himself. But you don't need a bug to eavesdrop, Wallace. We've got stuff that can pick up a conversation through the carpet if necessary."

Forsyth looked down at the floor, which was covered in shiny vinyl. The tip of one leather Oxford was scuffed and he rubbed it against his pants leg. "You say 'we' like you know who is on whose side."

"Everybody's on my side," Burchfield said. "Some of them just don't know it yet."

Satisfied with his reflection, Burchfield turned to face Forsyth. "We did everything we promised," he said. "We leveled the

Monkey House, sold that 'limited contamination' story in the press, hid the bodies, and pretty much let everybody else go on with their lives."

"Even though they might snitch you out?"

"You've been reading too many spy novels, Wallace. Most people aren't looking for intrigue or danger. Most people are scared as crap that they're going to be noticed. Then they'd have to act like their job is vital, that they don't cheat on their taxes, and that they know all the words to the Pledge of Allegiance."

"Have you ever considered, Daniel, that you're far too cynical to be the president of the United States of America?"

"Yes, I've considered it. But they say if you scratch a cynic, you find a frustrated idealist. And, I confess, I am idealistic. I love this country. I still think we're the best in the world, and that we have a sacred duty to shape the future."

"'Sacred duty'? Sounds like you're starting to cater to my crowd." Forsyth smiled inwardly.

"Don't worry, Wallace. Federal support of religious non-profit groups is a done deal. And it won't even be a fight. I've already got a nod from the House leader."

"You're assuming the Republicans will control the House next year?"

"Change is in the air. Change is always in the air during troubled times."

"Some would say your actions have helped make them troubled." Forsyth knew the devil's hand was involved, but Burchfield wasn't as true of a believer as he played it in public.

"Look, I didn't start any wars. The people wanted them. We have a moral imperative. Where governments are corrupt and people are oppressed, we lend our might. That's been true since the Monroe Doctrine."

"Only when it serves our corporate friends."

"Don't make me use up all my best material right before an interview, Wallace. Right now, we need to tie up this Halcyon thing before the primary. That's all we need, to let one of the neocons catch wind of it, or that goddamned Utah governor."

"He'll carry his home state, but as long as you bring up the word 'Mormon' in every press conference, the Internet bloggers will do the job for you."

Burchfield, who stood a good four inches taller than Forsyth, slapped the wispy-haired man on the back. "You've been catching up to the Digital Age," he boomed, with the boyish grin that guaranteed him an extra 10 percent among women voters. "Good man. Before you know it, you'll be running your own Facebook page."

There was a knock at the door, and a woman's muffled voice came from beyond it. "Five minutes, Senator."

Burchfield adjusted his tie again and nodded at Forsyth to continue. The senator had been in bed with Big Tobacco before the historic settlement had gutted that lobby's power, and then he'd eased over into Big Drugs without a hiccup. As senior member of the Senate health committee, he'd exploited killing and healing with equal success.

Now Burchfield had said the one word that had been on both their minds since receiving the same text message earlier in the day: *Halcyon.*

"Our boys have Dr. Morgan under surveillance, but we don't see her conjuring up anything," Forsyth said. "Her current research project might as well be June bugs in a jar, as far as we can tell."

"You think she backed off Halcyon completely?"

"She didn't get on the president's council by being a dummy. She knows we got eyes on her."

"And Mark Morgan?" Burchfield's face darkened with the memory of betrayal. Mark Morgan had been a staunch ally in the pharmaceutical game, but he'd chosen his wife over his career, and then added insult to injury by refusing Burchfield's offer to join the campaign team. And now, unaccountably, he was training to be a cop.

"I checked on his performance at Durham Tech," Forsyth said. "Solid Bs, mediocre marksmanship, generally well-liked by his teachers but considered town-cop material at best. He won't be enrolling at Quantico any time soon."

"And that Underwood guy is still locked away in the loony bin?"

"They've got him juiced on so many drugs, he can't tell daffodils from dandelions. You don't have to worry about him talking none."

"The other two, the art teacher and the drunk?"

"They moved up to the North Carolina mountains and turned into hillbillies." Forsyth was getting a headache from Burchfield's cologne and hair gel. "They do some of that Internet stuff but it's all above board, nickel-and-dime web business. All art and no politics."

Burchfield chuckled. "Well, that takes care of them. They'll be on food stamps before Election Day. In today's America, you either buy in, sell out, or get on the gravy train. Free thinkers learn the hard meaning of 'free' sooner or later."

"We're monitoring them anyway. E-mails, phone calls, we're even scanning some of their postal mail."

"Spoken like a true paranoid patriot."

The knock came again. "Three minutes."

Burchfield looked at the door as if speculating on the chances of a romantic rendezvous with the young production assistant.

Burchfield had gotten married six months before, enlisting a charming and guileless former debutante he'd dated at NC State. The wedding fulfilled the voters' need for perceived stability in their leaders, although it had done nothing to dampen Burchfield's lascivious nature.

Which brought them to the last survivor of the Monkey House trials: Anita Molkesky, known during her porn career as "Anita Mann."

"And the one that died?" the senator asked, reaching for the glass of water on the makeup table.

"Nothing surfaced," Forsyth said. "As far as the world knows, she was just another messed-up kid with a drug problem. The only wonder is it took her so long to OD."

"And she wasn't...helped?" Burchfield searched his friend's eyes.

Forsyth kept his face as stolid and stony as he had while practicing law in Clay County, Kentucky, moving from divorce court to civil litigation before making a successful run for district attorney. From there, he'd risen quickly through the party ranks and, with his drawling brand of hellfire and brimstone mixed with down-home values, he settled into eight consecutive terms in the U.S. House before the last Democratic sweep had dumped him to the curb.

Burchfield had kept him close as an advisor, since Forsyth knew all the snake handlers in the capital, as well as most of the snakes. But some things, even Forsyth didn't have the stomach for.

"Our people weren't involved," he said. "As far as I know."

Burchfield looked off in the distance, perhaps fondly recalling his disgusting behavior on that long-ago night, when he'd rutted sinfully with Anita while under the influence of Seethe.

If he ever needed a reminder, Forsyth had stashed away a video recording, the one Burchfield had assumed was destroyed with the rest of the facility.

"Collateral damage is sometimes necessary," Burchfield said. "But we need to nail that down and make sure the autopsy shows no foul play. Primary season is when those little rumors start percolating. And I have a few hand grenades of my own, but I need to lay out some landmines and tear gas first."

"The Monkey House is ancient history, Daniel," Forsyth said. "Hell, I barely even remember it, and I was *there*."

"But somebody remembers besides the CIA. And we better find out who it is, before Fox News and MSNBC and that goddamned Diane Sawyer get wind of it."

"We got a saying back in East Kentucky. It goes, 'If you don't stir in the outhouse, it don't stink so much.'"

"If we could fit that on a bumper sticker, we'd have this thing won already," Burchfield said.

The knock came again.

"I know, two minutes!" Burchfield shouted. CNN had tight live programming, as did all the cable news networks, and Burchfield's swing through Atlanta had allowed him a chance to drop in on the Centers for Disease Control. In addition to providing a great photo op of a somber Senator Daniel Burchfield talking with medical researchers, he'd been able to buttonhole a few of them and inquire about any breakthroughs in drugs treating post-traumatic stress disorder.

While the inquiries sounded like those of a leader concerned about the country's combat veterans, it was also a chance to see if Sebastian Briggs's experimental compounds had somehow entered the black market and made an end run back into the system.

Since Forsyth wasn't officially a candidate for anything, he didn't have to campaign, and thus could devote time and energy to working behind the scenes and tracking potential threats.

But it also meant retrofitting the past, making sure Burchfield was spotless, no matter how much whitewash it took. And some of that wash might be red if necessary.

"Scagnelli's snooping around the NSA, FBI, CIA, the usual," Forsyth said. "I'd say you have about eighty percent support there, which means nobody's likely to knock your legs out from under you. But there might be a rogue agent somewhere, somebody who wants to freelance on the side."

"Be sure to check out Scagnelli, too," Burchfield said, straightening his tie for the third time. "He's an opportunist just like the rest of us. He might have learned something and decided to turn it into a lottery ticket."

"He learned that your last consultant died from a sudden heart attack," Forsyth said. "But that may not work again, because Scagnelli ain't got a heart."

"Whoever is behind it, before we take them out, I need to know one thing." Burchfield's face grew serious, and even the Botox regimen couldn't diminish the hard wrinkles around his eyes.

"What's that?"

"Whether or not Seethe and Halcyon still exist. I'm not even sure they were real."

"They're real. Those drugs have changed you."

"How?"

"You're more intense now. It goes over as passion. And I think you can ride that to the White House if you can keep a lid on it."

"I am in control." Burchfield brushed past him and opened the door, where the pretty production assistant was waiting to outfit him with a wireless, clip-on microphone. He grinned boyishly as she attached it to his breast pocket.

"Be careful, I'm ticklish," he said.

"Bet you say that to all the voters."

"Only the pretty ones."

She blushed and finished the job, giving him an extra pat to make sure the wire was completed concealed. Burchfield's smile stayed with him as he was escorted before the bright lights and cameras.

Forsyth watched from the wings in admiration as Burchfield masterfully fielded questions about his foreign policy, budget plan, and the all-important controversy over whether the Tea Party was going to fracture the Republicans and create an opening for a third-party candidate.

When Burchfield deftly dodged questions about a potential running mate, it was Forsyth's turn to smile.

Seethe and Halcyon changed both of us, Daniel.

CHAPTER EIGHT

"Dr. Morgan?"

Alexis looked up from the computer, where X-rays of Mark's brain were scattered across the screen. Even though the images were filed under a pseudonym, she was careful to intersperse images of other volunteer subjects so anyone cracking into the vector machines wouldn't notice an obsession with any one case.

But she instinctively minimized the window anyway, leaving up images of four other brains.

"What is it, Haleema?" she asked her graduate assistant.

"Have you seen my laptop? I left it here yesterday when I had an appointment with my advisor."

Alexis flashed to the memory of the two men who'd raided the lab. She'd conducted another search that morning and hadn't noticed anything out of place or missing. She'd settled on the story that the men were after drugs, which made pharmacies and medical facilities popular targets for addicted, desperate crooks. Lying to herself had become easier with practice, and denial was one of the most basic survival mechanisms.

"I haven't seen it," Alexis said. "Are you sure it was here?"

Haleema pointed a slender brown hand toward a narrow cubicle where volunteers filled out their paperwork. "It was on the table. I meant to come back and pick it up last night, but I got tied up by my boyfriend."

Alexis tried not to smile, and the young woman recognized the double entendre. She might have blushed, though her skin was too dark to reveal the rush of blood to her cheeks.

"I mean...he took me to a play on campus. So I couldn't get back here, and I figured the lab would be locked anyway."

"I left early, and no one else should have been in here," Alexis said. Haleema, an honors student planning to become a brain surgeon, wasn't authorized to enter the lab without Alexis present. Alexis had very briefly wondered if Haleema was involved in yesterday's raid, but Haleema would have had to illegally copy one of the few existing keys to the door. Besides, it wouldn't have been hard for Haleema to steal while Alexis was consumed with her research.

Maybe she stole things that didn't need to be carried.

"I can't afford another laptop," Haleema said, eyes misting in frustration.

"I'm sure it's around here somewhere," Alexis said. She left her chair and checked her desk drawers and cabinets, repeating the search she'd conducted earlier.

Haleema checked the cubicle again, adding, "It's not just the computer that worries me. All my research was on it, too."

Haleema had been correlating images for the brain-stimulation study, handling a lot of the grunt work of noting the before-and-after differences in the brain scans. Since most of the images revealed only minute changes, her job was to create the median from which the deviations could be measured.

"It's backed up on the vector machines, isn't it?" Alexis asked, browsing a shelf filled with binders and journals to make sure the laptop hadn't been tucked among them.

"Most of it," Haleema said. "I didn't get a chance to upload yesterday's data."

"That's okay," Alexis said. "We can go to the last update and catch up from there. But that laptop probably cost a few thousand dollars. I know we don't pay that much, and it would suck for you to take out another student loan."

"Some of the data may be saved," Haleema said. "I e-mailed thumbnails of the image batch to my university account so I could work on them from the library."

"I told you to keep it off the networks, damn it! It's hard enough to keep electronic information private on dedicated devices, but anything sent over a network is fair game for anybody to steal."

Haleema drew back, cowering a little. Alexis realized she'd better not let her rage run wild, or Haleema might start wondering about the real nature of the work.

"Sorry," Haleema said, lowering her gaze to the floor.

The subjects had been assigned numbers to protect their privacy, and when the results were published, no names would be revealed. But during the analysis, Alexis was running both names and assigned numbers to avoid mistaken identities. If someone had hacked the records, that would have led them to take a closer look.

Or raid the lab.

"Anything particular you were correlating?" Alexis asked, more calmly.

"I was working on the Ds," Haleema said. "Four or five, if I remember correctly."

Davis.

Alexis forced her voice to remain steady. "And you e-mailed them all?"

"Yes." Haleema picked up a stack of manila folders to check behind it.

"With names and numbers assigned?"

"Yes, the way we did all of them."

Alexis pretended to keep searching but she knew the laptop was gone. Whoever had been watching her must have hacked into Haleema's e-mail. It wouldn't even be that difficult, since the university had a large IT staff devoted solely to maintaining the networks, any of whom could have opened her e-mail.

Or granted password access to an interested bidder.

You're getting as paranoid as Mark. Nobody cares about the brain chemistry of college students besides the Miller Brewing Company. I've been very careful.

Still, the Donnie Davis files couldn't be a coincidence. She'd lumped Mark's scans in with the others so they wouldn't be identified as anomalies, and Haleema was too inexperienced to notice the tiny lesions that only a skilled eye could detect.

"I don't think it's here, Dr. Morgan," Haleema said, worried and depressed.

"Maybe you left it in your dorm room, or your boyfriend's apartment. Have you checked with Lost and Found?"

"No," Haleema said. "Should we call the campus police?"

"Let's not do that yet," Alexis said. "It's got to be around here somewhere."

She said the words vacantly and automatically, knowing it had walked out of the room yesterday afternoon under the arm of one of the intruders.

But why didn't they steal the vector machines or my desktop? Sure, those would be much harder to carry away without attracting notice, but then they would have had a better chance of tracking my digital footprints.

Whatever the reason, Mark's brain scans were now in some-body else's hands, and whether they knew what they were looking at or not, the covert thieves held the early evidence of how her husband had changed since the Monkey House exposure.

Evidence of how *she* had changed him.

CHAPTER NINE

National Clandestine Service Officer B.H. Gundersson had spent all his life trying to make up for being born with the name "Byron." Back before he was old enough to know it was a dorky name, he liked it. Then in the sixth grade, some wiseass kid had called him "Lord Byron," and one of the teachers said it was the name of a Romantic poet, and the boys rode his case until high school, when he got big enough to crack a few skulls if necessary.

And he'd found it necessary.

To make matters worse, he kind of liked poetry, although he preferred Shelley to Byron. Even worse than that, he was a little chubby and squishy, and girls often thought he was gay. Maybe the boys, too, but he was big enough to keep their mouths shut. Then one day he'd made the mistake of wearing a gold T-shirt and a black leather jacket, and some girl had called him "Bumblebee," and that drew a few laughs and caught on for a while.

Finally, he'd settled on "Bee," even writing it on all his homework until that's how it appeared in the football program, which his dad thought sounded tough and his mom said she could live with, though he'd always be Byron to her.

The kind of shit you think about when you're sitting in a tree. Should've just gone with my middle name in the first place.

But Horace was even worse than Byron, as evidenced by the army captain at the Citadel who'd referred to him as "Horse," a slightly better nickname than Bee and a little higher up the food chain.

Luckily, the CIA let him go by his initials and, as a core collector for the CIA's National Clandestine Service, he was just as happy as B.H. Gundersson, although a couple of times they'd issued him false identities for some domestic work. But all the name games had been a waste of time, because Field Director Harding referred to him as "Gundy."

While ostensibly the NCS was charged with coordinating information across all the different intelligence agencies in the post-9/11 U.S., it hadn't taken Gundersson long to realize the creation of a new agency had simply snicked another wedge out of the pie. Occasionally the juice from one piece leaked over to another, but some top dog always had a fork jammed hard in the center of his particular slice.

As a patriotic American, he prayed that there would never again come a time when thousands of civilian lives depended on communication between people whose mouths were full of pie.

But it was a little ironic, in a Bruce Willis–movie kind of way, that the NCS was established for foreign intelligence yet spent a good deal of time snooping on its fellow agencies.

He looked through the binoculars again, sitting twenty feet up a young maple tree. His view wasn't quite as interesting as it had been last night, when the couple had given him quite a show through the infrared binos, but it appeared they were finally stirring along with the birds around him.

Gundersson hadn't spent the entire night in the tree. He was a targeting officer, not paramilitary. The killers were on covert missions overseas, handling assault weapons and explosives in locales where there weren't many trees. People like him were usually chained to a desk, poring through e-mails, financial records, and questionable Google habits, but they also made good field workers because no one knew they were field workers.

Compared to dodging rockets in Islamabad, staking out a couple of reclusive hippies seemed like an easy gig.

The only thing that bothered Gundersson was why the CIA was wasting time on these guys when al-Qaeda was still Code Red and the next Timothy McVeigh was probably stopping by the feed store for a truckload of fertilizer at that very moment.

The guy, Roland Doyle, rolled out of bed first and went flopping toward the bathroom and out of Gundersson's limited view. The woman peeled down the sheets and stretched, and he was disappointed to see her grab a robe from the floor. She stood and Gundersson thought she was headed after hubby, but instead she slipped into the robe and came right to the window.

Then she looked directly at him and he froze.

No way. I'm in camo and a hundred feet deep in the woods, and all this April foliage is thick enough to hide an army.

Then she glanced left and right before pulling the curtains closed.

Gundersson finally released a breath. They said sixth sense was a bunch of baloney, but in his experience, people often expressed discomfort when they were being observed, even if they didn't quite understand why. Something just felt different.

But the house was quiet and still, and the pair was likely in the shower, rinsing off last night's dirty play with a round of aquatics.

From his briefing, he'd learned that these two were involved in some sort of secret drug test. Harding, a Desert Storm vet, stressed that it hadn't been a CIA drug test, like when they'd given hallucinogenic drugs to civilians in the MK-Ultra experiments during the Cold War. Harding made it clear he didn't like that "wavy gravy shit," and that Gundersson wasn't to engage the targets. Somebody way up the chain, somebody so high that Harding could merely roll his eyes heavenward, ordered that the pair be monitored until further notice.

With the curtains drawn, Gundersson figured he was done for the day. The couple's routine was to eat breakfast on the porch, feed the gaggle of hens they kept in an open pen behind the cabin, take a little walk along the creek, dig in the garden for maybe an hour, and then rest a little before lunch. After lunch, he'd log onto his computer and she'd get out the paints and brushes.

Gundersson zoomed in on the painting currently drying on the easel.

Sure looks like some drugs involved. Freaky stuff like that, it's no wonder they kicked her out of the university. Couldn't have her warping the minds of our next generation of grade-school teachers.

But he'd not observed any drug use of any kind, not even a bottle of cooking sherry. For crazed, anti-American hippies and possible threats to national security, they sure seemed docile.

He was just getting ready to climb down from the tree and head back to his camp on the edge of the national wilderness area when the couple came out on the porch.

Gundersson slowly lifted the binoculars again.

Shit.

Roland Doyle was armed, wearing nothing but boxer shorts, a black revolver dangling at his side. He clearly wasn't trained with it, because he carried it like somebody in a movie. Wendy Leng hunched behind him in a bathrobe.

"Where did you see it?" Doyle asked, not bothering to lower his voice.

She pointed about thirty feet to Gundersson's right.

Roland marched down the porch steps, across the narrow skirt of ragged grass, and into the forest. Leaves crunched and scuffed under his bare feet. Gundersson was armed but he didn't dare move, although he gently let the binoculars rest by their strap against his chest.

Harding said Roland Doyle was "a nothing," despite a few alcohol-related legal troubles in the past. The unspoken message was that Gundersson was on a babysitting errand and it was time to just shut up and follow orders. Wendy Leng was even cleaner, despite her subversive art. On the surface, they were just intellectual rebels, maybe a little too liberal for their own good but certainly not plotting to smuggle nuclear weapons.

But Gundersson was trained to believe nothing was as it appeared on the surface, and Harding's directive of "Don't ask questions" had certainly spawned a lot of questions.

Roland moved between the trees, not bothering to muffle his footsteps. He didn't look up, either, which meant Gundersson hadn't been spotted.

He was in Gundersson's line of sight now and headed toward a small clearing. Roland raised the pistol in front of him and moved aside a birch sapling. Gundersson calculated how long it would take to draw his Glock from his shoulder holster. Being in such an awkward position might slow him and it would be hard to do so silently.

"Do you see it, honey?" Wendy called from the porch.

"No," he said. "You sure it was out this way?"

"It ran from behind the pen straight down that little trail."

It. She's calling it an "it." Which means it isn't me.

Still, Gundersson remained tensed and ready for action. Roland had a furtive aspect about him, as if he was enjoying the hunt.

The shrubs to Roland's right exploded with motion and Roland raised the pistol, squeezing off three shots in rapid succession. The sudden thunder boomed across the hills. Gundersson had the impression of a sleek, dark animal bounding away, but it was the bushy red tail that helped him identify it.

A fox?

The animal couldn't have been more than ten feet from Roland, which reassured Gundersson that the guy was too liberal to practice his marksmanship. The fox, instead of bolting deeper into the woods, took a detour and splashed up the creek. Roland fired one more wild shot, sending a ricochet off a rock that *zizzed* through the woods. The fox slowed and trotted up the creek about twenty more feet, almost taunting its attacker, and then vanished in a thick tangle of laurels.

Roland gave chase for about fifty yards, lost from Gundersson's view but traceable by the commotion. Roland apparently gave up at that point and returned to the clearing, where he brushed twigs and leaves from his feet.

You have to admire the little critter. Even in danger, it still takes the time to double back and trick out its scent so it can't be followed.

That was probably a good lesson for federal intel agents as well. Gundersson wondered if he'd been diligent in covering his trek from the tree to his camp, as well as a couple of other reconnaissance points he'd established—a massive tumble of granite slabs on the south side of the cabin and a dense thicket of rhododendron near the chicken shed.

But he was more of a desk jockey than anything, a little out of shape, with curly, unkempt hair that didn't fit the ramrod stereotype, and a freckled complexion. Nobody would mistake him for a secret agent of any kind, and someone spying him in the tree would have taken him for a redneck poacher. Hell, he'd barely even made it up the tree, skinning his elbow in the process.

He probably had been a little less careful than he would have been on a real assignment, checking up on an alleged KKK militant or scouting transfer students from the Middle East. And mistakes like that could get you killed. Mistakes like that were why the clandestine service was needed in the first place.

"Did you get it?" Wendy asked from the porch.

"No," Roland called back, irritated.

Roland bent and stirred around in the leaves a little, plucking something from the ground where the fox had been. Still clutching the pistol, but relaxed now, he headed back to the cabin.

When he reached the porch, Gundersson raised the glasses. He could see the feathers in Roland's hand as Wendy reached for them.

Fox must have been raiding the henhouse.

The couple went back inside the cabin. It was time for breakfast. Gundersson was hungry himself. Eggs sounded real good.

But he'd be eating out of a can instead.

He made his way down the tree and, taking a hint from the fox, he navigated a new route back to his camp so that he wouldn't create a trail that Roland might follow.

Sly as a fox. I hope I'm quick enough to dodge four bullets when my time comes.

CHAPTER TEN

"Morgan!"

Mark snapped alert. His Basic Law Enforcement Training instructor was in his ear, leaning into the sedan.

"Yes?" Mark asked, avoiding the automatic "sir" he was compelled to add. While most of the students were in their early twenties, Mark was close to the same age as Derrick Frady, a former sheriff's deputy who'd lost his job during a political housecleaning. Frady, who made up for his diminutive stature with a militaristic zeal, was of course nicknamed "Frady Cat" by the students, but none of them dared call him that to his square, flinty face.

"The suspect just ran another car off the road during the chase. It looks like a probable PI. What do you do?"

"PI" was the police code for "personal injury." Mark was faced with the choice of continuing his pursuit of the suspect or serving the public he was sworn to protect.

Well, I haven't sworn anything yet. I still have another two hundred hours of training to go.

Mark figured that a real cop faced with such a dilemma would punch the accelerator and indulge in the adrenaline rush of a high-speed chase. Because that was Mark's first impulse, he figured it was probably the wrong one.

"What's the Ten-Twenty of my backup?" Mark asked. He was in the back parking lot of Durham Tech, behind the wheel of a dummied-up police cruiser. The car sported a two-way radio, siren, bar lights, and all the accessories of a real cop car. It even had the black-and-white, two-toned paint job, although it bore no emblem or insignia of any kind.

"Half a mile behind, but the neighboring department has a road block a mile ahead," Frady said.

"I pull off pursuit and check on the collision victims," Mark said. "Calling it in, of course."

Frady pulled a twisted crease in one side of his mouth, an expression that passed for a smile. "Serve and protect," he said. "The first word is *serve*." He slapped the top of the sedan. "Good enough."

A series of orange cones were arranged across the empty parking lot. Mark had negotiated the obstacle course in just under three minutes, burning a little rubber off the tires but managing not to tip any cones. He'd scored an 87, which wouldn't have him busting Vin Diesel in a *Fast and Furious* sequel anytime soon, but at least he hadn't skidded into the chain-link fence that surrounded the lot.

Several students waited their turns on a weedy courtyard between the lot and main campus building. They were all dressed in the loose black athletic pants and gray T-shirts that bore the BLET logo. The outfit was part of the indoctrination, a sort of junior varsity uniform to prepare them for blues and badges. Two women were in the class, and they were both as tough as twisted rawhide.

Mark had not beaten the women at anything yet, although he suspected it would be his turn to shine when they trained for presenting evidence in court. If only he could keep his head straight and concentrate.

"All right, Morgan, we need a braking maneuver and a full turn in pursuit," Frady said.

"Which way?"

Frady smirked. "Listen to the radio, rookie. Now wheel it to the start."

While Mark navigated the cruiser to the end of the hundred-yard lot, he eyed the crumbling asphalt. The roads wouldn't be in any better shape once he pinned on a badge, given the sad state of infrastructure funding. Fortunately, government leaders didn't dare cut law enforcement budgets, so he should be able to land a job even if he didn't make top of the class.

Frady had a short-range CB radio system set up in the court-yard. The receiver in the cruiser was set to a channel used infrequently but sometimes prone to interference. Frady's reasoning was that real-life emergency communications often featured overstepping and crowding, so an officer should be skilled in filtering out the noise.

"How's it looking, Unit Seventeen?" Frady's broadcast voice issued from the dashboard speaker, using Mark's assigned number to simulate on-duty patrol.

"Looks like asphalt's a little—"

"All units, Ten-Thirty-two!" Frady barked. "Armed robbery suspect heading west on Tree Street."

"Unit Seventeen in pursuit," Mark said into his mike, gunning the engine and accelerating. "Tree Street" was the name of the straightaway where the students practiced accelerating, braking, and dodging obstacles. The route had a series of four exits, each at a different angle and all named after various species of trees.

As Mark pushed the cruiser to sixty, he fully expected Frady to throw the 90-degree left turn at him, which was the most difficult. He braced for the fake name of "Dogwood Avenue" to come over the radio.

"Suspect in a maroon SUV, armed and dangerous," Frady said, spitting the words like staccato bullets.

"This is Unit Seventeen. I'm Ten-Eighty with suspect in sight," Mark replied, talking fast but steadily. Even though the situation was make-believe, he couldn't help the surge of adrenaline coursing through him. Part of the drill was to maintain control with only one hand on the wheel, the other busy manipulating the mike.

Mark glanced to the side where Frady stood by the radio unit, the students gathered around as if part of some frat prank.

He zoomed past Dogwood. *Goddamned Frady. Trying to show me up. He'll probably throw Birch at me just to keep me off balance.*

"Suspect turning onto Cedar!" Frady said.

The fuck?

Mark slammed on the brakes, and despite triggering the antilock mechanism, the rubber bit at the pavement with a squeal of resistance. Cedar was two streets back, the first left turn.

"Suspect still in sight, Unit Seventeen?" Frady asked, artificially maintaining urgency.

Instead of replying, Mark dropped the mike, yanked the wheel wildly to the left, and cut a donut. *I'll show that asswipe.*

As he leaned into the turn, fighting inertia, his body pulsed with a rush of warmth. The glow was exhilarating and heightened his senses. The tires wailed in a symphonic scream, the surrounding fence glinted like sunlight dappling the surface of uneasy water, and the vehicle was like a sled riding soft snow beneath him. He could even smell the stale cigarette smoke from some prior student's law-breaking indulgence.

He rolled out of the circle, startled by his own mastery of the move. He'd not even broken the painted boundaries of Tree Street. By the time the wheels quit complaining, he was already up to forty and headed for Cedar, which was now on the right.

"Goddamned, Morgan," Frady said, breaking protocol. "What in the hell are you doing?"

Mark felt the grin fixed on his face like a skeleton staring stupidly at its own epitaph. He yanked the mike into his fist by its cord and thumbed it on. "I'm Ten-Eighty on Tree Street," Mark said, wondering if the students could see him through the tinted windshield.

Mark realized he'd already botched the assignment, because he'd forgotten to engage the bar lights and siren. Not that the criminal cared, and it wasn't like Mark needed to warn vehicles in a deserted parking lot.

He communed with the roar of the engine, 250 horses galloping toward hell. As he thrust the accelerator to the floor, he was dimly aware of the unexpected pleasure of power. In high school, while the jocks were picking up chicks in muscle cars and hot rods, he'd driven a rusty Toyota, reading *Forbes* instead of *Car and Driver*. Now, here he was, hunched over the wheel and wanting more juice.

He got it.

And it felt good.

"Break off pursuit, Unit Seventeen," Frady ordered.

Instead of slowing, Mark whipped the cruiser to seventy and veered between the painted lines that designated Cedar Street. The "street" was only forty yards long, ending in a fence, and beyond it was a strip of lawn and landscaping that buffered the college from the highway.

Now where's that suspect?

Where are you hiding?

Officer Morgan has a surprise for you.

Armed and dangerous. That was an excuse to shoot him, right?

Mark tossed the mike away, barely aware of Frady's frantic jabbering on the radio.

Mark reached below the seat to where the Glock was strapped above his ankle. Sure, the college didn't allow concealed weapons, but how did they expect Mark to keep the streets safe if only the crooks had guns? What was he supposed to do, write a warning ticket?

The baggy pants that had disguised the bulk of the weapon were a barrier, and Mark nearly let go of the wheel in his haste to free the pistol.

"Break off, Morgan!" Frady shouted, one last attempt to restore order.

"Fuck off, Frady Cat," Morgan shouted to the sky.

The fence was dead ahead, approaching fast, and Mark glanced around, surprised. The suspect was nowhere in sight.

You're not getting away that easy.

The cruiser plowed into the fence, jerking Mark forward. He bounced against the seatbelt and the passenger's-side air bag exploded. The chain links stretched taut with a brittle *skreee*. Then Mark was through, peeling the fence loose from its posts as metal grabbed at the cruiser's flanks. He bounced over the uneven terrain and plowed through a stand of flowering shrubs. By then, he was sufficiently slowed to merge with the midday traffic.

The other cars miraculously made way, even slowing to the speed limit so Mark could easily move through them. Going with the flow, Mark was able to free the Glock and lay it on the seat beside him.

He checked the side and rearview mirrors, then peered through the windshield.

Somewhere there was a maroon SUV that had made the mistake of stepping out of line while Officer Mark Morgan was on duty. It would be a mistake the crook would live to regret. Or maybe *not* live. Whatever.

He was humming, glowing, flushed with heat as he clicked off the chattering CB radio.

It felt good to be a cop.

CHAPTER ELEVEN

Dominic Scagnelli didn't like the way this was going.

That wasn't unusual.

He hadn't liked the goddamned Drug Enforcement Agency. He hated the FBI. And this new gig as a fixer for Danny-Boy Burchfield was about the bottom of the fucking barrel.

The bitch of it was, this new job paid better than any of them. At least on the numbers reported to the Internal Revenue Service. But the IRS could roll up those check stubs and cram them up their puckered little buttholes, for all he cared.

They were all part of the same machine, the upper end of the trough. And people like him were paid to stand guard while the hogs fed.

Simple as that.

And in a way, he was getting his share of the swill, too.

Scagnelli reached into his pocket to touch the metal tin of "breath mints." *You've got to hand it to that two-faced bastard, Wallace Forsyth. He really knows where to score some good shit.*

Scagnelli glanced out the car window. He was parked in a handicapped space near the rear exit to the neurosciences building. He wasn't sure when Dr. Alexis Morgan would make her daily trek to her car, but it was close to lunchtime and that was as good a bet as any.

He drifted into that semi-alert state of surveillance and was startled when someone knocked on the driver's-side window.

Holy fucking guacamole on a crispy corn fritter.

He glanced over to see a young woman, college-aged, wearing a bright orange vest and holding a little booklet. He was getting soft. What if that had been a punk with a gun?

He rolled down the window. She was cute, but he didn't like cute. He smiled anyway. "Good morning, miss. Nice day, huh?"

She glanced around as if noticing it was daylight for the first time. "You're in a handicapped spot, sir."

Scagnelli nodded and pointed at the sign. "Fine of two hundred and fifty dollars. That's a lot, considering half the people with handicapped stickers are faking it."

She fanned herself with her ticket book, a little perspiration on her flushed skin. She was a brunette with television hair and a body that would go to cheese in about five years, right after she married some dumb frat boy with a business degree. "The spot's for people with stickers," she said.

"We've established that."

"You don't have no sticker."

"We've also established that."

"Are you picking somebody up?"

"You might say that." Scagnelli's eyebrow twitched. He'd only taken one hit of speed this morning. He didn't like to get too wired while he was on a stakeout, but he also didn't want to drowse off, either.

"There are metered spaces over by the parking deck," the young woman said, the first sign of exasperation entering her tone. She had a little two-way radio on her belt that squawked and fell silent.

"If I wanted to be in a metered space, I'd be in a metered space. I want to be here."

"Sir, university parking regulations requires a civil penalty of—"

"Yeah, I know."

She looked into his aviation sunglasses as if trying to read his hidden eyes. "I'm afraid I have to write you a ticket if you don't leave."

He nodded. "Yeah. That's your job, right? You should always do your job to the best of your abilities. That's what they teach you here, right?"

You and the other fucking corporate slaves.

"Yes, sir."

"What do they pay you to be a Parking Nazi? Minimum wage plus a quarter, but you turn around and give it all right back to the Man."

She glanced around as if deciding whether it was easier to fill her quota elsewhere, or maybe she was debating hitting her little radio and calling in the university rent-a-cops. Scagnelli didn't want the hassle of showing his federal badges and playing the one-up game.

"Go ahead and write your ticket," Scagnelli said.

She was nearly in tears now, and relief washed over her face as she walked to the rear of the rental sedan. Scagnelli monitored the building's exit again, glancing once in the rearview mirror to make sure she was writing it all down. The pedestrian traffic had picked up, and Scagnelli wondered if he should change his plans.

The traffic monitor came back to the window and ripped a copy of the ticket free, then stuck it out toward him. He brushed his lips—speed made his skin itch—and then popped open the briefcase on the seat beside him. His guns were stuck inside padded mailing envelopes, and a few papers were clipped together on top to make it all look legit. He reached into a fold and pulled out a handicapped sticker. "Sorry, miss. I forgot I had this."

She stood there with the ticket held out to him, still a foot away from the window, as if afraid he'd grab her wrist and pull her into the car.

Good instincts. You'll make a great soccer mom. I see lots of Jennifer Aniston movies in your future.

"I can't void a ticket in the field," she said. "Once it's written, you have to go through the appeals process."

"I don't have time for an appeals process." He smiled.

"I'm sorry, sir. It's in the regulations."

"That's always the answer, isn't it?"

She forgot she was an official representative of the University of North Carolina at Chapel Hill's Department of Public Safety and became just another ex-teen. "Huh?"

"It is what it is," he said. "Rules of the road. The way the game is played. Love it or leave it."

"I'm sorry, sir, I'm just doing my job."

"Hitler was just doing his job. Osama bin Laden was just doing his job. Ted Bundy was just doing his job. That's the problem with this fucking world. Everybody's just doing their jobs."

She stepped forward and thrust the ticket inside the window, letting it flutter into his lap. "The appeals process is on the ticket," she said, hurrying away, hunched as if expecting a bullet in the back, or at least a shouted insult.

Scagnelli smiled. All she had was a fake license-plate number on a rental car.

Have fun explaining that one to the boss. Because, guess what? I'm just doing my fucking job.

The encounter had entertained him past noon. Dr. Morgan was late. Young students were streaming in and out of the building, and he struggled to track each face. The dossier had contained photographs of an attractive woman with nice shoulders. He didn't go for cute, but attractive was a different matter, and she was worth looking for.

The federal files on Morgan listed her as a person of interest, making references to a Dr. Sebastian Briggs who had died in a chemical explosion. Briggs was implicated in the illegal manufacture of drugs, with the FBI drawn in because of suspected trafficking across state lines. Morgan had been his graduate assistant at one time.

Scagnelli knew the FBI files were bullshit. It was the kind of information available to all clearance levels, and nothing important was ever made widely available. Within the security departments, knowledge was the currency through which the power games were waged, careers made or broken on the ability to gain access.

The real Briggs files were Sensitive Compartmentalized Information, a wonderful murky phrase that kept the info on a "need to know" basis, an ever-shifting clusterfuck of smoke and mirrors that guaranteed nobody would possess the whole truth.

But truth is just another layer of smoke, like the smoke Forsyth is blowing up my ass. If he says this Seethe and Halcyon stuff are threats to national security, what he really means is they're a threat to Danny-Boy's bid for the nomination.

Scagnelli had hacked the e-mails the two CIA agents had shared after "discovering" the laptop in Morgan's lab. He'd gone through all the research files and hadn't found anything suspicious, but what did they expect? He was a goddamned fixer, not a brain surgeon.

A bearded man started to enter the building, then stepped back and held the door open. A woman exited and nodded thanks at the courteous gentleman, who "You're welcomed" her by glancing at her ass as she walked away. It was Dr. Morgan, he was sure, her figure rolling smoothly inside her skirt suit as her heels clattered on the sidewalk.

She was carrying a briefcase. After her encounter with the two undercover agents the day before, she wouldn't be stupid enough to have incriminating records with her, much less the Seethe or Halcyon compounds.

Scagnelli started the rental sedan and eased out of the handicapped spot. The game plan was to follow Dr. Morgan and see if she made any slips or had any interesting appointments. If she wasn't synthesizing the compounds in the university labs, she was working with someone off-site. Scagnelli had wanted to break into the Morgans' house, but Forsyth said Mark Morgan was armed and possibly unhinged. Violence was the course of last resort because bodies always led to questions and more dummied-up dossiers.

Unless they could be handled like he'd handled Anita Molkesky. In a case like that, you were performing a public service and giving the people what they wanted. It was a job that brought a little pride and satisfaction.

The parking lot was crowded but the congestion gave Scagnelli an excuse to drive slowly. He could have followed her on foot, but he'd have been too easy to spot. Nobody expected a stalker to use a car. That wasn't how it worked in the movies, and people could no longer tell movies from real life.

Dr. Morgan was wearing sunglasses and her suit was navy blue. Scagnelli liked the sleek curves of her calves, which were encased in dark hose. He was glad she didn't have thick ankles. He hated stalking women with thick ankles.

She'd parked her late-model Lexus in the satellite faculty lot that morning, and Scagnelli expected her to walk straight to it and drive away. Scagnelli passed the cute traffic monitor, who was busy writing a ticket and didn't see him.

Dr. Morgan turned her head suddenly in his direction, and Scagnelli wondered if she had somehow sensed him. He fought an urge to speed up. While she would be on her guard after yesterday's encounter, she would be looking out for two dark-skinned men, not a swarthy, smiling white guy.

Scagnelli silently applauded Forsyth's little shell game, which would have her suspecting the lab raid had been connected to terrorists or international espionage instead of federal investigators.

But you only sold me a bowl of smoke, didn't you? Just doing your job as Danny-Boy's advance scout.

Scagnelli planned to circle the lot as if unable to find a parking space, and then loop behind her when she hit the highway. He was easing forward, checking her in the rearview, when a black-and-white police cruiser wheeled in front of him, skidding and swerving.

"Fucking townie!" Scagnelli shouted, braking and cutting hard right, narrowly missing the cruiser's fender. The cruiser didn't slow at all.

Weird. No siren, no lights.

Town police were usually the most by-the-book because they were often the newest to law enforcement, the lowest on the totem pole in any cross-jurisdictional investigation, and the most likely to be reprimanded or fired. One citizen report of reckless behavior could be enough to send the mayor crawling up the chief's ass.

Scagnelli watched in the mirror as the cruiser spun into the satellite lot toward Alexis Morgan a hundred feet away. The cruiser slowed and the cop apparently said something to her, because she stopped walking and stared in surprise.

Hold the guacamole. That damned cruiser doesn't have any insignia.

Town departments often employed one of two looks for their fleet, usually reflecting the current chief's personality and philosophy. The first was the two-toned, old-school, black-and-white look if the chief believed in visibility and crime prevention. The second was tinted windows and sleek, unmarked cars designed for stealth and intimidation. That was the theory. In practice, limited funding often meant departments had a mix of each.

But Scagnelli had never heard of a department whose marked cars didn't sport departmental emblems on the doors. The cruiser was almost like a movie prop. He eased his own car forward, keeping one eye on the mock cruiser as a pickup truck pulled in behind him. The ticket girl had also noticed the cruiser and was watching with her beady little tattletale eyes.

Alexis Morgan walked toward the cruiser, her confident gait now stilted and unsure.

If Forsyth cut another agent in on this deal, I'm going to yank his rubbery old ears down around his neck, strangle him, and shove a Bible up his ass. Except he'd probably enjoy it.

By the time Scagnelli had negotiated a three-point turn, Alexis Morgan had climbed into the passenger side of the cruiser. The ticket girl scrawled a little note on her pad, probably the cruiser's license plate number. Scagnelli's anger cooled a little as he realized his job had just gotten a whole lot easier.

I'll let that clown cop do all the heavy lifting, and I'll just walk in and pick up the winning lottery ticket. A guy acting all erratic like that, the suspicion will fall on him when she turns up dead.

He popped one of Forsyth's gift amphetamines to celebrate.

CHAPTER TWELVE

"Every four hours," Roland said.

"What's that, honey?" Wendy said. She sat curled on the window seat, between the maidenhair fern and the wax begonias, sketching in the midday sun. Her T-shirt was a Jackson Pollock mess of spilled paint and stains.

"Does that mean anything to you? Every four hours?"

"Sounds like a TV commercial."

The cabin didn't have a television. If they wanted to watch something, they had to rent a Redbox movie and huddle around the laptop. Not that Roland cared. That made movies a good excuse for snuggling and popcorn and then some dangerous erotic play.

What he did care about was Wendy's memory of the Monkey House. As a long-time alcoholic, he understood obliterating chunks of consciousness. And he'd done it by choice, at least as far as drunks had any control in their own self-destruction.

Wendy, however, had been an innocent victim of Briggs's drug experiments. Seethe had scrambled her senses and driven her into a confused, hedonistic hurricane. She hadn't been herself when she'd fallen for Briggs's sick seduction.

Yeah. Keep telling yourself that. Just like you only killed Briggs in self-defense, not because he was fucking your wife. So much for a twelve-step program built on honesty.

Roland tried to tell himself the Seethe had driven him to murder, but he remembered the pleasure he'd felt in pulling the trigger and watching Briggs leak. Sure, Seethe was designed to evoke such a reaction. But just like a drunk on a blackout was still acting from a core impulse, no drug could totally alter personality.

All Seethe had done was make him more like himself.

Wendy paused in her sketching, noticing he'd dropped the conversation. "Why are you talking about 'every four hours'?"

"One of my clients is using it for a book title," Roland said. "I have to wrap the words around a picture of a scantily clad woman."

"Tough duty, huh?"

"Beats selling billboards." He opened his e-mail program and looked again at the message he'd received that morning. Just like the first one, it had the subject line "Every four hrs or else" and was from the same National Clandestine Service address.

This one also had a message in the body of the e-mail. It said, "Surely you didn't think we could let you live, after what happened."

"Is she cuter than me?" Wendy said.

"Who?"

"The scantily clad woman."

"It's a cartoon. Old pulp-fiction style. Boobs the size of watermelons and a waist like Gandhi."

"Blonde?"

"If I paint it that way."

"Make her blonde so I don't get jealous."

"You never get jealous." *Only me.*

"Yeah, out here I guess there's not much competition." She tucked a leg under her rear in a motion of feline grace and continued with her work.

Roland studied the e-mail for clues, but he couldn't read anything between the lines. First the "David Underwood" trick and now this new threat.

On a whim, he hit "Reply," and when the message window opened, he typed, "Maybe we can help each other." He paused, then typed "David Underwood" as a signature beneath the message and hit "Send."

"What's it about?" Wendy asked.

Roland jerked upright. "What?"

"The book. *Every Four Hours*. That sounds familiar."

"It's by a new mystery writer." He waited. "David Underwood. You haven't heard of him."

"There are too many writers in the world. Who can keep track of them all?"

"Not like you artists. Supply perfectly matches demand."

"Hey, smarty-pants." Wendy perched her sketchbook on the ledge of the bay window. "Come over here and kiss me."

"I'm working," Roland said, watching his e-mail to see if a response was forthcoming. The message hadn't bounced, so it must have been routed to someone's inbox, although he doubted it went to the CIA.

Wendy curled up on the window seat and gave a fake pout. He grinned at her and went back to his laptop screen.

"Ro?" she whispered.

He ignored her. Work was work, and even pretending to work was work.

"Honey?" she said, louder.

He logged out of his e-mail program, annoyed. If somebody was playing cat and mouse, he wanted to be the cat. "What?"

"Something's moving out there."

"Is the fox back?" Roland had reloaded the pistol and returned it to the bedside table because he hadn't expected the fox to return. The creatures were most active at dawn and dusk, and it was rare to see one in full daylight. That's why he'd suspected the one he'd shot at that morning had been rabid.

He'd hated to kill it, because it was just trying to survive, and it might even have a pack of kits in a den somewhere. But he and Wendy had grown fond of their chickens, treating them like pets and also enjoying the fresh brown eggs. It was part of their new game of playing hillbilly homesteaders.

"I don't think it's the fox," Wendy said. "It's bigger."

What could be bigger than a fox? A stray dog? A deer? A bear?

Roland set his laptop on the sofa and went to the window. He peered into the woods, scowling. Wendy leapt up and grabbed him around the neck, pulling him down.

"Gotcha!" she squealed with a laugh. They wrestled as she giggled, and Roland finally pinned her against the window seat and kissed her.

"Who got who?" he whispered, running his hands over her hips.

He glanced out the window again, glad they were out in the country and didn't have to worry about Peeping Toms and—

Shit. Was that a reflection?

The light flashed again in the woods, its distance difficult to gauge. Hunting season was long past, but hikers might be exploring the Blue Ridge trails, wandering away from the nearby national park.

"Come on, zookeeper," Wendy said, unaware of his unease. "Tame your tiger."

"Shh," he said, still on top of her but no longer pressing his weight against her.

"What's wrong?"

He moved toward the glass, peering out. "Something's out there."

"I already used that trick," she said. "You have to come up with your own."

"No, really. I saw a glint of light, like the sun bouncing off of metal."

Wendy rolled up beside him, leaning on the ledge. "I can't see the forest for the trees."

Roland glanced down at her sketchbook. *What the fuck?*

It was a slightly surrealistic treatment, with distorted and oversized eyes, but the portrait was unmistakable. David Underwood. The older, psychotic David, as they'd found him in the Monkey House, hollowed out from Briggs's deranged experiments, not the teen David from the original clinical trials.

The sketch caused Roland to realize just how much they'd all changed since the first trials. But some had changed more than others.

"Who is this?" Roland asked, tapping the pad.

"I don't know," she said. "Just a face."

"Not bad." He studied her dark eyes, looking for any sign of confusion or suspicion. "He looks familiar, though."

"Maybe it's like your book title. Everything's been done before."

Roland gazed into the forest. Nothing there.

Don't tell me I'm cracking up. I thought peace and quiet was supposed to calm your nerves.

He moved away from the window, shrugging off Wendy's half-hearted attempt to lull him into a kiss. "By the way, honey, have you been using the computer?"

"Not since yesterday." Her tone barely hid the hurt of rejection. "Why?"

Because I wonder if you've been sending me e-mails. The enemy within. That's how they get you. That's how it always goes bad.

"Nothing," he said. "It's just been a little glitchy."

"You've been acting a little glitchy yourself. Where are you going?"

"To get the gun, just in case that fox comes back."

CHAPTER THIRTEEN

Burchfield made a campaign stop in Charlotte, speaking to a women's group about the importance of funding early-childhood education, addressing a Rotary Club crowd at breakfast, stopping by the city library for a photo op, and giving a short interview to a *Charlotte Observer* beat reporter.

Wallace Forsyth admired the way the man slightly adjusted his personality to fit each situation while maintaining the polished veneer of the career politician. Forsyth was no political slouch, but playing folksy, down-home politics in East Kentucky was a much simpler game than prepping for the national stage.

Now, as they drove northeast toward Raleigh on I-85, Burchfield studied the morning edition of the *Observer*.

"Only down six points," Burchfield said. "Thank the Lord for Tea Party wackos fracturing the base."

"Now, Daniel, they're a vital part of your constituency," Forsyth said. "Besides, you've got plenty of time to make a push. The Iowa caucus is still seven months away. Lots can happen between now and then."

"Yeah. Like some goddamned TV celebrity could enter the race."

"You got 'em all beat on looks," Forsyth drawled. "And you got most of 'em beat on money. Just keep beating that donkey with a stick and it will start braying like a jackass."

Burchfield softened slightly at the compliments. He flapped the newspaper, folded it, and tossed it on the back ledge. The driver, a Secret Service agent named Abernethy, was separated from them by a layer of soundproof glass. The back of the limousine had become an informal Command Central for the campaign, although the official headquarters were in Burchfield's hometown of Winston-Salem.

They'd be setting up satellite offices around the country, but North Carolina was one of the few Southern Red states that occasionally swung Democratic. It was important for Burchfield to make a stand on his home turf, even if he had to fend off a pack of well-heeled conservative challengers in his own party first.

"Any news on the Morgans?" Burchfield asked.

Forsyth fished his cell from the inside of his jacket. It was some fancy BlackBerry and did all kinds of tricks that scared him half to death. Burchfield had forced him to learn to text and operate the pager system, but that was about all Forsyth could handle. He was afraid he'd hit the wrong button and send out some top-secret memo or one of those slips of the tongue that the media would twist out of shape.

But since it wasn't government-owned, Burchfield had assured him, nobody could file a public-records request on his messages.

"Why don't we just check up on them, if I can figure this thing out," he said.

"Careful you don't trigger the Star Wars missile defense system," Burchfield teased.

"Maybe I could send a bomb into San Francisco and make the world a better place."

"Now, Wallace, they're American citizens just like the rest of us. If there's any killing to be done, let's keep it in the Middle East where it belongs."

"California's a lost cause, anyway. Unless you hog-tied Schwarzenegger as your running mate."

Burchfield smirked. "You know the rules, Wallace. Never pick a sidekick who's more macho than you are."

"If I was younger, Daniel, I'd be mighty offended."

"Don't worry. The 'elder statesman' thing is in. Cheney, Biden, people kind of like a VP who stays in the background."

Forsyth laboriously punched in the numbers. The limousine ride was smooth, but Wallace hadn't eaten since the Rotary Club ham biscuits, and his blood sugar was a little low. When he thought he had the numbers right, he waited for the ring and the terse response: "Scagnelli."

"It's Wallace. What you got going on?"

"Doing my job."

"That's reassuring. And what exactly do you imagine that is today?"

"One thing I need to know. Do you have other agents on this job?"

"Just the CIA agents were brought into play." Which was true, if Wallace considered the "job" to be keeping the Morgans under surveillance. "How did she react?"

"The doctor's just going about her business. Well, she *was*. Then hubby went a little over the top."

"Damn," Wallace hissed, drawing a cocked eyebrow from Burchfield, who rarely heard him cuss. "Is he violent?"

"Well, not quite. He's apparently stolen a car belonging to the Durham Technical Institute where he's taking his cop classes."

"That's all we need, for the local police to get in on this."

"No problem. Just call up the head of the program, tell him it's a matter of national security, the whole bit. They won't be too anxious for the media to get hold of the story. Talk about a black eye for your cop program."

"Where are you now?"

"The Morgans are together, traveling away from town in the stolen car. No stops since he picked her up in Chapel Hill. I'm tailing them, but it's not high-speed."

"Good. Keep it below the radar as long as you can."

"Let me handle it solo, and I can guarantee it. Bring in any others and it's not my problem."

"Do you know where they're headed?"

"They're heading north out of Chapel Hill."

"Stay with them and call me when you find out the destination. Is he armed?"

"Wouldn't you be?"

"That means Dr. Morgan's at risk. She must be protected at any cost."

"Yesterday you wanted her dead at any cost."

"That was yesterday. Those records the CIA hacked suggest she may be onto something. I want to know what it is."

"Yes, sir."

"*Any* cost."

"I heard you the first time." A pause. "Sir."

Forsyth rang off and prepared his response, wondering how much he wanted to tell his friend and political ally.

"That didn't sound so good," Burchfield said.

"Dr. Morgan probably has Seethe. Her husband's as addled as a frog in a butter churn."

"Goddamn it." Burchfield punched the back of the seat with the bottom of his fist, causing Abernethy to slow and check the rearview. Burchfield gave an impatient wave forward and the driver accelerated again. "I didn't trust them to destroy it, but I didn't think they'd start playing with it."

"Maybe this is a good thing, Daniel. If she's cooked some of it up, then it didn't die with Sebastian Briggs."

"But we've searched her labs and her house and her office, checked up on all her associates, and tracked down every web search she's made and every journal article she's checked out. Lots of pieces, but no goddamned puzzle."

You don't know about the piece named Darrell Silver.

"Dr. Morgan learned a lot from Sebastian Briggs," Forsyth said. "And she learned that you can't trust nobody, especially when you're in the business of scrambling people's brains."

"I want it," Burchfield said. "And I want them buried." He stared out the window. "I should have dealt with all this last year. That industrial accident could have just as easily claimed half a dozen more lives."

"'The quality of mercy ain't strained, it drops like the gentle rain from heaven.'"

"Shakespeare? I didn't know you could quote from anything but the Bible."

Forsyth actually was quoting Barney Fife from an episode of *The Andy Griffith Show*, but he let it go. Someone like Burchfield valued book smarts over real-world wisdom, and it was one of his weaknesses. But Forsyth was cunning enough to exaggerate his slow drawl and backwoods upbringing, because it always led people to underestimate him, especially his opponents.

And Burchfield might be one of them soon enough.

"Scagnelli's one of the best," Forsyth said. "And he won't talk once it's over."

"How can you be so sure?"

He couldn't. But he'd given the consultant enough amphetamines from the labs of Darrell Silver that Scagnelli would gobble just about anything Forsyth handed him.

"I've known Scagnelli since his DEA days," Forsyth said. "He can play both sides of the fence as good as anybody."

"Okay. Keep him close. Everybody who gets near this stuff seems to want a piece of it."

"Heaven forbid."

"And if this new Seethe works as good as the stuff Briggs made…" Burchfield trailed off, apparently casting about for dim memories of the Monkey House calamity. Forsyth's own memories of that night were of a lurid encounter with Satan, a vision that fully convinced Forsyth that the final days were upon them. Satan not only walked the Earth, but he was drawing ever closer to the nation's capital.

"Dr. Morgan is quite talented, Daniel," Forsyth said. "And she's also smart enough to know we're watching. That's why she's kept her guinea pig close to home."

"Mark?"

"That would explain a lot. He used to have a lot of sense. We had high hopes for that boy, despite him having an uppity liberal for a wife. But if she's been feeding him that monkey juice, it's no wonder he cracked."

"You don't think she'd do that to the man she loves, do you?"

"No. Only the one she married."

"What's that supposed to mean?"

"Seethe. If ever the devil was put into a pill, that's what he would look like. There ain't no morals with that stuff, and that's why the world better not get a hold of it."

"Wallace, I respect the hell out of you, but sometimes you're just a little too holier than thou. You don't have to frame everything as a moral issue."

"Well, somebody better. The only place the government's able to use the word *God* anymore is on money."

Forsyth was loyal enough to deliver Burchfield a powerful weapon for his Oval Office arsenal, but he wanted to ensure his own place in the administration first. And he wanted collateral in case Burchfield backed off his plan to start a war in Pakistan, igniting the tinderbox of Afghanistan and Iran, opening the door to massive U.S. military involvement and God's final battle. That's why he'd triggered the CIA investigation into the Morgans while making it appear Burchfield had started the inquiry.

"If Dr. Morgan has Seethe, how do we get it without killing everybody in sight?" Burchfield asked. "And what do we do with her afterwards?"

"There won't be any 'afterwards' this time," Forsyth said. "Scagnelli will make sure of that."

Alexis Morgan had been his philosophical adversary on the president's bioethics council, defending the benefits of what she considered "humane neurochemistry" to treat mental conditions. Forsyth saw the brain as God's domain, the seat of reason and choice, and its sole purpose was in making the decision to believe in that which had created it.

Intelligence existed to manifest temptation. Logic existed to lead humans to faith.

And God had shaped Wallace, guided him toward this destiny, and the president's council seemed like a distant dream on a long-forgotten night. Wallace had a role to serve, and he'd been placed in the perfect position to fulfill the prophecies.

After all, revelations weren't an option if God put them right into your head.

Which is where Dr. Morgan had it all wrong. Believing in God was not only natural, it was the highest purpose of brain function, whether that brain had evolved from monkeys or whether it had sprung full-blown into the world.

But she'd answer for that, for she'd never repent of her sorceries.

"You've got a campaign to worry about," Forsyth said to Burchfield. "Leave Seethe and Halcyon to me."

CHAPTER FOURTEEN

Alexis figured she'd better just play along.

The pistol was in the seat between them, but she ignored it. Mark was in the gray T-shirt and baggy athletic pants he called his "Dirty Harry warm-ups," and he wiped at his forehead as if cobwebs had collected there. He focused his gaze on the road ahead with an intensity that alarmed her.

"Class end early?" she asked.

"I was on call."

"Is that part of the training?"

"Everything's part of the training, honey."

Even his voice was slightly off, a clipped monotone that he might have used if talking to himself. She glanced at the mock police radio that had been installed below the dash. Wires had been ripped from it and the handset was lying in the floorboard in three pieces.

"Nice of them to let you take the car home," she said.

"We're not going home."

She glanced at him, but he didn't blink. "I have to be back in the lab this afternoon."

"They've been watching the house."

"We don't know that, Mark. We have a lot of research that corporate spies would love to get their greedy little paws on. I think the lab raid was about something else, not Seethe."

"It's always about Seethe."

They had crossed Franklin and Rosemary streets and were heading into the suburban outskirts of Chapel Hill, where Colonial-style homes were tucked behind fences beneath old oaks and towering pines. They passed a county patrol car coming from the other direction, but it didn't slow, much less follow them.

"Where are you going?" Alexis asked.

Mark's hands tightened on the wheel until his knuckles were white, and he looked at her for the first time since he'd insisted she get in the car. "You know."

"No, I don't."

"Where it all started."

A second surge of panic rolled through her. A hundred stories and images fought for attention, but they were like broken strips of film reassembled at random: the original Monkey House trials, where she'd been nothing but a diligent graduate assistant; the trials themselves; and one bloody and battered face—had *she* been part of that?

No. Remember it the way it happened. You were Briggs's assistant and that woman fell down the stairs and struck her head. A tragic accident and nothing more.

But the fresher waves of memories were harder to fend off. The events of a year ago had been carefully reconstructed, both externally and internally, and they stirred beneath a gently roiling surface. If Mark took her back to the Monkey House—or what was left of it—then they might rise in a psychotic tsunami and sweep away the levees and bulkheads of her defenses.

And nobody wanted the truth, least of all her.

"Mark, we can't do that. They might think we know something."

"Do we?"

"They've split us all up. Anita's hanging by a thread. David's locked away. I wouldn't be surprised if Wendy and Roland are out of the way, too. Maybe their move to the mountains wasn't voluntary."

She glanced at the gun. She couldn't risk provoking him in this state. The effects of Seethe could spin him in several unpredictable directions, and she realized how foolish she'd been in thinking she could treat the unknown.

I'm just as arrogant and deranged as Sebastian Briggs.

The realization stunned her because she'd been acting through a coherent scientific method. But if she couldn't trust her own motives and thought processes, how could she be confident she was doing the right thing? Maybe Briggs had been his own guinea pig, the first subject of the Monkey House trials, and his contamination by Seethe had led to his later madness.

God, what if I'm running past the fun-house mirrors myself? What if Seethe and Halcyon changed me in ways I can't even recognize?

"Lex?" Mark said, his tone normal but concerned. He took his right hand from the wheel and, for a moment, she had the image of him grabbing the gun and putting the barrel to her temple. Instead, he gave her a reassuring stroke on the forearm. "What do you remember about that night?"

"Just like we told each other. Briggs tricked us into coming back to the Monkey House and then he tried to kill us. But the federal agents got there first. There was an explosion and four people died."

"And we took the last of Briggs's Halcyon. They thought it was all destroyed, but we had it, didn't we?"

Her pulse accelerated, and she wondered if the lie would somehow show on her face. "You flushed it. You didn't trust anybody with it, even me."

He looked at her, dangerously ignoring the lunchtime traffic on the highway. "I can't remember. I might have given it to you. I love you, remember?"

He squeezed her arm with passion, but then the grip tightened until it hurt. She moaned and tried to pull free, but he dug his fingers into her soft flesh. He yanked her closer and the car swerved, causing car horns to blare around them.

"You're sick, Mark. Seethe did something to you. You don't see it, but you're changing."

He shoved her away and she bounced against the door. As he regained control of the cruiser, he took an exit ramp onto I-40, heading west.

"Why in hell should I believe you?" he said. "You think I don't know you've been in bed with them ever since Briggs revived the experiments? You think I didn't see the hunger in your eyes when you thought you could steal his work? And the goddamned government had you right in their sights, because they saw it, too. How goddamned hot for it you were."

Her lungs hurt and she could barely force air into them. *Paranoia. He's cracking apart and he doesn't even know it.*

"You're not making any sense, honey," she said. "You said yourself the government was watching us."

"No, not 'us.' Just me. You're right about one thing. I'm changing, and I can't think straight anymore." He pounded the wheel with one fist. "If only I could think straight, I'd figure this out."

The interstate traffic moved steadily, with consistent spacing. Otherwise, Mark's erratic driving might have drawn more attention. As it was, the weaving combined with the car's official appearance kept other motorists both well away and near the speed limit.

"Slow down and pull over," Alexis coaxed. A neurochemist by profession, she'd had her share of psychology classes. The first step was to calm him and then maybe he'd listen to reason.

If the Seethe exposure had permanently affected him, then he'd become more unstable by the minute, especially if his amygdala was hyperstimulated by anger or fear. And her Halcyon supply was on the middle shelf of the refrigerator back home. If she could get him there in one piece, they might have a chance.

"I have to know what happened," Mark said.

"The Monkey House is gone," she said. "The explosion caused a toxic spill and they had to level it."

"Maybe, but the truth is there somewhere."

"But we don't even know how to get there."

"I do. I remember more than I ever admitted." His face was dotted with sweat, his jaw tense, eyes wide and lit by a manic gleam.

"How could you remember, Mark? Halcyon wiped most of it away."

"That's what they all say." He cast a demented grin. "But since you've been dosing me with Seethe, it's all coming back to me."

She covered her mouth with her hand. "Honey, honey, honey," she whispered, scared and sad.

Signs of paranoid schizophrenia, manifesting as sociopathic rage. One of Briggs's suspected outcomes of end-stage exposure.

And not just "suspected." Desired.

They exited a side road into the Research Triangle Park, and the first of the glass-and-steel research and manufacturing facilities came into view.

"It all makes sense," Mark said, and his newfound rationality was even more unsettling than his earlier rage. "You and CRO and the feds get rid of Briggs, who was in everybody's way and uncontrollable. You take over, and Burchfield ties everything up with a nice bow so it looks like Seethe and Halcyon never happened. And the work goes on without a hitch, except now you've got all the backing you ever wanted and you've got your test monkey where you can keep an eye on him at all times."

"No, Mark, that's the Seethe talking—"

"Of course it's the fucking Seethe talking! That's what I am. That's what I do. That's what you've turned me into. You didn't need a fucking Monkey House, all you needed was a monkey."

His roar caused her to shrink away, and she considered opening the door and taking her chances on the grassy shoulder. But she was *his* only chance. She loved him so much, she could never abandon him when he needed her most.

Even if he didn't know it.

When you loved somebody, you lifted anchor and rode the tsunami with them.

Mark drove with purpose, the route apparently still clear in his mind although she only dimly recognized the scenery. She wondered how many times he might have driven out here, seeking answers as the lesions in his brain pulled apart all the memories and experiences that had shaped his life and made him Mark Morgan.

Alexis risked a glance at his profile, the sheen of his moist forehead, his unkempt hair, his curled upper lip. *How much of my husband is still left in there?*

He fell silent after his eruption. His mood swings were getting more erratic by the minute. She'd miscalculated terribly. The Halcyon she'd been administering had not been helping him. Instead, it had only masked his deterioration and allowed her the placebo of helpfulness.

He turned off the highway onto a narrow, crumbling access road. Visible through the surrounding pine trees was a chain-link fence running parallel to the road. It was topped with barbed wire. Alexis strained to see beyond it, but the foliage was too thick.

Still, she knew they were approaching the Monkey House.

"I was telling the truth," she said quietly, trying to sound reasonable.

"We'll see about that."

"If I was working for the government, do you think they'd let you kidnap me? Wouldn't I be far too important to take the risk of your killing me? And would I have told you about the lab raid?"

Mark glanced in the rearview mirror. Then he shook his head. "Here's the deal. They need you, but they need me, too. Right? You know how the brain processes it, the theory behind it, the molecular structure, but I am living and breathing the shit. I *am* Seethe."

They came to a steel cable strung between two poles embedded in concrete. Beyond that was a gate set in the fence, tangled with honeysuckle and poison sumac. It hadn't been used in a long time.

Not since the cleanup a year ago.

Mark stopped the car, collected the gun, and motioned her out. When they were both standing by the steel cable, Mark said, "In there's where it all happened."

"There's nothing here, Mark."

"Then you don't need to worry, do you?" He knelt and rolled up the leg of his athletic pants, revealing a holster strapped inside his ankle. He slid the gun into it and smoothed his clothes.

Alexis followed him through the weed-choked entrance to the gate. Beyond it was a stand of scrub pines, and in a clearing was a blackened circle, a few piles of masonry rubble, and deep gouges in the red clay. A dented "No Trespassing" sign leaned to one side in the center of what had once been the Monkey House. She released a breath she hadn't realized she'd been holding.

"That's what happened to the people we used to be," Mark said. "That's where we died and didn't know it."

CHAPTER FIFTEEN

Butner was a small town about fifteen miles north of Durham. It had been known as Camp Butner during World War II, an army training facility that later became a home for injured veterans. The town of nearly six thousand people had maintained that institutional identity ever since, housing several prisons, a federal correctional facility, some state agency headquarters, and the largest mental hospital in North Carolina.

Forsyth had driven himself to Butner after leaving Burchfield in Winston-Salem. He could have used Abernethy and the limo, since Burchfield planned to spend the night at home, but Forsyth didn't want anyone to know of his movements, especially the Secret Service.

He was just exiting I-85 when the cell phone rang and he had to fumble through several jacket pockets to find it. "Forsyth here."

"Scagnelli."

"Do you got anything?" Forsyth didn't bother with correct grammar when he was away from the press.

"No. They headed out to the Research Triangle Park, and I figured they were working with somebody out there. Thought I'd get lucky and they'd lead me right to the secret lab."

"You might as well expect a wild hog to grub up a truffle and drop it on your dinner plate," Forsyth said. "You ought to know by now that 'secret' means everybody don't know about it."

"Well, the Secret Service has a Twitter account. That's hardly a good way to keep secrets."

Forsyth knew Twitter was some kind of Internet thing, and he was happy to stay away from it. As far as he could tell, all it did was get people in trouble when they said things they shouldn't.

"You don't have to worry about what the Secret Service does. You'd better be worrying about what Dominic Scagnelli does. Don't forget who you work for."

"You say that a lot."

"Because you work for *me*. Where are the Morgans now?"

"They're walking around an abandoned lot. I checked out the property on my laptop. It's owned by CRO Pharmaceuticals but apparently it was shut down after a fatal industrial accident last year."

"You don't say."

"Morgan worked for CRO. Real high up the ladder, a guy just doing his job. And he gave it all up to become a cop?"

"No, he gave it up for his wife. He just didn't know it at the time."

"Women. They sure know how to fuck up a good thing. The most selfish creatures on God's green earth."

Forsyth winced a little. He'd been married once. He'd lain his lovely Louisa to rest fifteen years back, and he'd never found her equal. He was content to finish up his time here and be reunited in heaven with his monogamy still intact.

Scagnelli sputtered on, the amphetamines fueling his tirade. "After the nuclear holocaust when all the dust settles, first will come the cockroaches, and then some cats will pussyfoot out of their holes. And then a few women will crawl out of the rubble. If ever you want to learn about self-preservation—"

"Did the Morgans see you?"

"Of course not." Scagnelli sounded offended, which was exactly what Forsyth intended. "He looks a little jittery but otherwise they're just hacking through the weeds like they're looking for a way inside the fence."

"Monitor them but don't take no action."

"What if they find something?"

"There ain't nothing left to find."

"Okay, I'll just send you a text."

"Why don't you Twitter it?"

"Tweet."

"Whatever. Or ram it up a carrier pigeon's butt and have it sing 'Dixie' on the way over."

Scagnelli laughed, taking Forsyth's gruffness for folksy humor. Forsyth could tell Scagnelli was underestimating him. Just the way he liked it.

He clicked the cell phone dead and turned into the parking lot of Central Regional Hospital. It had once been named Umstead Hospital after one of the state's endless series of mental-health reformers dating all the way back to Dorothea Dix, whose own namesake hospital was nearly dead.

Two and a half centuries of meddling in people's heads and they still ain't got things right.

The hospital was two stories at ground level, although it was set on a gentle slope that allowed for a lower floor at the back end of the building. The flat roof and glass façade suggested a 1990s-era design, back when architects didn't realize how quickly their futuristic designs would look bulldozer-ready. The lot was relatively empty, since the hospital didn't get a lot of visitors. Many of the patients were of the sort that no one wanted to acknowledge, much less spend time with.

The assistant director was waiting by the front desk, wearing a crisp pants suit. She was of late middle-age, her hair white and fluffy, although her face was relatively unlined. She greeted him with a smile and shining blue eyes that suggested unflagging optimism in the face of her grim duties as a shepherd of the lost and hopeless.

"Mr. Forsyth," she said, shaking his hand like a man. "I'm a fan of your work. Except for that proposal to cut federal support for mental health services. I'm Paula Redfern."

"A real pleasure, Dr. Redfern. And about that—"

"I know you're a busy man, so let's not waste your time. Besides, I don't vote in your district."

As she led him down the hall and into the labyrinth, Forsyth found himself admiring her spunk as she described the various missions of the hospital. He liked the graceful way she moved, too, but he was wise enough to keep it on an aesthetic level, like a man watching someone else's thoroughbred gallop through a meadow.

"We focus on interdisciplinary approaches individualized to each patient's desired therapeutic outcomes," she said.

"I ain't sure what that means," he said, "but your funding just went up a million dollars."

She laughed and kept on with the tour. Forsyth was pleased the hospital had honored his request to keep the tour private. Because every entity receiving public funding was now in intense competition with all the other entities, people grabbed any advantage they could. Everybody in the country was in favor of smaller government until it came time to take a pay cut themselves.

"We're not just a treatment center, we have research and forensic wings as well," Dr. Redfern said. "UNC and Duke conduct research work here."

"I know a few researchers down this way," Forsyth said. "As you know, I'm a close friend of Senator Burchfield's and—"

"I vote against him every chance I get, but I am sure he's an honorable man in private."

They were entering the Acute Adult Unit, where psychiatric patients with little hope of release were confined. Dr. Redfern continued on with her chipper presentation in wholesale denial of the fact that the ward wasn't much of an upgrade from the mental asylums of old. The main differences were better lighting and a diverse array of designer drugs, plus the fact that the public couldn't pay admission to derive some cheap entertainment.

Forsyth signed in with an armed guard while Redfern blathered airily about the "pathophysiology and psychosocial precipitants of mental illness," getting an extra lift when she started in on "comprehensive community-based intervention modules."

The first patient they passed, a shuffling young man in paper slippers with a strand of drool dangling down to his chest, looked like he could care less what the community thought.

Forsyth nodded at him out of rote politeness but the man simply took another sliding step away from reality and toward whatever mercy God granted the deranged.

The patients in open confinement were largely clean and passive. A bald black man sat playing checkers with himself, although there was no board on the coffee table. A woman in street clothes stood looking out the barred window as if waiting for a bus that would never come. Another woman with palsy muttered to herself over and over, and it took Forsyth a moment to realize she was faithfully reciting the Gospel According to Luke.

Then they entered the ward with the private rooms. These resembled regular hospital rooms, although through the doors of the unoccupied ones, Forsyth saw padding on the walls and restraint devices made of steel and leather. An occasional wail reverberated from a distant hellhole, a sound as lonely of that of a barn owl in the October night.

"What's your interest in Mr. Underwood?" Dr. Redfern asked.

"One of those researchers I spoke of asked me to look in on him," Forsyth said. "A cousin. Just between you and me, I suspect he's afraid that sort of thing runs in the family."

A few howls stitched themselves together into a caterwauling melody. It wasn't until the sounds repeated that Forsyth made it out. The old western folk song "Home on the Range."

"Mr. Underwood is one of our more...*interesting*...cases," Dr. Redfern said. "He's clinging to a persistent delusion that he's the subject of a secret government experiment. He was connected with a clinical trial during his college years, and one of the subjects died. Apparently the guilt and trauma lingered, triggering a latent schizophrenia."

Forsyth probed her a little in case David Underwood's psychotic ramblings had aroused any suspicion. "I thought schizophrenia was genetic."

"There are certainly links," she said. "But current research is focusing on neurobiology. Drug use could worsen such a condition."

"What kind of drugs?"

"Anything mind-altering or mood-altering."

Then they were outside the room from which the wailing came. Forsyth wondered if Underwood would remember him. But the great thing about a nutcase, nobody believed anything they said.

They peered through a glass observational window. Underwood sat on a cot, hunched forward and staring at the floor. His hair was clipped close and his ill-fitting gown was draped over his gaunt frame.

Forsyth noted that Underwood's present circumstances were not that different from when he'd been held captive in Sebastian Briggs's lab and used as a test monkey. The only thing that had changed since then was the name of the zookeeper.

"Is he responding to medication?" Forsyth asked, making conversation.

"He's on several new antipsychotic drugs," Dr. Redfern said. "He's also presenting anxiety and depression, and because he's such a risk, I'm afraid he doesn't have much hope for release. He's got the major first-rank symptom of schizophrenia."

"What's that?"

"The belief that his thoughts are controlled by an external force. In his case, he believes he's been brainwashed by the government."

"I could make a grand joke of that, but it doesn't look like a laughing matter," Forsyth said.

"Still, he deserves the same compassionate care that Central Regional aspires to administer to all its patients," Dr. Redfern said, once again lapsing into a robo-cheerleader for her facility.

"Of that, I've no doubt," Forsyth said. He took one more glance at David Underwood and was surprised he didn't feel a twinge of sympathy for the man.

Too goddamned long in politics. Your heart is the first thing to go, and then you lose your soul. God help me. God help us all.

"Did you want to see him personally?" Dr. Redfern asked, eager to please.

"No," he said, making a show of glancing at his wristwatch. "Is Darrell Silver available?"

Redfern's mood darkened a little. "Of course. Federal inmates under treatment place a particularly heavy burden on a facility like ours, as you can imagine."

Add another million to that funding request, Doctor. Maybe we should put you on Daniel's staff. You would make a mighty fine health secretary and I'd bet you'd say whatever it took to make the administration look good.

And being pretty don't hurt a bit.

"I understand Silver's been charged with drug manufacturing and conspiracy," he said.

"This way." Redfern led him down the hall and around a bend, passing rooms in which involuntary patients spent their time until the next dose, meal, or change of underwear.

Alone with nothing but their thoughts. Satan has truly been loosed for a season and his millennium is coming up.

Forsyth's Pentecostal upbringing had softened a little in the face of political realities, melding into a more palatable fundamentalism as he became entrenched in Congress. Extremes of every kind tended to get blunted by the forge and hammer of the corporations, lobbyists, and party leaders.

Still, he felt Armageddon was near—not in the literal sense of a climactic battle in the Middle East, but in a general erosion of the human spirit. Where others saw Satan's armies attacking from the field, Forsyth believed Satan delivered destruction from the inside out.

Just like those drugs, Seethe and Halcyon, did.

Forsyth wondered if that was more than a coincidence.

Redfern was blithely enumerating all the funding challenges in the face of rising costs and the threat that national health care posed. Forsyth mumbled assurances that one of Burchfield's top priorities was to revise the landmark legislation, although they all knew that entitlements were nearly impossible to take away once people got used to them.

Soon they came to a thicker door with a security camera and keypad. After Redfern logged in and was identified, they were buzzed into an antechamber where an armed and uniformed guard staffed a desk, surrounded by security monitors and alarm systems. Both of them had to sign another log, and then they entered a second door.

The rooms on this floor were a cross between prison cells and hospital rooms. Another armed guard patrolled the hallway, a tall, sunburnt man who greeted Redfern by name and gave Forsyth a sideways grin.

"Tell Senator Burchfield I'm voting for him," the guard said. "I've voted for him in every election since he ran for the State House, and I'm not about to stop now."

"I'll do that," Forsyth said. "And thank you for your vital service here. Is Mr. Silver ready?"

"In interrogation like you requested."

Redfern beamed in satisfaction at the show of efficiency. The guard led the way to the room as Redfern explained, "Usually lawyers meet their clients here, and if the inmates are deemed competent, they are sometimes asked questions by investigators."

Forsyth didn't want to ask who did the "deeming," but he was sure the taxpayers were footing the bill for some egghead to write big words that added up to either "Nuts" or "Probably guilty."

Darrell Silver was seated at a table, shackled to a steel bar that was welded to the table's edge. He appeared calm and was relatively clean, although Forsyth was surprised the man was allowed to keep his beard and unhealthy-looking dreadlocks. He could have passed for a street musician if not for the orange scrubs and his spasmodically twitching right eyelid.

"Where's my lawyer?" Silver asked.

"It's okay, Mr. Silver," Redfern said. "We're not interrogating you. Mr. Forsyth is touring our facilities. He's a member of the president's bioethics council."

"Are you being treated well, Mr. Silver?" Forsyth asked, sitting at the table across from him. Redfern joined him while the guard waited at the end of the room.

"Not too bad. They have some awesome drugs in here," Silver said.

"I understand you worked with Dr. Alexis Morgan," Forsyth said, watching the way Silver's eyes narrowed like those of a cornered animal's. "She served with us on the council for a while."

"Yeah, I did some research for her."

"What were y'all working on?"

"I thought you weren't going to ask any questions."

Forsyth held up a palm and smiled. "Just making conversation, Mr. Silver. No need to go getting riled up."

"Well, if you ask me, she ought to be the one in here, not me."

"Is that so?"

Dr. Redfern gave Forsyth a sympathetic look, as if Silver had just revealed his own paranoid delusions. "Mr. Silver also believes he's involved in a secret government conspiracy," Dr. Redfern said.

"Sounds like a contagious idea," Forsyth said, staring fully into Silver's eyes. "What did Dr. Morgan do that was so terrible?"

"*She* did it. She gave me the formula, asked me to cook it up for her."

"A formula? Some secret government drug?" Forsyth gave Redfern a surreptitious wink.

"Yeah. She called it Halcyon. It's supposed to make you forget stuff. I played with it, put my own spin on it. That's my style."

Dr. Redfern cut in, speaking as if the inmate wasn't present. "Mr. Silver has a record of illegal drug manufacturing. LSD, methamphetamine, OxyContin. His diagnosis states chronic drug use has damaged his perceptions of reality."

"You call it 'damaged,' I call it 'superduperfied,'" Silver said, swinging his dreadlocks in his exuberance. "What's in a name, right? I mean, if they called MDMA 'Funny Puppy' instead of 'Mad Dog,' everybody would be taking it. It's all about marketing, man."

Forsyth ruminated while Silver finished his rant, and then said, "Do you think you could recreate this Halcyon?"

"No prob, dude."

"You have a vast range of experience, Mr. Silver," Forsyth said. "I think we can work something out."

He gave a lopsided grin. "You think I don't know what's going on here?"

"What?" Forsyth asked.

"You guys are in on it. This Halcyon stuff. She said I had to be careful because important people were watching. People all the way up to the top."

"That's what I'm worried about," Forsyth said. "If people in the government have secret drugs, then they can take away anybody's rights at any time by making you think a certain way. By changing your mind. Why, they can even make you crazy, right?"

Silver's eyes narrowed again, as if he was figuring Forsyth's angle. "I tried some of that stuff. I can't remember what it was like."

Dr. Redfern's face furrowed in deep concern and solemn sorrow. Forsyth was sure she'd refined that look in a mirror.

"Did Dr. Morgan ever mention a drug called Seethe?" Forsyth said.

"No, but it sounds cool," Silver said. "Upper?"

"It doesn't exist," he replied. "But we got reason to think Dr. Morgan may be under a bit of…strain. As you can likely appreciate, her previous post as a presidential advisor means her actions reflect on all of us. If she needs help, she deserves the finest treatment and…" Forsyth turned to Dr. Redfern. "What did you call that?"

"Continuum of care," she said, pleased to contribute.

"She didn't talk about Seethe, but she did seem a little freaked out," Silver said. "I offered her some weed to help her chill, but she said she didn't do drugs." He gave a sudden bark of laughter. "Doesn't do drugs. Now that's what I call *crazy*, man."

"Thank you for the information. Mr. Silver," Forsyth said, rising from his chair. "I'll be sure to put in a good word for you with the federal prosecutors."

"But this wasn't an interrogation, right? If it was, I'd have had a lawyer and stuff, right?" As they retreated, he raised his voice to yell at their backs. "Unless my lawyer's in on it, too."

After the guard let them out, Dr. Redfern said, "We have more secret government drug conspiracies per square foot than any facility in the country, it seems."

Forsyth gave an understanding smile, one full of paternal concern and a veiled promise of support. "Just between you and me, I think it's the aliens and their little mind-scrambling ray guns."

Dr. Redfern granted him a coy and unprofessional titter.

CHAPTER SIXTEEN

Roland checked the entire cabin, which wasn't large, but he had to be careful not to arouse Wendy's suspicions. The cabin was basically one open floor with a loft bedroom. While Wendy collected painting supplies for her afternoon session, Roland searched under the bed and the tiny closet.

He wasn't sure what he was looking for, but he couldn't shake the feeling that someone had been in the cabin. It didn't make sense, because they hadn't been anywhere except for their usual afternoon walk. They would have heard a car on the long gravel driveway, and the remote rural area held little attraction for burglars and thieves.

His laptop was on the table where he'd left it, and they didn't have a television or other items easily pawned for cash. And they certainly didn't have any money or jewelry.

The gun.

He jogged toward the loft stairs, nearly slamming into Wendy at the landing.

"Hey!" she said, gathering her paints in her arms.

He ran to the bedside table, cursing himself for letting down his guard. He should have been carrying the gun on the walk.

However close or far away, somebody was watching them. And they could be *very* close.

"What are you freaking out about?" Wendy called from below.

"Shh," he hissed, sliding open the table drawer. And there it was.

He pulled out the gun as Wendy joined him in the loft. "Did you see the fox?"

"Yeah." He hurried back down to the open door and gazed into the woods, feeling a little stupid. A breeze played through the leaves, making a sound like faint laughter.

After a moment, he sensed Wendy behind him. "Maybe you should practice with that thing," she said. "You're not going to get many more chances."

She nudged past him and he made room for her, looking at the .38 revolver. As she spread her paint tubes around the easel, he glanced back at the table.

The laptop.

It was still there, but was it in the exact same position he'd left it? He tried to recall his last online activity. He'd been working on some lettering for a proposal. That had been before lunch.

Roland opened the laptop and powered it from its sleep. The Photoshop file came up, just as he'd last saved it. He knew the hard drive contained fingerprints of all commands the computer had ever performed, but such a search was well beyond his technical skills.

He looked at the USB ports on the side. Someone could have slipped a zip drive in and quickly downloaded his files.

But why? Maybe Wendy's right. You're getting paranoid.

But the e-mails were real. Even if it was the aftereffects of Seethe that were making him paranoid, that didn't change the fact that someone knew about the Monkey House. And probably that he was a murderer.

National Clandestine Service, Burchfield, the enemy within.

God, grant me the serenity to—

Ah, fuck it.

He went out on the porch, the gun concealed in his pocket. Wendy made graceful strokes with her brush, powerful and confident gashes of dark red. She was in one of her moods.

Maybe it was guilt, subconsciously revealing itself in the figure huddled in a dark corner.

"Wendy?"

"Just a minute," she said in that distracted, annoyed manner of the self-absorbed artist. She'd changed her style, slapping out lines and curls in a type of calligraphy. She worked until she was satisfied with the red, then she dabbed her brush in a jar of water.

She turned and put an impatient hand on her hip, the brush dripping onto the porch. "I hate it when you interrupt me."

"This is important."

"So is *this*." She stabbed the brush toward the painting. "I'm getting close, I can feel it. What I'm trying to say."

"I know what you're looking for in there."

She laughed. "You're not going to start that stuff about conspiracies, are you?"

He wanted to grab her by the shoulders and shake her awake, describe how the drugs slept inside her like a pair of evil twins, one committing dark deeds and the other enabling. But his few attempts at honesty had ended with his feeling slightly unhinged, like a drunk emerging from a blackout in total denial of all the accompanying sins.

"No," he said. "I was just wondering what you were painting."

"What I'm always painting," she said. "The monkey we left behind."

"I see that. Can I ask you something?"

Wendy made a pantomime of looking around to see if he might be talking to anyone else. "Just between you and me?"

"Yeah. I got an e-mail yesterday. And another one this morning."

"You get lots of e-mails."

"The first said, 'Every four hours or else.'" He watched her face to see if her expression was any different this time.

"I know. That book cover you're working on." She appeared bemused but slightly annoyed at having her work interrupted.

He tried the next one on her. "'Surely you didn't think we could let you live, after what happened.'"

"Is that from the book, too?"

Wendy was genuinely confused. Roland relaxed a little, willing to let her off the hook. Of all the survivors of the Monkey House, she was the most detached and innocent. Alexis had explained the drugs caused individualized reactions, not surprising considering Briggs had been scrambling with a big chemical spatula, but even Alexis didn't seem to remember the real effects of Seethe and Halcyon.

Roland sure as hell did. Because he could still feel them inside his skull, fighting for control. Seethe commanded him to wipe that naïve look off his wife's face forever, because the mask disguised all her hideous, carnal behavior. Halcyon kneaded his memories like Play-Doh until he was no longer sure exactly which sins she'd committed.

He wondered if his alcoholism had created a special response to the two drugs. He often thought of his alcoholism as a living entity, a shadow creature lurking inside him and compelling him toward self-destruction. His addictive nature might have opened up inviting paths, and just as an alcoholic was one drink away from a lifelong binge, lying might be keeping the drugs active inside him.

Maybe it was time for a little honesty.

"It's from the Monkey House, honey," he said. "That night in the Research Triangle when I killed Sebastian Briggs."

She grinned as if he were joking. "You couldn't kill a fly."

"Somebody thinks we know something," he said. "That we remember."

"Well, they're wasting their time."

"I think they're after us."

"Are you okay, Ro? You're looking a little pale."

He felt a little shaky, but he refused to believe the chemicals in his head were changing him and causing delusions. Compared to a decade of heavy drinking, this was even scarier, because with drinking, you could always stop one day at time. But *this*—this tap stayed wide open forever, gushing barrels and barrels of its poison.

"I'm sorry, honey. I tried sparing you from it." He staggered toward her, his arms wide. She stepped back from his embrace.

"Whatever it is, we can face it together." Awareness flashed across her face. "Oh, God. You started drinking again, didn't you?"

He shook his head. It was natural for her to assume the worst, because with a drunk like him, the worst was just a matter of time.

He reached for her as she withdrew. "They've been sending me e-mails, and I think somebody was in the house while we were gone. You told them, didn't you?"

"Stay back," Wendy said, holding up her brush like a weapon. "Alexis said this might happen."

"Have you been talking to her?"

Wendy's eyes gave a furtive flick left and right, looking for the correct lie. "She's been…coaching me. About how we could make it through this."

"Why the *fuck* didn't you tell me?" He could feel the cords tighten in his neck as the sudden rage swept through him.

"*Look* at you," she wailed. "You're a goddamned time bomb. How am I supposed to tell you anything?"

He stopped, two feet away. She was pinned against the porch railing beside the easel. "You're one to talk about trust," he said, hissing the last word like an accusation.

"You said you loved me the way I was."

"The only fucking lie worth telling." The anger was a live, palpable force, a red entity invading his limbs. He panted as his pulse accelerated. He was dizzy, high, disoriented to all except that one bitching, conniving face in front of him.

The courage to change the things I can…

Her eyes widened in fear, her small mouth an O of shock and disappointment.

Roland had one last fleeting thought—*it's not me, it's the Seethe, it's always the Seethe*—but just as whiskey trumped reason every single time, his self-righteous fury infected him with the obsessive fever of revenge.

"Alexis was right," Wendy said.

That's not what I want to hear, honey. What I want to hear is that you're sorry, that you didn't mean to make me murder for you. I want you to apologize for being a slut, even if you can't help it.

He thrust his hand toward her face, meaning to grab her hair and twist until she submitted, but she was faster. She scooped up the jar of rinse water and splashed it toward him, and the dark gray liquid slapped him in the face like a rag. She shoved past, knocking over the easel as she fled.

Roland wiped his face with his shirt sleeve and let out a bellow of anger. Eyes stinging, he kicked at the painting, and the toe of his leather boot went through the huddled monkey on the canvas.

He drew the pistol as he ran, but she was already in the woods by the time he regained his vision.

The bitch painted me. Well, there's a price for that. Yeah, we're going to have us a talk about respect and submission and surrender.

A long, long talk, the kind that would make Sebastian Briggs proud.

Leaves rattled ahead of him. So he'd be hunting a tiger instead of a fox. Seethe didn't care one way or another.

As he entered the woods, he forgot all about government conspiracies, mysterious e-mails, and death threats.

It was the worst of both worlds, but then again, with Roland, the worst was always just a matter of time.

CHAPTER SEVENTEEN

Gundersson had been caught by surprise when the couple returned early. Their walks were usually twenty minutes, and over the last three days, he'd taken the opportunity to search the downstairs and the bathroom. He'd been searching the loft, looking for any signs of Seethe, when Roland's boots banged on the porch below.

Gundersson had lifted the screen from the window above the bed, swung it up on its hinges, and climbed through, dangling by his fingers to lessen the distance of the drop. Still, it was good twelve feet, and when he hit the ground, his ankle twisted on a tree root. The chickens had squawked in alarm, and Gundersson hissed a quiet curse of pain.

He heard them talking inside the house, ignoring the chickens, and he made his way into the woods. The pain was worse by the time he reached the trail. He crouched beside the creek and massaged his ankle, waiting to see if someone would notice the window. He was good at leaving no trace, a real Boy Scout.

The forest immediately around the cabin was dense with laurel tangles, crabapples, and blackberry vines, pocked here and there with old-growth oaks and maples like the one he used as a surveillance post. He didn't have time to reach the tree, and he wasn't sure he could climb it with his game leg, anyway.

Then the argument had started, and he figured he might overhear something important despite the gurgling of the water over stones. He caught "Sebastian Briggs" and he figured "Alexis" referred to Dr. Morgan, which suggested the couples had been in contact. But the sudden explosion of Roland's anger caught him unaware, and now Wendy was running right toward him.

He rolled to his feet and lightning raced up his leg. He put weight on the injured ankle and realized he'd never make it to concealment.

Might be broken.

His orders were clear: Avoid detection at any cost. He couldn't afford to blow this mission through overconfidence. And he'd been warned what would happen if he was forced to leave corpses.

I'll chew your ass like bubble gum and leave you stuck on the director's toilet seat, Harding had said.

Wendy was coming up the trail about twenty yards from Gundersson, slapping at limbs and panting hard as she ran. He glanced around and saw a tiny recess where water had washed away soil beneath a hemlock's roots. He lay down in the cold, shallow water and wriggled into the damp crevice. He wasn't completely concealed, but he hoped they were too preoccupied to notice.

"I know you're in there!" Roland shouted, just now entering the woods, apparently moving a little more slowly than she was.

Is he talking to me? Shit, if he saw me—

"Wendy!" Roland sounded more angry than concerned.

Ah, a lover's spat. With firearms.

Through a gnarled web of exposed roots, he watched Wendy jog along the trail, lithe and graceful but gasping for air. She was dressed in her stained painter's frock, a psychedelic camouflage that would hide her in a Phish concert but not here in the Blue

Ridge forest. Then she was gone, and Gundersson lifted himself from the bone-chilling water.

Roland had stopped yelling for Wendy, so Gundersson couldn't place his location. The bracing water had numbed his ankle a little, so he hobbled onto the opposite bank and found refuge in the scrub. He considered drawing his weapon, but that wouldn't fit his cover story.

After a full minute, he got curious and wriggled like a snake until he could peer through the low willows. Some wild mint crushed beneath him, mixing with the fecund, earthy aroma of the creek. He gingerly pushed a blackberry vine aside and saw Roland scanning the spot where Gundersson had tended his ankle. After a moment, Roland bent down and picked up something from the ground.

Gundersson felt his pants pocket. *Shit.*

He'd placed three tiny wireless microphones in the cabin, but the place was so small he hadn't needed the fourth. And it must have worked out of his pocket while he was rolling around in pain.

So much for getting answers the easy way.

"Wendy!" Roland shouted again, the anger leaving his voice. "I found something."

After a moment, he added, "I'm not going to hurt you."

Wow. If you actually have to say those words, it's not a good sign.

Judging by the awkward bulge in Roland's pocket, he would probably hurt if he had to. And he wasn't hunting foxes this time.

"Wendy!" Roland called again. "It's not you. It's *them.*"

Gundersson ground his teeth together. On the bright side, at least Wendy was unlikely to find his camp. He'd have to scuttle the mission, and Harding would be an unhappy camper as well, but at least he'd avoided disaster.

All he had to do was wait it out, then limp half a mile through the woods and collect his gear, and—

"I know," Wendy called.

From right behind him.

Gundersson rolled up on his side and considered going for his gun. She was unarmed, standing above him with flared nostrils and darkly intense eyes. She wasn't menacing, given her small stature, but she was crouched and tense as if ready to explode. He wondered if she knew *jiu jitsu* or karate, and figured that was probably racist, because she was more American than Asian.

He decided to wait on the gun until Roland decided for him.

"Over here," Wendy called to Roland.

As Roland splashed through the creek, Gundersson managed a smile. "I hope I wasn't trespassing," he said to Wendy.

"I hope you weren't, either. My husband is a little paranoid."

Gundersson started to agree, but then remembered his cover story. He adjusted his tone to sound casual and a little rural. "I'm a travel writer, doing a piece on backwoods hiking for *Appalachian Today*. I followed this trail up from Buffalo Bald," he added, remembering a colorful name from the map. "Twisted my ankle and fell in the creek."

"Where's your camera?" Wendy said.

It was in his watch, but he couldn't tell her that. "I just take notes," he said. "They send the photographer separately. I can't even take a mug shot without getting my thumb in the way."

He tried a disarming smile but her oval face was hard as jade. Roland crashed through the shrubs along the creek bank and gave Wendy a glance before looking down at Gundersson.

"I was just telling your wife here—"

Roland gave him a hard kick in the ribs that drove out both his words and his breath. He raised a hand to ward off the next blow, examining Roland's posture.

I'd lay four-to-one odds I'll get my gun out before he does. But then I'd have to kill her, too.

"Who owns you?" Roland said.

"Excuse me?" Gundersson wheezed, giving diplomacy one last feeble attempt. "A magazine, like I told your wife."

"He said he's a travel writer," Wendy said.

"No notebook, no camera, no laptop?" Roland said. "Unless you have a zip drive in your pocket. Do you have a zip drive?"

Gundersson was relieved that Roland hadn't fished for his gun. He decided he had only one chance to buy some time and maybe even complete the mission.

He sat up, brushing blackberry blossoms from his arms. "Okay," he said. "Would you believe me if I told you I was a federal agent?"

"Great," Wendy said. "Tell the most unbelievable lie possible."

Shell game. Half the truth.

"I'm with the Central Intelligence Agency," he said, looking directly into Roland's eyes and not blinking. "We know you've been targeted by the National Clandestine Service. And we're conducting an internal investigation to find out why."

"What's he talking about, Ro?" Wendy said.

Roland raised his hand to quiet her, a big change from a minute ago when he'd seemed intent on brutalizing her. But she'd calmed down as well, as if learning to ride out his wild mood swings. He handed her the tiny microphone he'd found.

"Yeah, we got some e-mails," Roland said. "It made references to the Monkey House trials. If you're really a fed, you probably know about those."

Gundersson nodded. He couldn't believe he was winning Roland's trust so easily. Uncle Sam might save a few bucks on ammunition today.

"Yeah," Gundersson said. "Can you keep a secret?"

"That's our full-time job," Roland said, with a bitter laugh. Wendy eased over to her husband's side and gripped his arm in loyalty, as if she'd already forgiven his homicidal rage.

Jesus. I'm glad I've never been in love. Talk about shell games.

Gundersson thought about standing, but he didn't trust his ankle and Roland would consider him less threatening if he maintained an inferior position. But he also wondered if copperheads or water moccasins might be sliding through the weeds and rotten leaves.

"The NCS thinks you guys have the drug Dr. Briggs was testing on you. I'm not supposed to tell you this but…"

Gundersson licked his lips. Neither Roland's nor Wendy's faces expressed eagerness. But neither did they show fear. If half the stuff in the file was true, they had faced down more torments than a normal person would undergo in Dante's nine circles of hell.

He continued. "Somebody in the NCS wants you dead."

"Yeah, I got the memo," Roland said, drawing a confused look from Wendy.

"They said it was all destroyed in the fire," Wendy said. "And we don't remember anything anyway. The other drug, Halcyon, wiped it all away. At least, that's how Alexis explained it."

She said it with such hope, with such a fervent desire to believe the trials had never happened, that Gundersson almost regretted having to drag it all out again. Roland must have worked hard to protect her, but his instability was a lingering effect of the drug exposure.

Another reason why half the truth could get us all killed, including me.

"Look," Gundersson said. "My job is to keep an eye on you so the NCS doesn't get what they want."

Roland's hand crawled to his pocket, where he cupped the outline of the gun like a teen jock flaunting his package. "And you expect us to believe the U.S. government is interested in protecting the rights and the lives of ordinary American citizens?"

Gundersson saw that brand of bullshit wouldn't fly. So he decided on another half-truth. "If I find Seethe, then I take it back to Washington, the heat follows me, and you guys live the rest of your lives out of the spotlight," he said. "Once it's not a secret—at least, not *your* secret—there's nothing the NCS needs to take from you."

"And no need to kill us to keep us quiet."

"Maybe you need to talk to Alexis," Wendy said. "She said somebody's been watching her."

Gundersson's heart skipped a beat. *Fuck. I knew there were free agents working the case, and I wouldn't be surprised if the CIA wanted a piece of the action, but maybe somebody's closer than Harding told me. In which case, I can't even trust my own people.*

"Hush, honey," Roland said, the supportive husband again. "Let him talk."

"Can I get up first?" Gundersson said.

Roland took out his revolver and pointed it at Gundersson's chest. "As long as you can do it without making me nervous."

CHAPTER EIGHTEEN

Dominic Scagnelli took a sip of his Pike Place Roast and glanced around the Starbucks. The shop was redolent of scorched beans, old newsprint, and a faint chocolate odor that lay over it all like fudge sauce. At the table across from him slouched a Japanese chick with a purple Mohawk, obligatory painful-looking nose ring, and a stained white wifebeater that clearly revealed she was braless.

Is it a "wifebeater" when a woman is wearing it, or do they call it a "tank top"?

The way America was headed, she very well *could* have a wife, and she very well could be beating her like rented mule. He was tired of Chapel Hill and its post-grads with no job prospects and a deep fear of leaving such a haven of the chronically hip. He was ready for a change of scenery.

Still, he didn't like Forsyth's new plan.

Killing was easy and usually led to a lackluster, by-the-numbers investigation. Murder was so common that unsolved cases didn't seem to bother anyone except the victim's family. And once those tears dried up, or fresher tears erupted, the media packed their tents and hit the next freak show.

Plus, Scagnelli had ways of eliminating people that left no fingerprints. Anita Molkesky's death had probably been discovered by now, but it hadn't raised any public alarm. For all their prurience, the media had an unwritten code of not covering suicides, their one bit of false morality disguised as sensitivity to the feelings of the survivors. Since her death was unattended—as far as investigators knew—the ME would be called in for an examination, but given Anita's history and the copious amounts of drugs in her system, it would be a simple matter of documenting a foregone conclusion.

Scagnelli wouldn't take the same route with Mark Morgan. If he had his way, he'd go with an automobile mishap of some kind. After Mark's little exhibition in his law-enforcement class, his reckless behavior created the perfect cover story. Hell, even a self-inflicted gunshot wound would have done the job.

But kidnapping was complicated compared to murder.

For one thing, a corpse was easy to handle. But a living person tended to kick, scream, and generally make a fuss. Corpses could show up eventually, particularly if they had been processed with care, but kidnapping victims had to stay hidden. Corpses inevitably brought closure to the cops, the press, and the justice system, but a kidnapping stayed an open book that commanded attention and effort.

Plus, if he was going to kidnap somebody, he'd rather do Dr. Alexis Morgan. Not that he ever played around on the job, but all things being equal, if he had to drug, bind, and wrestle somebody, he'd just as soon have a pretty victim with soft curves. Mark probably stank of the kind of cologne they marketed in *Sports Illustrated*, and he'd try some macho, psycho shit like he'd pulled on the driving course.

Which is what he was trying to tell Forsyth on the phone, but the man wasn't used to having his orders questioned. Considering Forsyth was chief bottle washer and towel jockey for Senator Burchfield, such an arrogant attitude seemed a little excessive.

But Forsyth had the two qualities guaranteed to fuel his self-righteousness: a career in politics and a fervent belief in Jesus Christ as the world's only redeemer.

"Assuming I can pull it off, where I am supposed to stash him?" Scagnelli said.

"The place where you followed them would have done perfect," Forsyth said. "But the Monkey House is ancient history now."

Scagnelli made a mental note to dig around in that history a little more. He knew about Halcyon, since it had been registered for a clinical trial with the FDA to treat post-traumatic stress disorder. But no case outcomes had ever been recorded, and no patents were filed on the compound. All he'd uncovered so far was the same stuff everybody already knew.

"If we know Dr. Morgan has the Seethe formula, why do we need her husband?"

"Bait," Forsyth said. "Dr. Morgan's two weaknesses are pride and love."

"Hell, that's true of just about any woman, but I don't see how we can crack her."

"You're like the city slicker who comes out to the farm to buy mule eggs," Forsyth said. "I could sell you any old thing and call it 'mule eggs,' and you'd never know the difference. You ain't the kind to ask questions."

True enough. But I've never been this curious before. And I've never been this close to the White House before, either.

"Okay, just tell me where to dump him and it's done."

"Umstead Correctional in Butner. It was a center for young hooligans but it closed two years ago. Minimum security, no fence, no surveillance. You'll find the warden's brick house at the back of the property."

"I assume it's ready for occupancy."

"All it needs is a guest. There's food, entertainment, and a little bonus for you. The kind you like."

"Mule eggs?"

"Let's just say they're little and white and make you kick up your heels."

"Consider it done."

"The key's under the mat."

"Of course."

Forsyth rang off.

Scagnelli tossed his half-finished coffee in the trash and went to the parking lot. Before entering his rental sedan, he dropped his prepaid Tracfone on the ground and then stomped it with his foot. He then collected a few of the pieces, leaving some on the ground. That's what he sometimes did with bodies, too. Spread them around to a lot of different places.

He reached the Morgans' house in fifteen minutes. After Mark's little rampage wore off, he'd dropped his wife at the neuro-sciences building. Apparently she had a lot of work to do on her Halcyon research, and Forsyth was content to let her finish before he swooped in for the harvest. Mark had driven the faux cop car home and it now sat in the driveway, facing the road like a real cop would park in case of an emergency call.

Scagnelli cruised the street, turned around in front of an ugly Tudor-style house with a "For Sale" sign in the yard, and rolled past his target once more. This neighborhood looked a little too upscale to pull the old "utility worker" trick, plus Scagnelli liked to vary his routines.

Dusk was approaching, and it was the time of weekday when late commuters would be pulling into the neighborhood. Even though the Morgan home was relatively isolated for such a densely populated area, Scagnelli didn't think a simple drive-through club-and-run would work. Mark was armed, minimally trained, and on edge, a combination that could end in a firefight.

While Scagnelli was okay with that, Forsyth wanted the guy alive and was willing to pay for it.

Scagnelli wished he had a dog. Hook up a leash and that gave you purpose. A jogging suit or gym shorts would also work, but he hadn't packed for such a cover and the shopping district was on the far side of town. He wanted to finish the job before the missus got home.

In the end, he decided on a combination of delivery boy and lost out-of-towner. The corner gas station had a restaurant attached called Papi's Italiano, and despite sporting the green, white, and red color scheme of Italy, its menu was about as authentic as a can of Chef Boyardee. Scagnelli had them box up a plastic-looking cheese pizza sitting under a sun lamp, paid his twelve dollars, and took it to his car. He removed his jacket, undid the top buttons on his shirt, and mussed his hair. Then he drove back to the Morgan house with the food filling the car with its oily stench.

His rental sedan didn't match the job, and he was fifteen years too old to be a stoner delivery boy, even in this economy, but he didn't think anyone would notice. The best thing about the current Congress and its complete destruction of the American standard of living was that everyone was focused on their own misery.

Parking beside the fake cruiser, he hustled to the front door, whistling. The pizza was a prop with one purpose only, to buy that one second of surprise in which to gain entry. Even though the front door gave him the most exposure to scrutiny, it would be the only way to make a grand entry. He knocked twice and glanced impatiently at his watch, all while hefting the pizza box above his left shoulder. Then he rapped with the brass knocker.

"Pizza!" he called, just to get in the mood.

He expected Mark to peek out the window and then cautiously open the door to tell him he had the wrong house. Mark would likely be armed, but he wouldn't want to show the gun because he couldn't risk a police report. Scagnelli enjoyed working with people who also had a lot to hide. In a way, it put hunter and prey on equal footing.

So Plan A was to wait for him to open the door, go through the "Order a pizza?" and get the confused denial, look at the receipt, and come back with "Sir, is this 417 Tanglewood?" and then, when Mark's suspicion gave way to the normal desire to be helpful, Scagnelli would shove the pizza box in his face, push him inside, and subdue him before Mark could wield his weapon.

But Plan A went mildly awry when Mark didn't answer the door after the third set of knocks. Scagnelli kicked over to Plan B, which would be to try the door himself, then go through the same routine, acting stoned and goofy to counter Mark's paranoia at least long enough to get the element of surprise.

But the sharp, hard jab against the back of his ribs announced Plan C.

A voice, presumably Mark's, murmured close enough to chill his earlobe. "I've been expecting you. And so has this Glock."

Damn. Looks like the guy's cop training is paying off.

CHAPTER NINETEEN

The visit to the Monkey House had jarred Alexis, and even though the old brick factory that loomed in her nightmares had been leveled, she could still smell the rot and rust of the interior despite being back in the antiseptic confines of her research lab. Odor was the most evocative sense because it had the most direct route to the brain, and the molecular memory had also carried the scent of blood. Whatever had happened that night, it still slept deep inside her.

But she didn't dare wake it, because all that mattered was her mission. Silver's formula wasn't effective enough, and she had no hope of working with him to refine it. Alexis didn't care that *they*—federal agents, drug-company spies, terrorists, they were all the same obstacles and enemies of science to her—were monitoring her research, and even if she unlocked Halcyon for them, all that mattered was that Mark had a chance.

Never mind that you lose your own chance.

She compared Mark's files from the previous week with the latest she'd managed the day before her lab was raided and Haleema's laptop was stolen. The lesions had made significant progress, the leaking fissures of blood leaving dark blotches on his MRI scans.

It's almost as if his brain is attacking itself. Committing suicide. Destroying parts of itself it doesn't like.

And she fought memories of her own, hooked and reeled from the depths of her subconscious by the return to the Monkey House. The antiseptic cleanser used in the lab was common to all university buildings, and its penetrating aroma swept her back to graduate school, when she'd been excited to become Sebastian Briggs's assistant and engage in exploring the mind's vast frontiers. Their first clinical trial had ended with Susan Sharpe's death, but that had been an accident. Last year, when Sebastian Briggs had lured the five survivors back, they had undergone…what?

The images came in a syncopated rush: *Mark's battered face, the oily-mold odor, the front of her own blouse wet and warm with blood, Anita naked and wild-eyed, Briggs lying dead on the stained concrete floor, the steel tool in her hand heavy and powerful, the primal power surging through her—*

No. That wasn't the way it happened.

She'd never remember, because Halcyon wouldn't let her.

She wouldn't let herself.

The only evidence she had of those events was the scars on Mark's mouth and her arm and the one Halcyon pill she'd concealed before Mark made her destroy the remaining stock. She almost wished Sebastian Briggs was still alive, because he might be the only one who could save her husband.

No. Halcyon is yours now. You've sacrificed too much to turn back now.

No, it wasn't completely hers. Darrell Silver knew, as well. Along with whomever the geeky drug fiend might have told.

Her cell phone rang and she grabbed it, worried that it was Mark with an emergency. Instead, she was met with a vaguely familiar female voice. "Dr. Morgan?"

"Yes?"

"This is Hannah Todd. Anita's therapist."

Dr. Todd had an office on the seventh floor, and it was odd for her to call since they often bumped into one another in the hall. Alexis suppressed the alarms in her head. "Is something wrong?"

There was a pause. "Haven't you heard?"

"What? Is this about Anita?"

The therapist's voice stayed cool and professional, almost aloof. "I'm sorry to be the one to tell you, but Anita committed suicide yesterday."

Something rolled over and kicked inside Alexis's chest. "That's impossible," she heard herself saying, although it was not only possible, it had always been just a matter of time. "I just talked to her a few days ago and she seemed fine."

"She is—was—a rapid-cycler manic depressive," Dr. Todd said. "Her mood could go from heaven to hell in a heartbeat."

"What happened?" Meaning, *Which method did she choose this time? The final time, the method that worked?*

"She overdosed on several kinds of drugs, mostly depressants," Dr. Todd said. "The ME determined she fell asleep in the bathtub, no foul play, but he wouldn't rule it accidental because she had razor blades lying on the edge of the tub, and several empty bottles of pills. She intended to go, one way or another."

"But she's intended before and…" Alexis recognized the foolishness of her own argument. And her survivor's guilt hit. She hadn't warned Anita when the man on the phone had threatened her and the two men raided her lab. She'd selfishly assumed they were after her Halcyon research, not the Monkey House subjects.

But how could those ever be separated now? The drug Sebastian Briggs had developed to help traumatized war veterans had mutated into a virulent cancer of an idea that infected everyone it touched.

"I thought you already knew," Dr. Todd said. "She considered you one of her closest friends."

Proof of just how isolated she'd become. "We've been a little out of touch lately," Alexis said, feeling defensive. "I've been busy with an important research project, and my husband isn't well."

"No one's blaming you. If anyone, I should blame myself, but I know better. I thought we were making progress, even if she disliked the antipsychotic drugs I prescribed."

Alexis glanced at the most recent scan of Mark's brain and wondered if similar damage had occurred in Anita's brain. She'd been so obsessed with curing her husband that she hadn't considered the rest of them. Or herself.

"But there was something strange she said to me in our last session," Dr. Todd said. "Since she listed you as a legally responsible person, I can break my confidentiality if it might help someone else."

"Anita said lots of things. She lived a life of fantasy, after all."

"True, but this was odd. Anita said someone called her and said, 'Surely you didn't think we could let you live, after what happened.' She couldn't identify the voice."

Alexis tensed. "I thought you said the ME suspected no foul play."

"Well, it's not something I'd ordinarily report, given her long history of suicidal tendencies. But I wondered if she might have said anything to you about it."

"No." Deception got easier with practice, and Alexis recognized that her own risk-reward center might be scrambled by Seethe and Halcyon. "She was always saying crazy things like that—sorry, I know 'crazy' isn't kosher anymore."

"She was also sharing an elaborate fantasy about the Monkey House, a place in her past where she'd committed shameful acts. Of course, I took that to be a metaphor for her career in pornography."

"I'd agree with that diagnosis, Doctor," Alexis said, remaining aloof, embracing the numbing sadness and shock.

"I just thought you ought to know that she mentioned you in connection with the fantasy. In her version, you were a murderer."

The metal piece of machinery, my hand warm and slippery, the tip plowing into meat and bone...

"We were in a couple of psychology experiments together," Alexis said. "We were simulating fear response."

"Yes, the Susan Sharpe tragedy. I remember reading about that, although Anita wouldn't share it. And you were assisting Sebastian Briggs at the time, correct?"

The "friendly" phone call was beginning to sound like either an interrogation or a therapy session, and anger boiled in the base of Alexis's brain. But she couldn't respond to anger, because she was unsure how it might evolve.

"Anita always felt responsible for Susan's death," she said. "We all did. Even though it was an accident. I've always believed that was a breaking point for Anita, because she started abusing drugs after that. Which led to...other things."

"I've read all her files, of course," Dr. Todd said. "And this outcome was almost inevitable, as much as I hate to admit failure. But that's my own ego speaking, as a therapist. We all think we have the answers."

Alexis relaxed a little. The conversation wasn't about Anita or the Monkey House at all. It was Dr. Todd's attempt at closure.

"Maybe her fantasy of me as a murderer was about killing our friendship," Alexis suggested. "The experiments put a strain on all of us. And it's why I've become so dedicated to unlocking more of the mind's mysteries. Not to minimize what you do, but as you must know, the brain is a complex biological organism that we've only begun to understand."

"I agree, and we're on the same team," Dr. Todd said. "This time, we lost."

Alexis nodded, then remembered she was on the phone. "Anita took herself out of the game."

"I'm sure I will see you at the funeral."

"Yes. I'm sure."

There was a pause. "Alexis?"

"Yes?"

"It's okay to grieve, even if this isn't a total shock."

Shock? I'll show you a shock, you bitch. Come into the Monkey House with me and we'll see how science kicks your touchy-feely ass.

But she realized Dr. Todd was reacting to her composure in the face of the news. No trace of sorrow. Which wasn't surprising. Leeches like Hannah Todd sucked at the misery and pain, grew rich on bankrupt souls, and sat on their thrones smug in the certainty that they always knew best.

If I could introduce you to Seethe, you'd find out what you're hiding inside. It would shrink you down to the manipulative whore you're dying to be if you only had the guts.

She was frightened by the surge of manic zeal, so she covered by saying, "It's so hard to believe. It just hasn't sunk in yet."

"Come see me if you need to," Dr. Todd said. "Faculty members have priority on my schedule. And I get them all sooner or later."

So will Seethe, bitch.

"Thank you, but I'll be okay," she said. "And thanks for letting me know. Good-bye."

She clicked off and studied her husband's damaged brain one more time, along with the time stamp and the false patient name of "Donnie Davis" in the corner. She didn't want him to die like Anita had.

Surely you didn't think we could let you live, after what happened.

Anita might have wanted to kill herself, but not that way. Not yet.

She called her husband. She needed to warn him.

Seven rings. Eight. No answer.

Maybe Mark was the next one they couldn't let live.

She shoved the MRI images into her satchel and hurried from the lab.

CHAPTER TWENTY

They were sitting on the porch as the first hush of dusk settled. The birds had found their roosts for the night, and the crickets had yet to take up their instruments. A tumble of clouds brushed the ridge tops, but white outflanked the gray and would likely bring no rain. The moist air was rich with a mix of green vegetation and humus, rebirth and decay dancing on the same ancient Appalachian dirt.

"Here's what we know," Gundersson said. "Somebody wants you both dead."

"Nothing new about that," Roland said.

Roland placed his revolver on the hand-carved table, where it would be easy to reach. He hoped his show of power would keep the agent in check until he figured out how to approach the situation. Of course, he'd also taken Gundersson's weapon, which the agent had voluntarily surrendered as a ploy to gain trust. Not that Roland was ready to trust anyone, much less somebody claiming to be with the government.

"We know about the original Monkey House trials and Dr. Sebastian Briggs," Gundersson said, sipping the iced herbal tea Wendy had served. "We're not sure how it all ended, but we suspect that someone came away with Briggs's formulas for Halcyon and Seethe. The files say they were destroyed in the industrial accident that claimed Briggs's life, but it's hard to imagine he'd have kept the details of something like that to himself."

Wendy touched Roland's arm and spoke before he had a chance. "We don't remember anything," she said to Gundersson. "That whole week was like a big blank."

Roland studied his wife. As much as he wanted to believe her, he could never be sure she wasn't simply covering her shame and regret. Not that she'd done much wrong, besides submitting to Briggs's sexual games. It wasn't like she'd killed anyone.

Not like him. And not like Alexis Morgan.

"Halcyon wipes out memories, so that's not surprising," Gundersson said. "And plenty of powerful people would love to have Halcyon just for that purpose."

"You can't trust something like that out in the world," Roland said. "Sure, they dress it up as medicine, a way to treat veterans and accident victims and help them rejoin society. But every fucking evil masquerades as good, at least until it's got a foothold."

Politicians fall back on the words "the right thing to do" like I fall back on the Serenity Prayer. Grab a mantra you don't have to explain.

"I agree, Roland, we need to move cautiously, but I also believe the U.S. government is the body that should make those decisions," Gundersson said.

"You've been drinking the Washington Kool-Aid too long," Roland said. "How can we trust your judgment?"

"It doesn't matter anyway," Wendy said. "We can't help you. We already told you we don't know anything."

"*You* told me," he said to Wendy before shifting his gaze to Roland. "But your husband hasn't said anything about what happened that night in the Research Triangle Park."

"Because I don't know who you are," Roland replied. "Sure, you can give me a blue ID card with 'CIA' stamped on it, and the name you give me conveniently matches the name on the card. And you're the guy in the photo. But anybody can trick up an ID card."

Like Briggs made me think I was David Underwood when he framed me for murder last year. Killing an innocent woman just to mess with my head. Worst of all, it worked.

And maybe you'll sell me out to the cops for that crime. Then who'd watch out for Wendy?

"I gave you my gun," Gundersson said. "And here's another reason you can trust me. You received two e-mails the past two days that the CIA intercepted. One said, 'Every four hours or else,' and the other said, 'Surely you didn't think we could let you live, after what happened.' Right?"

"What's he talking about, Ro?" Wendy said.

"Nothing," he said, unable to come up with a satisfactory lie.

"Why didn't you tell me? Those sound like threats. And you said 'Every four hours' was the name of a client's book."

"Don't you remember what that means?" Roland asked her. After she shook her head, he said, "That's how often we had to take Halcyon to keep from going crazy."

Wendy's lips pursed in anger. "I told you, I don't remember anything."

I don't blame you. I wouldn't, either, if I could help it. And if I was the enemy within, I'd be lying, too.

She must have read the accusation in his eyes. She pushed away from the table and went to the tipped-over easel, where she tried to restore the canvas Roland had shattered during his rampage.

"How do I know *you* didn't send those e-mails?" Roland asked Gundersson.

"We hacked into your e-mail account, I'll admit. But it was to protect you."

"Every fucking evil masquerades as a good."

"I don't blame you for being paranoid—"

"I'm way past paranoia. All the evidence I see says that everybody's going to do whatever it takes to unlock Seethe and Halcyon. You, the NCS, the FBI, Santa's little elves, and whoever's left alive in the Jackson Fucking Five, not to mention Senator Burchfield and no telling how many other warmongering right-wingers and socialist liberals."

"This isn't political," Gundersson said. "Our government wants to make sure it doesn't fall into the wrong hands."

"What if all hands are wrong?"

"We have information that Dr. Alexis Morgan is developing a Halcyon formula."

Wendy paused in her restoration work. "Lex wouldn't do anything like that. Not after what happened."

I thought you didn't remember anything. Gundersson's eyes met Roland's.

"Susan Sharpe," Wendy said. "From the original trial. She died in that accident."

"Dr. Morgan was Briggs's graduate assistant," Gundersson said. "Wouldn't it make sense that he'd entrust her with the formula? Maybe she even contributed to the research. Maybe she was involved all along."

Roland recalled the crazed rage of the woman as the Seethe swept over her and she killed Briggs's bodyguard with a rusty tool. She hadn't looked like a disciplined woman of science then. She was like a feral animal, taking prey that she had no intention of eating.

Or protecting a secret.

"Why are you bothering us, then? I can't even cook a pot of coffee, and Wendy's an artist, not a brain surgeon." He ignored her glower. "You ought to be watching the Morgans. Her husband was tied up with CRO Pharmaceuticals."

"They are...under observation by the CIA," Gundersson said. "But other elements in the capital believe you two are hiding out because you know something."

"What about you, Secret Agent Gundersson? What do *you* believe?"

"Off the record, the CIA is not happy about getting our nuts snipped in the aftermath of Nine/Eleven. There was enough blame to go around for everybody, but the competition really got rolling at that point and it's harder than ever to know who you can trust."

"Tell me about it," Roland said. "Put J. Edgar Hoover in a skirt and he still comes out Hitler. As far as I'm concerned, the government is doing what the terrorists couldn't: destroying this country from the inside. Best thing that could happen to protect our freedom is a big fucking asteroid blazing down Pennsylvania Avenue."

"I respect your libertarian principles, and I even share some of them, but I've sworn loyalty to the United States," Gundersson said. "It may be a mess, but it's the best mess in the history of human civilization."

"And you can fix the mess by getting answers from us."

"More importantly, I can help *you*," Gundersson said, glancing at Wendy to exploit Roland's protective streak. "Both of you. Give me what you know, and the official word goes around that you know nothing."

"Why should we believe that anybody trusts the official word?"

"Because it will be one of those secrets that people are allowed to discover. You know, the secret that nobody's supposed to know but it's hiding right there in plain sight."

"Boy, DC is an even bigger clusterfuck than I figured. The only way they'll accept the truth is if you disguise it as a lie."

Wendy was dabbing violet paint around the gash in the canvas, using it as a foundational feature. She worked with savage strokes, using bold straight lines with a geometric precision. "Secret messages," she said, her back to them, not pausing in her work. "All you have to do is add more layers, change things around. Illusion is your friend."

"No, honey," Roland said. "Illusion is your lover. Reality is your husband."

She turned, letting the brush splash acrylic on the rough pine planks. Roland looked at the Rorschach pattern on the porch and decided it was Sebastian Briggs kneeling between his wife's naked thighs.

Then again, he read that image into everything.

What a bargain. Wendy gets lost in Halcyon while Seethe makes me obsess over every memory. God, if ever you feel the need to let me accept the things I cannot change...

Gundersson cleared his throat to break the tension in the air, but the clumsy guttural noise only heightened it. "Mr. Doyle, I doubt aiding the government inspires you, but you have my personal guarantee that you'll come to no harm. I am under orders to protect you until this situation is all clear."

"And just when would that be? It looks like the only way to clear it would be to find your precious drugs and then kill us both."

"There are powerful elements—"

Roland swept the .38 into his hand and banged its butt on the table. "*I'm* a powerful goddamned element. I can take care of us."

"No offense, Mr. Doyle, but I saw you shoot at the fox yesterday. Four rounds at twenty paces and you didn't come close."

Roland's gaze dropped to the gun. "It was beautiful. I couldn't…"

"What makes you think your aim would be better if the fox is shooting back?"

"He's no killer," Wendy said, storming her painting, applying a second swollen breast. "A woman knows."

Keep on loving the illusion, honey. That's all you get of me anyway.

"One question," Roland said to Gundersson. "If it wasn't the CIA that sent the e-mails, then who did?"

"National Clandestine Service. One of those new federal agencies gone a little rogue. The great bait-and-switch was that they were created to monitor overseas threats, but we all know how that goes, right?"

"The enemy within," Roland said. "That's the one that gets you."

He pulled Gundersson's gun out of his waistband, where it had been digging into his skin. He slid it across the table. "Your move."

Gundersson left the gun lying there between them. "Tell me what you know."

Roland sighed. The truth—at least, the truth as Seethe remembered it—had haunted him like those shadowy figures in Wendy's paintings. Maybe if he exorcised it, he could sleep at night without lying next to his wife and imagining squeezing her throat until the images went away.

"I'll tell you both what I remember," Roland said. "But I'm not sure I know anything."

CHAPTER TWENTY-ONE

Wallace Forsyth entered the abandoned youth correctional facility an hour before dusk, using the gravel service road he'd scouted earlier in the day.

In better economic times, the center might have been renovated into a different type of institution. But Butner already housed two prisons, and the town's population wasn't big enough to support an extra school. Apparently the guards and nurses weren't breeding fast enough to expand the tax base.

As it was, the center had taken on a seedy, neglected look despite only recently being mothballed. Forsyth welcomed the seclusion. Mark Morgan was removed from the influence of CRO's bottomless pockets and deaf to whispers of money, and therefore he was unpredictable. Forsyth hadn't survived so long in Washington by doing business with unpredictable people.

Scagnelli's rental sedan was parked beside a holly hedge that a warden had once planted to imitate the landscaping of a real residence. The little house was of the same brick and small, white-framed windows as the main barracks, the kitchen, and the wing where young offenders likely sat through group therapy while plotting to smuggle in drugs or alcohol or sexually abuse their weaker peers. Forsyth was willing to bet that 90 percent of the hooligans had since graduated to the federal or state penitentiaries down the road.

Forsyth pulled his car beside Scagnelli's. Despite having no official government employment at the moment, he was sure he could talk his way past any local cops that suspected trespassing. Given the small size of the town and its high inmate population, and the fact that inmates with nowhere to go often stayed where the jail doors had last opened to eject them, the police were probably understaffed and overworked, too busy to worry about decaying state property.

Forsyth had one call to make before he confronted Mark. He reached Burchfield on the third ring.

"They're asking about you at the arts gala," Burchfield said, with a string quartet and laughter in the background. "Apparently you're considered a great friend of the Winston-Salem Community Arts Project."

"They've been hitting the moonshine jug, then," Forsyth said. "But since you ain't announced your running mate yet, the media doesn't give a pig whistle about my whereabouts."

"You wouldn't believe what I'm doing right now."

"Drinking lemonade and grinning like a turtle eating saw briars?"

"I have my hand up a puppet's ass, and I'm making it dance."

"Good practice for handling your secretary of state."

"I can only hold this grin and this puppet for so long before this lovely lady at the podium demands a speech."

"Give 'em the old 'Arts are the foundation of a good community' line. They might conveniently forget to look at your voting record."

"I have maybe ten seconds before I seem rude."

"Furrow your eyebrows, Daniel. This call will seem critical to national security."

"This *is* critical. Where are we on this thing?"

"We're about to hog-tie it and make some bacon."

"I'll assume that's good news."

"That's the only kind you'll hear."

"Good. Thanks for that 'community' line. All politics is local."

So is sin. Forsyth hit END, slipped the phone into his jacket pocket, and walked across the unkempt lawn. The sky was low and the gray was gathering, promising a coming storm.

And a storm shall come to pass.

Unlike the Doomsday opportunists who sought to cash in on predictions of the Lord's return, Forsyth had never believed there was a single firm date for the end. The way he saw it, "End Times" were plural and might be well underway already. He felt no apocalyptic zeal, however, nor any particular urgency. All he could do was today's service and hope it would be enough.

The door was unlocked, just as he'd instructed Scagnelli. He entered, instinctively trying the light switch before realizing the power had been turned off long ago. Sunlight leaked through the partially drawn blinds, casting a serrated yellow path across the living room.

"You here?" Forsyth called into the gloom.

"In the back," Scagnelli said in a monotone.

Forsyth locked the door and headed for the narrow hallway. The small house couldn't have held more than two bedrooms, and Scagnelli's voice had come from the room on the right. Forsyth found a closed door as he entered the hallway.

He braced himself to confront Mark Morgan again. The man was a sinner, but his worst offense had been abandoning CRO, Burchfield, and the opportunity to serve a higher purpose by delivering Seethe and Halcyon. Satan walked the world not in a supernatural shape but in the troubled hearts of the selfish and the morally weak.

Forsyth entered the room, startled by its darkness. He'd been right to be suspicious of Scagnelli, who'd already proven he'd betray anyone at the first light knock of opportunity. Forsyth had ordered Scagnelli to have Morgan ready for interrogation, not to play hide-and-seek. But he suppressed his anger as he called out. "Where is he?"

"Right here," Mark said. "Right where you want me to be."

Forsyth pulled his Blackberry from his pocket and opened it, casting the room in greenish light. Mark was standing, while Dominic Scagnelli was sitting on what appeared to be a metal bed frame that had no mattress. Forsyth blinked and made out the weak glint of gray in Mark's hand. A gun.

As his eyes adjusted, he saw that Scagnelli's hands were bound to the bed frame with a short electrical cord. A surge of rage rolled through Forsyth, but he suppressed it, knowing Mark had the advantage.

For the moment.

"Hello, Mark," he said. "I'm glad you honored my request to meet."

"It would feel really good to kill you right now," Mark said. The coldness in his tone projected its chill into Forsyth's heart.

"I understand. I felt the effects of Seethe myself, remember?"

"Yeah. I remember. That's the problem."

Forsyth glanced at Scagnelli, whose shoulders slumped in defeat. "I see you met the protection we assigned to you," Forsyth said to Mark.

"I don't need no fucking bodyguard. I can take care of myself."

Forsyth calculated a couple of options, deciding diplomacy still had a chance. And diplomacy worked best as a tool to get fools to lower their guard. "Obviously," he said. "But it's your wife you should be concerned about."

Mark emerged from the shadows of the corner of the room. His eyes were wild and his gun hand was quivering, the scar on his mouth imitating a reckless grin. "What about her?"

"Haven't you heard? Anita Molkesky is dead. An apparent suicide, but you know how things work when corporate assets are at stake."

"Anita?" Mark wiped his mouth with his sleeve. "She was…it was just a matter a time."

"It's a matter of time for all of us, Mark," Forsyth said in the soothing tone he'd once used to win over witnesses for the prosecution and voters for the moderate conservatism he'd projected. "But CRO doesn't give up easily when millions are at stake."

"They said they were done with Seethe and Halcyon. We all agreed—"

"CRO never agreed to anything. We live in a corporate police state, Mark. The government was stolen from the Christians and given to the corporations. And all of us are bottle caps on their checkerboard. You, me, Senator Burchfield, your wife, Dominic there—"

"I tried to tell him," Scagnelli said, causing Mark to swing the barrel of the gun in his direction.

"Shut up," Mark said. To Forsyth, "What about Alexis?"

"CRO got to her. They have her working on Halcyon. She's their new Sebastian Briggs."

"Bullshit. I would have known. I live with her. I *sleep* with her."

Forsyth gave a sad shake of his head. "But ain't you wondered why you don't feel right? Feeling a little unsteady, blacking out, getting eat up by sudden rages? And it's getting worse, ain't it?"

"I—I'm fine." The gun lowered a little.

"It's Seethe. Your wife has been using you as her guinea pig. It was too risky for a full-scale trial, after what happened in the Monkey House. But there were still refinements to be made. And once you left CRO—"

"How do you know all this?"

Ah, the shadow of a doubt. A liar's best friend.

But Mark was unstable, so the diplomacy game could turn in the blink of an eye. Or in the time it took him to squeeze the trigger.

"That's what I've been looking into," Scagnelli said, and Mark didn't swing the gun at him this time. "Burchfield had to distance himself from the whole deal. Once you run for president, you can't go near the dirt. We hacked your wife's research records and found out Halcyon was still in play."

Forsyth picked up the narrative thread, pleased that Scagnelli had caught on to the con game. Despite Scagnelli having botched the snatch of Mark, Forsyth might yet have to give the man a bonus, assuming they survived this encounter. Of course, right after the bonus, he'd probably have to fire him. Or silence him another way. Scagnelli was good, but there were dozens of Scagnellis out there, and all of them would be only too happy to eliminate their failed predecessor as on-the-job training.

"Senator Burchfield obviously wants to tear down the Monkey House once and for all," Forsyth said.

"I know, and he wanted to bury us monkeys along with it," Mark said.

"He's none too happy that CRO started this back up again," Forsyth continued, deliberately overlooking the senator's threats to kill the trial subjects a year ago. "And he's worried that CRO will back one of the other candidates. He may lose his health-committee chair if he gets the nomination, and they'll be looking for stronger allies who'll introduce their legislation."

"I used to write that legislation, remember?" Mark said. "You don't have to preach to me about the corporations running the country. I don't trust CRO and I don't trust *you*."

Apparently Seethe had infected him with a special brand of paranoia. Forsyth still vividly recalled his own journey through hell after exposure to the drug. It had left him on his knees and praying for deliverance, certain he was in Satan's grip. And he had a calling to inflict that hell on others.

"None of us can afford to let the word get out," Forsyth said. "Especially your wife."

Mark gripped his forehead as if fighting off a migraine or mild seizure. If Forsyth were a man of action, he would have taken the opportunity to dive for the gun. But Forsyth was sixty-five, and he trusted his brains more than his muscles.

"If you kill us, there will be a major investigation," Forsyth said. "Your wife and I served on the president's bioethics council together, and you and I are both connected to CRO. It wouldn't take long for enough of the truth to come out. And you know what your wife did."

"She didn't kill anybody!" Mark's outburst echoed through the empty house.

"Of course not," Forsyth said. "But we know easily *they* can fabricate evidence."

"And she isn't developing Halcyon and Seethe for CRO. She's not like Briggs."

Forsyth had come to believe Briggs and Dr. Morgan were very much alike, because he understood the ambitions of each. But they both shared the moral weakness of serving science instead of the Lord, and so were destined to fail. But Satan's work could inflict a lot of suffering before the final redemption.

The trick was in making the Archangel's sword look like the devil's tool.

"We want to protect her from CRO, Mark," Forsyth said. "And we want to protect you from her."

"I don't need any protection."

Scagnelli made a feeble attempt to rise, but Mark stabbed the gun toward him. "For the record, I don't like cheese on my pizza."

He stormed past Forsyth, bumping into his shoulder hard enough to hurt.

"They're watching you, Mark," Forsyth called after him. "We can help."

After the front door slammed, Scagnelli lifted one hand, dangling the electrical cord he had worked free. "I could have jumped him and wrung his scrawny little neck," Scagnelli said. "But I figured you need him alive."

"For now," Forsyth said. "Only for now."

CHAPTER TWENTY-TWO

When Alexis found the house empty, her first realization was that she had nowhere to turn.

The wall of secrecy she'd built, and the fear of failure, had isolated her more than she'd let herself believe. She'd carried on with her regular research work and her teaching duties, but she'd become so obsessed with cracking Seethe and saving Mark that she'd created yet another Monkey House.

And it was the house in which she was standing, the one she shared with her husband. The relics of a past life that decorated the living room—degrees, awards, golfing trophies, photographs of happier times—served to mock her now. She couldn't go to the police, she couldn't trust the government, and she couldn't even count on the one person she'd vowed to keep no secrets from.

Because their life together was a lie.

She didn't bother trying his cell phone, because it was on the couch, the silent TV flickering with last night's sports highlights. The BLET car he'd taken was still in the driveway, and she wondered if he'd been arrested for taking the college's property.

No. Someone would have called.

Maybe the same person who threatened to kill me.

When her own cell launched into its "We Can Work It Out" ringtone, she fumbled it from her purse with held breath. The number was blocked, but that didn't matter. "Mark?"

There was no answer for a moment, and Alexis paced the living room, ruminating on places Mark might have walked, or who might have picked him up. But she couldn't imagine him leaving his phone while they were both under surveillance.

"Mark?" she repeated, going to the living room closet.

"Lex?"

She couldn't place the voice at first, and images flickered through her mind—*Sebastian looking down at the hole in his chest, Mark's bloody sneer, Roland holding a gun*—before her whisper seemed to fill the house. "Wendy?"

"We're in trouble."

Alexis opened the closet and felt along the top shelf. No gun. "I know," she said, but she didn't know how many people the "we" included.

"They're listening."

Of course they are. That's what they do. It doesn't matter if you e-mail, phone, or send by postal carrier, they get you whenever they want.

"They've got Mark," Alexis said, not wanting to believe it but unwilling to imagine anything worse. Like suicide.

"You have to come now," Wendy said.

"Where?"

"You'll know. The summer of green dresses."

Alexis was about to scream into the phone, tired of all the cryptic nonsense, but she couldn't afford to surrender to rage. She had to be strong for her husband.

"Summer of green dresses," Alexis repeated back.

"We have what you're looking for," Wendy said, her tone strangely flat, as if she'd rehearsed her lines and wanted to inject them with ambivalence.

"I'm looking for *Mark.*" Alexis noticed the assault weapon, that cruel, multi-chambered rifle she'd been afraid to touch, propped behind Mark's dusty bag of golf clubs. She didn't know if its presence was a good sign or not.

"What you've *been* looking for," Wendy said. "Since the Monkey House."

"Anita's dead."

"That's...my God...it's true. They're after us." There was no remorse. Wendy was a zombie, removed from it all, just the way she'd been that night—

The night that never happened.

But the images came again, of the rusty tool in her hand, the wet, slippery grip, the sickening but satisfying *thunk* as she drove the tip of it into Susan Sharpe's face—

"It was part of the experiment," Alexis said, pleading defense to an unleveled accusation. "We only *pretended* to kill. So Sebastian could measure our response."

"Summer of green dresses."

Then Alexis was holding the dead phone to her ear, staring past the walls of her house to a night that she could never fully remember yet never fully escape.

You didn't kill Susan Sharpe eleven years ago. She died in a fall down the stairs. Everyone said so.

And last year...she couldn't have killed again. She wasn't a killer. Mark would never tolerate a killer.

She broke from the obsessive cycle by clinging to Wendy's words. She'd only spoken to Wendy a few times since the Monkey House. Roland and Wendy had come over for dinner just before moving out of town, but they thought it was safest not to reveal their new location. Even back then, they were already sinking into mistrust and paranoia, with an unspoken agreement between the couples that they should distance themselves from one another.

Alexis had been one of the bridesmaids at Roland and Wendy's wedding eight years before. Susan's death had been far enough in the past that they could all ignore it, and the couple was determined to live happily ever after, even though Roland's drinking had already become impossible to ignore.

The bridesmaids—Anita and Roland's sister among them— had worn strapless dresses of emerald green. The ceremony had taken place on June 21, the solstice, and Roland had even joked that he was going to have to squeeze a lot of consummation into the shortest night of the year. He was well into the champagne before the wedding even began, and he didn't slow down during the reception.

At one point he'd thrown his arms around Anita and Alexis, hugging them close together, swaying with his full weight on them. "Shummer of green dreshes," he'd shouted in his slushy, drunken joy.

A lifetime ago. Frustration filled Alexis's belly with heat. *What did it mean?*

Then she remembered. During their last dinner, she and Wendy had been going through old photos while the guys talked libertarian politics. One of the photos was of the bridal party. "Summer of green dresses," Wendy had said with a mixture of embarrassment and nostalgia.

The photos were stored in a trunk coffee table. Alexis shoved away the magazines and lifted the table lid, pulling out the top photo album. She'd not opened the trunk since their visit, since most of her photos had been digitally scanned. She flipped to the wedding photo and saw the plastic film had been peeled back and the corner folded. She slid her fingernail under the film and removed the photo, glancing at their younger, more innocent faces.

She searched it for clues. She saw nothing to indicate the reason for Wendy's veiled hints, unless the goal was to show how much they'd changed. Then she tilted the photo in the light and saw the raised creases on the surface, made by pressure from beneath.

She turned it over. On its back was written an address. *161 Roby Snow Road, Creston NC.* Beneath that, in Wendy's artful but barely legible scrawl: *Just in case.*

She couldn't leave, not until she found Mark. But she wasn't sure whether Wendy's veiled invitation was for both of them. She'd said "We," and Mark and Roland had never been close. Mark was from "after." He wasn't part of Sebastian Brigg's original Halcyon trial like the rest of them, but it was unlikely they would have survived the Monkey House last year if not for his bravery.

Some may have forgotten what he did, but others hadn't.

Surely you didn't think we could let you live, after what happened?

Most importantly of all, *she* hadn't forgotten. At least, not completely. While that night was a psychotic rollercoaster of rage and pain, the inescapable result was that Mark had risked everything—his career, his sanity, and his life—to rescue her, and she would do the same for him.

Alexis returned to the closet and grabbed the assault rifle. Mark had tried to teach her to shoot it, though she didn't have the stomach for it. But she remembered his instructions, and the casual earnestness of his face as he'd spoken: *"Just press the trigger as fast as you can."*

She made sure the switch was on "Safe" before propping it by the door to her office. She retrieved her paper records with their coded notes, shoving them in a backpack with her laptop. The assault rifle had a canvas strap, so she shouldered it along with the backpack, then went to the kitchen, feeling like a soldier shipping out to the front.

War of a different kind. The war between the ears.

She collected the Halcyon-spiked bottles of water from the refrigerator and shoved them into the backpack. She was heading for the front door when she saw him sitting on the couch.

"Where the fuck do you think you're going?"

CHAPTER TWENTY-THREE

Darrell Silver squinted against the midday sunlight like a mole whose tunnel had been ripped open by an earthquake.

He kept shrugging the shoulders of his jacket, as if he were uncomfortable with the fit. More likely, he'd never worn a jacket and tie in his life, at least outside of a courtroom. Forsyth would let him change into his work clothes soon, but first they had to endure a dog-and-pony show for the U.S. district attorney. They'd arranged to meet at Central Regional, with Burchfield pulling enough strings to not only gain Silver's release but to have him declared mentally competent.

Forsyth was impressed by how much clout the threat of budget cuts could carry. His run in Congress had mostly been marked by growth and expansion, and the trough had overflowed. When everyone knew there was more than enough to go around, the fear factor couldn't keep people in line.

"We guarantee his full cooperation," said Silver's attorney, a liberal young female named Ivanevski who'd been planning a defense on the outlandish premise that her client had been the victim of a government frame-up.

"We'll review the charges," the DA said. "It's likely we can drop the interstate trafficking and conspiracy counts. But if the state chooses to indict, our hands are tied, you understand."

"Understood," the attorney said.

"What does that mean?" Silver asked. "Like, I'll be on probation or something?"

The DA scowled at the recently released inmate. "If you so much as take one bong hit, I'll have you back here in barbed-wire shackles."

"Dude, no need to get all Judge Dredd on my ass," Silver said. "You think I'm going to be doing much partying with *this* crowd?"

He waved his hands to indicate Forsyth, Scagnelli, and his attorney, who were also wearing suits, although Scagnelli's was a bit rumpled and his tie was loose.

The DA was a silver-haired man who'd achieved his position during the Bush administration, largely with the support of then-Representative Burchfield.

"Don't worry, Stan," Forsyth said to the DA. "We'll keep him in line."

"You'd better. People tend to get emotional over these drug cases, and I don't want to hear any rumors down at the country club."

"Don't forget, these alleged crimes were victimless," Silver's attorney said. "My client poses no danger to anyone."

Forsyth glanced over to the glass entrance of the hospital, where Paula Redfern watched with crossed arms and concerned glare. She had been upset over losing one of her government-conspiracy patients, adamant that the lack of community-based modalities would jeopardize Silver's rehabilitation efforts.

"Mr. Silver, please come this way," Forsyth said. Scagnelli, who had shown fake FBI credentials, took Silver by the elbow and led him to the rental sedan.

The prosecutor and defense attorney looked at each other like chess players who'd just agreed to a draw. Forsyth said good-bye, waved to Dr. Redfern, and joined Silver in the rear of the vehicle.

As Scagnelli wheeled the sedan out of the parking lot, Forsyth asked Silver, "Did you happen to meet a patient named David Underwood?"

"Underwood?" Silver tapped his forehead as if trying to shake a memory loose. "Was he that guy with the god-awful singing?"

"That would be the fella, yes."

"I heard he was a drug burnout." Silver gave a vacant, goofy grin. "Not like that's a bad thing, but some people just can't handle a buzz, you know?"

"I'll take your word for it."

"I still don't know what's going on. I'm sitting there like, 'Well, do I masturbate or do I meditate?' I mean, when you have all the time in the world, they both get a little old. Then here you guys come with this deal. The bitch of it is I don't have anything to give you guys."

"Oh, I think you do, Mr. Silver. Remember when I asked you about Alexis Morgan?"

The goofy grin tightened into a line, and Forsyth saw Scagnelli's eyes staring back from the rearview mirror.

"You said you were synthesizing drugs for her," Forsyth said.

"Just *one* drug, man," Silver said. "Now you're starting to sound like those feds, putting words in my mouth and making shit up."

"Halcyon. Right?"

"That's what she called it. Pretty cool name. The molecular structure was a little like roofies."

"Roofies?" Forsyth asked.

"Rohypnol. Derivative of nitrazepam. It got a bad rap as a date-rape drug, but that story's way overblown by the cops. You know how that goes. Scare tactics."

"Yes, I do know how that goes," Forsyth said. "Why does it have a 'bad rap'?"

"Blows out your short-term memory while it sedates you. Slip it in your date's beer, wham bam, thank you ma'am, and she wakes up sore and not remembering a thing. Well, that's the urban legend, anyway."

"Sounds…romantic. So how is Halcyon different?"

"An extra fluoride ring in the molecular structure. Freaky. Seems to kill the sedation factor and stretches out the amnesia. Probably some other heavy side effects but it would have to be tested. Say, where are we going?"

"You'll know when we get there," Scagnelli said over his shoulder.

"So you made some of this compound for Dr. Morgan?"

"We go way back. I had her for a few classes at UNC. Wait, do I need my lawyer for this?"

"You're done with lawyers if you work with us," Forsyth said. "Unless you'd rather spend the next two decades in a rubber room with David Underwood serenading you."

Silver gave Forsyth an awkward slap on the thigh. "Hey, I'm your man. Whatever you need, I can fix you up. Downers, meth, weed, acid—"

"Dr. Morgan is the only one who knew what you were doing?"

"Yeah. I didn't see any value as a recreational drug, but it was kinda weird, she coming to me and all, when she had that big, fancy lab and all those resources."

"So you made it for her?"

"I fixed her up a six-pack. Liquid form, mostly water. It was weak as shit. I planned a second-gen batch, but…well, somebody dimed me out."

Forsyth kept his face blank. After the CIA had connected Morgan and Silver, it had been a simple matter to fetch the DEA and from there to get the FBI involved. As a fringe benefit, Forsyth had also secured a decent supply of the seized drugs, which he'd used to keep Scagnelli happy. Silver was unaware that the man who'd "dimed him out" was sitting in the seat beside him.

"You have more of this drug?" Forsyth asked.

"Feds probably seized it, but I doubt they knew what it was."

Forsyth squinted against the glaring afternoon sun and smiled like a patient, kindly uncle. "I reckon you're a very talented chemist, Mr. Silver. I got some connections if you ever decide to go straight. And, just between you and me, with all these eyes on you, I'd go straight."

"Like, a square job? Shit."

"Of course, you'd need a haircut first."

Silver fingered one of his dreadlocks. After a moment of reflection, he said, "What does it pay?"

"First things first. This drug you made for Dr. Morgan. Did you know what she was using it for?"

"A good dealer doesn't ask questions. Give the people what they want, right? Keep them distracted and feeling good. Just like in politics. We're sorta in the same biz, man, if you look at it that way."

Forsyth mulled what it would take to control Silver and bring him onto the team. He'd have to stay off the official payroll because of the indictments, but the court documents hadn't made any reference to Halcyon or Seethe. Of course, the drugs didn't officially exist. And the arrest report hadn't mentioned any unidentified or counterfeit drugs, either.

Which meant they were probably still on site, if Silver was telling the truth.

They'd find out soon enough.

Scagnelli made good time on I-40, an hour ahead of the rush-hour traffic that clogged the university belt on weekday evenings. Silver was looking out the window when Scagnelli exited the highway, and he exclaimed, "Hey, you going to Chapel Hill?"

"We're *all* going to Chapel Hill," Forsyth said. "Time for you to earn your freedom."

For the next forty minutes, Silver entertained them with stories about his analyst at the hospital, a Portuguese named Rafael Rego who spoke very poor English. To make matters worse, Rego attempted to talk like Sigmund Freud, and Silver's imitation of the man's earnest inquisitions drew snickers from Scagnelli. Forsyth barely listened, reflecting on the different ways he could use Seethe, Halcyon, and a dark box of blackmail secrets to dominate the Burchfield Administration.

Where evil dwells, the Lord sends a servant.

They detoured around the UNC campus and entered the southern end of town, where rundown student apartments mixed with spotty commercial development and industrial lots. Soon they were pulling up to a concrete-block building whose white walls were mottled with mold. The former gas station featured large windows in the front bearing purple curtains, but the garage area had been sealed off with new cinder blocks that had never been painted. The raised concrete ovals where the pumps had once stood now contained Japanese maples, their burgundy leaves flapping in the spring breeze.

"Home on the range," Silver said.

"It's government property now," Scagnelli said, still playing the role of an FBI agent. "It's considered a drug asset and subject to seizure and forfeiture."

"Shit, man! Nobody can just take away your property like that! Whatever happened to the Bill of Rights?"

"The court will decide whether it was used to facilitate drug trafficking or if it was purchased with illegal profits," Scagnelli said. "I wouldn't hold your breath waiting. You think a criminal trial takes forever, wait until you start dealing with these civil procedures."

Silver turned to Forsyth with pleading eyes. "Man, this is my *pad*, man. I got a lot of memories here."

"That's what we're here for," Forsyth said. "To relive a few memories. Do you have your cell phone, Scagnelli?"

Forsyth didn't want any record of communication between his phone and Dr. Morgan's, and Scagnelli's rotating supply of pre-paid, disposable cell phones offered the best way to contact her. As they escorted Silver toward his home and laboratory, Scagnelli produced a key they'd secured from the DA. A rusty pickup rumbled by, honking its horn, and Silver waved. The driver must have realized that Scagnelli and Forsyth weren't typical drug customers, because the truck accelerated and burst down the street, setting off barking dogs next door.

"You guys are seriously bad for my rep," Silver said.

"All it takes is a haircut," Forsyth said.

Silver gave a desultory shake of his head that caused his dreadlocks to whip around his neck.

Scagnelli led the way as they entered the renovated living room, formerly the public end of the gas station where maps, soft drinks, and fan belts had once been sold. The aroma of grease, rubber, and mildew still lingered over the stench of forgotten garbage. The power was off, and Forsyth opened the curtains so they could see. Dust swirled as the sunlight revealed a ground-level living room with a '57 Chevy chassis suspended from the ceiling by steel cables. A rope ladder descended from the open driver's-side door. Scagnelli tugged on the ladder, causing the chassis to sway.

"My bedroom," Silver said with a smirk. "Wore out the shocks with my lady friends so I had to float it."

"I can see why," Forsyth said. "You're quite a charming young gentleman. What we called 'Sugar Britches' back in Kentucky."

Silver squinted at Forsyth, perhaps wondering if he was making a homosexual come-on, but Forsyth waved him to the garage area, passing through a tiny kitchenette and dining area that might have been salvaged from an RV.

"Did you do all this?" Scagnelli asked, unable to hide his interest. Forsyth took it as a kind of peer respect among criminals. The main difference between Scagnelli and Silver was that Scagnelli would kill his own mom for a buck, while Silver would rather drop acid and fantasize about world peace.

"Most of it," Silver said. "When you're a spiritual entrepreneur, you got a lot of free time."

The garage area was equally surprising, with Scagnelli switching on his long-handled police flashlight to augment the weak natural light. The garage was stocked almost like a real garage, with a bizarre array of pumps, belts, chains, and spare parts, but some animal hides were nailed to the walls, gray patches of bare skin showing here and there. Long wooden benches that looked like church pews were arranged across the floor, pointed toward a large-screen television. A mannequin in the corner was draped with a tattered American flag, and it held an empty bottle of whiskey in one stiff hand.

"Idle hands are the devil's playground," Forsyth said. One of the investigating agents had described the space, and the indictment had also mentioned Silver's clandestine lab. The room wasn't small, originally housing bays for two cars, but Silver had packed enough oddities to make it feel cramped.

The shag carpet was peeled back, revealing an opening in the floor where the second service bay would be. A thick piece of plywood was sitting off to the side. Silver hurried through the dim clutter, knelt and stuck his head down into the darkness. Scagnelli leaned over his shoulder and illuminated the space below.

"Bastards," Silver said. "They took it all. Some of that was legit."

"You know how it works," Forsyth said. "The government seizes all evidence and assets and sorts it out later."

As Silver descended via a metal ladder fixed to the wall, Forsyth stepped to the lip and looked past him to the refashioned service pit. Silver had applied his ingenuity by installing stainless-steel shelving and tables. Forsyth could imagine it full of flasks, trays, electron microscopes, computers, and gooseneck lamps. Silver settled into the metal office chair as if he were opening up shop again, the star of the show in the circle of Scagnelli's spotlight.

"So this is where Halcyon and Seethe were reborn," Forsyth said from above.

"Seethe?" Silver said.

"Dr. Morgan's formula."

"Bitchin' name. I like it."

"The good news is the drugs you were manufacturing for Dr. Morgan aren't illegal," Forsyth said.

"'Alleged,' dude. My lawyer said make sure the feds always use the word 'alleged.' Or did they take 'innocent until proven guilty' out of the Constitution while I was in the loony bin?"

Forsyth smiled. Darrell Silver was beginning to grow on him in a way. *A spiritual entrepreneur. Maybe we're not so different, after all.*

"The bad news is that the drugs can't ever exist, if you understand my meaning. They must remain our little secret."

In the orb of Scagnelli's spotlight, Silver's eyes narrowed as if embracing the existential possibilities. "Heavy."

Quietly to Scagnelli, Forsyth said, "Rig a recording device. Then call Dr. Morgan and invite her over. I want to get her and this knotty-headed hippie talking, to see how much they know."

"What about her husband? The guy who don't like cheese?"

"He's itching to explode. Once he hears she's been sneaking around behind his back, that's one less corpse for you to deal with."

"And then I deal with *him?*" Scagnelli squeezed his bony knuckles together in anticipation of revenge.

"No, I'll handle this end. Silver's already in my pocket. You have two CIA agents to put out of my misery. I don't want the senator to find out we've been cutting in line at his all-you-can-eat buffet."

CHAPTER TWENTY-FOUR

"Get out your scorecard, Chief," Gundersson said into his Sectera Edge, a clumsier but better-firewalled version of a cell phone. Gundersson normally relied on the device for e-mails and text messages, but the security classification of the Sectera rated higher for audio communication.

Plus, he wasn't sure he could have typed the entire message on the tiny keyboard without his fingers cramping.

Gundersson sat on a stump by the small ring of stones in which he'd built a fire of dry wood to minimize smoke. His camp was half a mile inside the Unegama National Wilderness Area, in a clearing that hadn't seen a chainsaw for nearly a century. His ankle throbbed after the long hike from the cabin, but it wasn't broken or he'd never have made it that far.

Roland and Wendy hadn't invited him to stay, not that he'd expected it. After all, having a federal agent walk out of the woods would make anybody a little wary, and if Roland's story was true, the couple had every reason to distrust him.

"What do you have?" Harding asked from his cramped NCS office in DC, sounding like his acid reflux was acting up.

"This is more than just busywork. Another agency is investigating, and the targets have received threats. Apparently it's connected to some secret drug experiment involving Burchfield."

"Did you say Burchfield? The senator?"

"Might be a smear job, right? But these guys swear Burchfield was behind several murders and a cover-up last year. Apparently Burchfield and CRO Pharmaceuticals were backing development of a drug that helped suppress memory."

"Shit, that's already been invented. It's called scotch."

The forest was settling into the first phase of dusk, with the birds falling quiet and a few insects issuing their high-pitched trills. Faint stars appeared through openings in the bright green canopy, and the dying sun cast a pinkish light over the clouds. It didn't look like rain, which relieved Gundersson, because he'd packed lightly and would have had to wear his poncho inside his tent.

"Doyle apparently got some e-mails with NCS as the sender. I told him I was with the CIA in order to get on his good side. I told him we were looking out for rogue elements in the NCS. Playing on all the interagency suspicion."

"A double agent within the same agency. Did he fall for it?"

"Enough. He opened up, but I don't know how much of it to believe."

Gundersson related Doyle's tale of how the couple and four of their college friends had been involved in a fear-response experiment eleven years earlier, where one of them had died. Then, last year, Sebastian Briggs had tried to recreate the experiment, testing a drug he'd discovered that caused the brain to shed its inhibitions and revert to primal functioning. According to Doyle, Burchfield was there when Briggs was killed, but nobody remembered what happened because Briggs had a different drug that caused short-term amnesia.

"That sounds like the biggest heap of steaming donkey malarkey I've heard since the WikiLeaks mess," Harding said in response. "Even if half of it is true, I'd guess Doyle was using that 'amnesia' card as an out."

"I don't know, Chief. These people don't really have anything to gain by lying. If they were players, why would they be hiding out in a hillbilly hollow?"

"I ran a background on Sebastian Briggs and not a whole lot comes up. That first experiment is on the books, and one of the subjects died, but it was apparently unconnected. Briggs was bounced from the UNC faculty, though, and he worked the fringe with some drug companies as a researcher, and then a whole lot of nothing. It's like the last five years of his life were erased."

"Big surprise. But there's one red flag."

"What?" Harding was growing impatient, annoyed that the job had gotten bigger and more complex than he'd counted on.

"No fake background was filled in for the last five years of Briggs's life. People who wipe out files usually put in some vanilla dates and places so the hole isn't so obvious."

"So whoever is behind this is either new to the game or is so goddamned big that they don't care who finds out."

Gundersson propped his sore ankle on a stone so it could cool. "And if somebody's playing connect-the-dots and wants to add more blank pages to the Seethe and Halcyon story, it's only a matter of time before they show up here."

"Or maybe they're already there."

The comment caused Gundersson to look around the forest, which already seemed wild and primal and threatening. "I better sign off, Chief. It's not so easy to recharge a cell phone by rubbing two sticks together."

"Okay. I'll dig from this end and find out who set up this mission. Be careful out there."

Right.

Gundersson hobbled to his tent and secured the Sectera in his pack, checking the clip in his Glock. He had been so engrossed in playing predator that he hadn't considered someone might be watching him watch *them*.

He made his way back to the fire. Even though it was April, the night was cool, with mist hanging low in the trees. Every snapping twig or flapping limb evoked images of a hunter creeping up on his camp.

He'd chosen a level clearing, preferring it to the rocky clefts and granite recesses on the ridge, thinking he might have to move quickly. Now he wondered if he'd left himself vulnerable, because he'd be exposed to anyone watching from the forest. And he couldn't shake the feeling that he was being watched.

Just the fox. Maybe even a black bear, but my food's suspended in a plastic sack. Nothing here to attract any nocturnal creatures.

But the shuffle of moist leaves just beyond the perimeter of the clearing indicated something big. Gundersson forced himself to remain casual. If a double agent was involved, or someone wanting Roland and Wendy all to themselves, then Gundersson would likely be already dead. One shot with a silencer and no one would be the wiser until Harding made his scheduled call the following night.

The NCS was clustered inside CIA headquarters four hundred miles to the north, but it might as well have been a million light-years. Harding would have to watch his step researching the CIA's involvement, since the agencies maintained an uneasy and oddly competitive relationship despite fulfilling the same basic mission. Harding had his own neck to protect. Gundersson was on his own.

He sat back down by the fire, keenly aware of the Glock thrust in the pocket of his windbreaker. He put his hands in his pockets, as if he were cold, and then realized that would look suspicious, since the fire was a better source of heat. He rubbed his hands over the flames, realizing how difficult it was to keep such a mundane gesture casual when you had to force it.

Depp and DiCaprio, you officially have my admiration for a change.

But good old Leo wouldn't sit there with a bull's-eye on his back. The script would tell him to do something cool like roll to the ground and come up firing toward the noise, squeezing off a chest-high line of lead that would result in a cry of pain.

Except he had no idea who was stalking him. It could be a real hunter, someone poaching deer out of season, or even a lost hiker. And killing the guilty was one thing. Killing the innocent was a lot harder to cover up, even for the National Clandestine Service, whose core mission was still officially classified. If Gundersson was the one who ended up tipping off the world that the NCS was involved in domestic actions, Harding would have him crucified, and the deputy director would make sure the nails stayed in place until the carcass rotted.

Gundersson opened the tin of pork and beans he'd warmed on a rock. He had no appetite but forced himself to eat a bite anyway. The syrupy odor immediately masked all the earthy, green smells of the woods.

He heard another clumsy footfall, a little closer and to the left, and he forced himself not to turn his head. He chewed slowly, staring into the fire, calculating distance.

Maybe I should casually stand up and saunter into the bushes as if I'm taking a leak. Except, if I assumed no one was around, I'd whip it out right here, wouldn't I?

Plus, I can't very well saunter when my fucking foot is about to fall off.

A night bird let out a piercing call, and it sounded a lot like a secret signal someone might make. Maybe there were two of them in the woods, closing in on him and cutting off any chance of escape.

The noise came again, and Gundersson decided it couldn't be a pro. Nobody with any level of training would be so careless.

Out of the corner of his eye, he saw the thin, fleeting flicker of a penlight beam. His stalker didn't have night-vision goggles, either.

Gundersson tossed the sardine can into the fire, the oil causing it to hiss and spit. He leaned back and worked his hands into his pockets, maneuvering the Glock so he could fire through his windbreaker if necessary.

Then the leaves parted and there she stood.

Her bathrobe hung open and she was naked underneath except for rubber flip-flops.

"You almost got yourself killed," Gundersson said after swallowing the lump in his throat.

"It's okay," she said. "I've been killed before."

She waited at the edge of the clearing, twenty feet away, and she was unarmed. She was "un" a lot of things.

Gundersson rose to his feet, remembering Roland's earlier rage. What if he'd tried to hurt her again? If Seethe had altered them the way Roland had claimed, then their behavior would be unpredictable even a year after exposure.

He had to admit, Wendy's behavior was certainly unpredictable at the moment.

"Are you okay?" Gundersson asked.

"Yeah." Her eyes were distant, but they held an animal cunning. "Can we talk?"

"Uh…I guess. Can I get you a blanket?"

"No. I know how to stay warm." She came toward him and knelt by the fire, spreading her legs as she crouched. The cool air had hardened her nipples to dark, blunted points. Gundersson forced his gaze away.

"Besides," she said with a girlish grin, tapping the penlight on her knee. "You don't want to be hobbling around on that sore foot of yours."

"I'm better now," he said, even though he was feeling much worse. What if Roland was after her, and was even now watching them from the woods? He might get the wrong idea.

But what was the *right* idea?

"Roland's going to be worried," he said.

"Don't worry, I can handle him."

"What he told me…about the Monkey House, and what happened to you…"

"I let him do all the talking because he thinks he remembers. But there are some things he always gets wrong. Like what happened between me and Sebastian Briggs."

Gundersson gulped. He didn't like meddling in other people's relationships. And he didn't need any new complications.

"Your husband is a jealous man," Gundersson said, choosing his words carefully. "And I don't know enough about Seethe and Halcyon to judge anyone's behavior. I'm just here to help."

"Why don't you start by helping me?"

She eased around the fire toward him, and Gundersson couldn't move. Her body moved with an animal grace that mesmerized him, and he involuntarily tightened his grip on the Glock.

"Here's the thing," she said. "Roland and me were separated at the time. So I could be with anybody I wanted, right?"

"Wendy, we have reason to believe that there are powerful elements—"

She reached out and placed a delicate finger on his lips, the touch of an artist. "Shh. I know."

She leaned closer, and her body heat was now rivaling the radiation of the flames. Her robe fell open wider and she let it.

"But you and Roland are back together now, right?" he found himself saying.

"Does it matter?"

He wasn't sure. He'd never been a cheater, but he'd never faced the opportunity before, either. And morality was a sliding scale based on current conditions and needs. He'd learned that particular lesson well in government service.

"We'd better get you back to your cabin, before…"

"Before what?" Her breath was on him, and the soft finger trailed from his lips to his cheek. The fire reflected in her black pupils, hell dancing against a deep, soulless night. Her Asian skin was radiant, and her frame, which had appeared skeletal beneath clothes, now seemed lush, soft, and rounded.

She gently pushed him backward until he was on the ground, the soles of his feet pointed toward the fire as she climbed along his length. His Glock jabbed into his kidney but he was afraid to move.

"You have to help me." She unbuttoned his shirt as he held his breath, and then she rubbed her breasts against his bare skin.

"I…I'll try."

"Sebastian Briggs wanted me to save Seethe. I can't count on Roland. So I need you."

"Is it Seethe that makes you this way?" he whispered, hoarse, feeling like a predator himself now, surging, hungry, utterly without remorse.

"Does it matter?"

It didn't.

CHAPTER TWENTY-FIVE

"I was worried," Alexis said to Mark, who was peeking through the curtains.

His sudden appearance had made her feel she'd done something wrong, that she was sneaking around behind his back. Of course, she was, but probably not in the way he thought.

"You ought to be worried," he said. "With your old pal Wallace Forsyth involved, it's hitting close to home. But I can't figure out what he wants. I mean, why would he have me kidnapped when he could have just killed me?"

Alexis was uneasy because Mark not only was carrying his pistol in his hand as he paced from window to window, but he slung the assault rifle over his shoulder. Luckily, he hadn't prowled through her backpack or she might have had to explain the bottles of "water."

"They obviously want something," she said. "First they raid my lab and steal my assistant's laptop, and now this. They won't kill us until they get it."

"So, tell me some *good* news," Mark said.

"Anita's dead."

"Anita? *Your* Anita?"

"It's been ruled a suicide, but it sounds suspicious. Especially with the timing."

"You don't seem too upset about it."

"Damn it, Mark, I'm numb. I've got so much to worry about…" She let her voice trail to a whisper. "I'm worried about *you*."

He spun, wild-eyed, one side of his lips twisted into a sneer as he waved the gun wildly in the air. "Me? I think I'm the only normal one left."

"Honey, you haven't been yourself lately. I think Seethe…I think what happened in the Monkey House…is still working on you."

"Is that so? Well, I happen to think it's the other way around. *You've* changed."

What a fool I've been. He's so far gone even Halcyon can't save him.

But she couldn't give up yet. She'd trained all her life, and she'd dedicated so much of the past year to finding a cure. But she had to rely on people like Darrell Silver to do the dirty work. The real frustration was that she couldn't do it alone. "Maybe if we—"

"Stop it." His face relaxed, and now he looked forlorn. "I can't take another of your lies."

"What are you talking about?"

"What you've been doing to me. The Seethe. Somehow, you smuggled a sample out of the Monkey House. Hell, for all I know, you were in with Briggs the whole time. He might have been your fall guy, while you kept right on cranking out the shit."

The words were like icicles driven into her heart. "Oh my God, Mark."

"Cute little story, about those guys raiding your lab. You knew Burchfield wouldn't leave it alone. If you make me think you weren't working on Seethe, then you can keep me as your guinea pig."

He stood as still as a statue, and that was more unnerving than his previous pacing. She leaned forward on the sofa, the backpack resting against her legs. She thought of Wendy's address scribbled on the back of the photograph. Their mountain cabin might as well be another planet.

"I never worked on Seethe," she said. "In the original trials, I didn't even know what it was. Sebastian Briggs tricked me just like he did the others. We didn't know we'd been exposed to it."

He wiped his chin with his Glock. He'd carried the gun for so long it had become just another appendage, a part of him.

"The worst part is that I can't kill you," he said. "I still need you."

"Don't you see? You'd never say something like that if you weren't Seething." She was talking fast, looking for a way out, but all the lies had chased her into a corner of the labyrinth she'd built.

He pointed the gun at her. "Where are you hiding it?"

"I don't *have* it," she said. She considered telling him about the Halcyon in the water bottles, but that would just prove she was a liar. If only she could remember all that had happened in the Monkey House, especially at the last, when she was collecting the pills. Had she somehow gotten Seethe from Briggs and didn't remember it?

And couldn't Seethe have worked inside her like a possessive demon, driving her to propagate it and spread it across the world? Didn't Seethe want to live, just like any organism? And wouldn't it do whatever it took to survive?

No. It's just a molecular compound. It's not alive in any real sense.

His gun hand was steadier than she'd seen it in days. "You hid the Halcyon after I thought it was all destroyed. I can't see you passing up your chance to change the world. You and Briggs had that in common."

"I swear," she whispered.

Then her cell rang and she flinched against the sudden noise, expecting Mark to pull the trigger. It rang four times, neither of them moving. Mark finally waved to her purse with the pistol.

"Get it," he said. "Might be one of your *friends*." He said the last word with a sneer.

Alexis dug into her purse and came out with the phone. The caller ID was blocked. "Hello?"

"Dr. Morgan."

No. It couldn't be. Darrell Silver's in...

Darrell Silver was in *federal* custody. That meant the U.S. government. And the government meant all bets were off.

"Mr. Silver," she said, trying to keep it on a formal footing. Maybe she could fool Mark into thinking it was a business call.

"I've got something for you."

Mark approached her, obviously wanting to listen in. She was tempted to terminate the call, but she had to find out. Silver had hinted he'd been refining the Halcyon, and if he'd synthesized a better version before being arrested, she needed to know. It might save Mark.

"I'm a little busy at the moment," she said, feigning calm. "Can we talk tomorrow? Maybe call me at my office?"

Mark was at the phone now, and she rushed out, "Okay, then. Fine. Bye," before clicking off.

"Who is 'Mr. Silver'?" Mark asked. "One of your secret government friends?"

"He's a former student who is doing some graduate research. We worked on some brain imaging together."

The phone rang again. Their eyes met. Mark smiled. He didn't even have to issue the command.

"Hu-hello?" Alexis said.

Mark put his ear near the phone. Alexis tried to pull away but he grabbed her by the hair and held her in place.

"Dr. Morgan," Darrell Silver said. "I have something for you."

"Tomorrow, like I said," Alexis said, but she couldn't keep her composure. The charade didn't sell, because Mark mouthed, "What?"

"You need to come pick up your groceries," Silver said, using the code name they'd developed for phone conversations to avoid mentioning Halcyon.

Mark jabbed the gun into her ribs. A small yelp burst from her lips before she could suppress it.

"What was that, Dr. Morgan?" Silver said.

"Is it…is it what we talked about last month?"

"Yes. The groceries have been delivered. Tonight."

Mark's lips pursed and curled as if he had all the proof he needed of her duplicity. He cupped a hand around the phone and whispered in her ear. "Tell him we'll be there right away."

He twisted the barrel of the gun deeper into her flesh as a motivator.

"Are you in the same place?" she asked after Mark removed his hand.

A bitter laugh came from the speaker. She couldn't tell if he was stoned, but knowing Silver, it was likely. "Home sweet home," he said. "Home on the range."

"What's that?" she said.

"Nothing. Some guy I met used to sing that all the time. Gets in your head, know what I mean?"

"I'll be there in half an hour," she said.

"Come alone, like usual."

She nodded. "Okay."

"'Like usual'?" Mark said after she hung up. "So, this is a habit."

She looked at the gun, which he'd forgotten to keep pointing. He smelled metallic, as if the corrosion in his brain had leaked out through his pores. Mark's grin made the scar on his lip stretch.

"I did it all for you," she said.

"That's what they all say." He motioned her to the door with the gun. "Let's roll."

She reached for the backpack, but he snatched it away from her and slung it over his shoulder with the assault rifle. He looked through her purse, evidently finding nothing suspicious.

He gave her the car keys and then the purse. "I'm in no condition to drive."

She didn't argue.

CHAPTER TWENTY-SIX

Scagnelli loved this kind of job, even if he'd rather be taking out the Cheese Guy.

The two CIA agents who had raided Dr. Morgan's lab were relatively fresh-faced. Or, at least, clean-shaven. They'd finished off their food at Bella Bistro on Franklin Street, each with pasta dishes, a plate of sloppy bruschetta between them. They were drinking a deep burgundy wine that probably cost ten bucks a glass.

They were dark-skinned, and besides the alcohol consumption, they could easily be taken for Middle Easterners. Azim, the one on the left, had been an overseas operative until he'd been made, at which point he'd been reassigned to the States. Of course, his stereotypical appearance aroused suspicion and thus he could only work in major metropolitan areas where his ethnicity wouldn't raise red flags.

Fortunately for him—at least up until tonight, when his fortune would go bad—Chapel Hill was one of the most international communities in the world.

Adrianus, the Greek sitting opposite, was also dark-skinned, and his radiant black hair and eyes also marked him as a foreigner. Scagnelli had actually met Adrianus once and had taken an instant dislike. Maybe it was genetic memory, dating all the way back to the Roman Empire, but Scagnelli had privately hung the nickname "Goatbreeder" on him.

Goatbreeder and Baby bin Laden symbolized all that was wrong with the nation's security forces. It was part of the reason Scagnelli had abandoned agency work. He wasn't a racist, naturally, but he saw the inherent flaw in using foreigners to preserve domestic policy.

"More *water*, sir," the waiter said. He was a college kid with sleepy eyes who carried himself with a sense of insouciant entitlement.

Scagnelli felt like dashing the remaining half of his water in the kid's face, but that most definitely would draw attention. Instead, he said, "What sort of wines are you serving tonight?"

The kid grinned, sensing a bigger tip, and hustled off to get a drink menu. Scagnelli, sitting outside on the patio at a small wrought-iron table, chanced another peek through the window to the restaurant's interior. Goatbreeder was laughing, swirling his wine around and taking a sniff of it before sipping.

Scagnelli wanted to kill him just for that irritating, pompous gesture if nothing else.

But he realized he was getting too emotional. This was just a job.

When the waiter brought his wine, he imitated Goatbreeder's gesture, trying to blend in with the well-to-do intellectual class that was sucking on the university tit and drawing taxpayer milk. He'd taken a second dose of amphetamines, and the speed was making his skin itch. He couldn't afford to get wired just before the job, so he gulped the wine instead of sipped, intending to mellow out the speed buzz.

A woman at the next table curled her lip at his performance as though he'd farted. Scagnelli toasted her and took another gulp. Her husband, a miserable-looking man who probably faced a dozen more years of ball-busting before mustering up the nerve to get divorced, caught her gaze, glanced over, and turned his attention back to his salad.

Inside, Baby bin Laden waved for the check, the agents apparently deciding to skip dessert. Goatbreeder took a last messy bite of the bruschetta, causing them both to laugh when a chunk of tomato tumbled free and plopped into his wine glass. Baby bin Laden paid with his credit card, scrawling his tip with a flourish when the water brought the receipt.

Goatbreeder fished the tomato chunk out of his wine with his finger. Scagnelli looked over at the scowling woman, hoping she would notice and launch into a fit of apoplexy. But she was griping at her husband, who gave his bobblehead "Yes, dear" nod, a motion so rehearsed it had created wrinkles in his neck.

At last, the CIA duo stood, and Scagnelli hurriedly downed the dregs of his wine. He stood, dug into his wallet, and slipped a ten on the table. He was hurrying around to the front, where the two agents would emerge, when the waiter called to him.

"Sir? Sir?"

Scagnelli frowned, with several diners now watching him. "I left my tab on the table."

"You left a ten, sir. Our Pinot Grigio is twelve dollars per glass."

Scagnelli dug into his wallet again. He wanted to shove the five in the kid's mouth, but instead made a small flourish of sticking the five in his vest pocket. He gave the kid's red bow tie a tug and said, "Keep the change."

By the time he got to the entrance, the two agents were gone. Scagnelli didn't want them to separate. Under ordinary circumstances, he would have preferred to divide and conquer, but the job had to be finished tonight.

He hurried to the parking lot, a dimly lit patch of cracked asphalt that was hidden from the restaurant by high tangled shrubs and a Dumpster enclosure that didn't smell any fancier than the garbage from a fast-food joint, Pinot Grigio or not. One of the agents was laughing, obviously in a good mood and secure in the belief that here in Chapel Hill, North Carolina, danger didn't dwell in every shadow and gutter.

Scagnelli kept his head down and marched purposefully in their general direction, but not straight toward them. Goatbreeder was talking about the Tar Heels, the university's basketball team that had apparently lost in something called "The Sweet Sixteen."

As Baby bin Laden mimed taking a hook shot, Scagnelli veered toward them and extended a friendly hand in a wave. "Adrianus? Is that you?"

Baby bin Laden froze in mid-motion, awkwardly standing with his arm curved in the air. The Greek turned with narrowed eyes. "Excuse me?"

"It's me. Dominic Scagnelli. We had that seminar together in the Pentagon."

"Scagnelli." Goatbreeder puckered his olive lips, his accent blowing any cover he might have used. "Maybe."

"Called 'Decoding the Obvious.' Remember that fat bastard telling us that if it walks like a duck and quacks like a duck, it's probably a pigeon?"

Goatbreeder gave an uneasy laugh. "Yes, yes. Now I do. Are you still with the Bureau?"

"Yeah, you know how it is. This gig, we're like monks, we're in for life." Scagnelli smiled to include Baby bin Laden in their brotherhood of government ineptitude, good guys trying to get through the day in a system that made no sense.

"Who's your partner?" Scagnelli said.

"Azim."

They shook hands. Baby bin Laden's was greasy, probably from the butter rolls. "So, what brings you to Chapel Hill?" Goat-breeder asked, clearly expecting Scagnelli to deliver the kind of lie typical for the profession—visiting an aunt, business conference, medical tests.

"I could tell you, but then I'd have to kill you."

Neither of them laughed. The joke was too old. Scagnelli continued. "I'm on this thing, some crazy shit. A researcher here is playing with a drug that opens people's brains like stripping away the layers of an onion, getting down there to the primitive impulses. Sounds like horseshit to me, but you know how the Puzzle Palace gets when they smell a chance at mind control."

Scagnelli knew he'd breached protocol. Even if they were all on the same case, a good agent never acknowledged that fact. The culture of subterfuge meant they all had to overlook the obvious.

"We're actually on vacation," Goatbreeder said.

"Golfing." Baby bin Laden gave an awkward swing, clearly revealing he'd never held a nine-iron in his life.

"Lucky bastards. Me, I got this intercepted e-mail from this researcher, she's working with a big-time drug dealer who cooks up his own poison. I don't know where the e-mail came from. May have been leaked from another agency. The CIA does shit like that all the time, right?" Scagnelli gave Goatbreeder a con-spiratorial nudge to the elbow, glancing around. The parking lot was empty except for a man sitting in a Lexus with a cell phone clamped to his ear.

"I don't know anything about that," Goatbreeder said. "Like I said, we're on vacation."

"Yeah, I understand. But I thought it might have been you guys, because somebody broke into the researcher's lab. They didn't find anything except for a laptop that had some copies of brain scans. And then *those* get leaked. The only agency I know that would deliberately let stuff get out is the CIA. Hell, even the Justice Department runs a tighter ship, and we all know how screwed they are."

Goatbreeder bristled a little at the criticism, but apparently he was well trained in restraining himself. Baby bin Laden, though, fidgeted, moving his weight from one foot to the other.

"Here's what I don't understand," Scagnelli said. "Why would the CIA want the Bureau to know about this particular researcher? I mean, we have different missions, right? Help me on this."

"I don't know," Baby bin Laden said. "All I'm thinking about right now is Whitehurst."

"Whitehurst?" Scagnelli said. "What the fuck is Whitehurst?"

"The golf course."

"You mean Pinehurst? Where they hold PGA events?" Scagnelli couldn't believe they let fucking foreigners traipse about on American soil like this, supposed defenders of democracy who hadn't even bothered to get their cover stories straight.

"He's newly assigned," Goatbreeder said, as if that was an excuse for being a stupid Arabian shitheel.

"Here's the weird part. My sources say it was two guys who raided the lab, and they were suspected terrorists. We all know what that means, right?"

Goatbreeder and Baby bin Laden looked at one another.

"I got nothing against people of any color or nationality, but even here in a college town, people have their preconceptions. I mean, they get cable here, right? Fox News? Brown people go boom boom?"

"What the hell do you want, Scagnelli?" Goatbreeder said. He didn't have much of a Greek accent anymore. He sounded like a college kid, like the waiter.

Damn. I'm really getting too old for this. Time to buy myself a compound in Montana and be done with it.

"I want what we all want," Scagnelli said. "Answers. The truth."

He had to bite the tip of his tongue to keep from snickering. He shouldn't have popped that second hit of speed. He was a little too buzzed for a job that required subtlety.

"The truth is a moving target," Baby bin Laden said.

"Then let's get moving." Scagnelli had his gun out before either of them noticed, yet more proof of their incompetence. He'd added a suppressor to the Glock's threaded barrel, which made it much longer and more difficult to conceal, but at least the agents would understand he meant business.

A couple had entered the parking lot and the woman was laughing like a sloppy prom date. Somebody was going to get lucky tonight.

Somebody including me.

"I need that laptop," Scagnelli said. "And I need to know who's pushing your buttons."

Goatbreeder kept on a diplomatic tack, his voice low. "If the Bureau is in on this, it means big politics. We can't compromise our mission of serving the president's policy objectives."

"Cut the rah-rah shit," Scagnelli said. "Where's the laptop?"

"You're not seriously going to shoot two innocent bystanders in public, are you?"

"Don't worry. No one will ever know. Or do you really think your regional director wouldn't bury you? I mean, you'd be a terrible embarrassment to the agency."

"Give him the laptop," Baby bin Laden said, barely hiding his nervousness.

Scagnelli wasn't surprised. He'd always figured Arabians had no grit, despite all the sand they'd eaten.

Scagnelli followed them to their car, already positive it was the silver Honda Civic, a car so painfully ordinary that it stood out even in a typical, middle-class parking lot. True to their nature, the agents had parked in the corner that was farthest from any streetlights.

He didn't know which one would go for a gun first. He figured neither. These guys were foreigners. No way would they put their lives on the line for the good old red, white, and blue.

Goatbreeder was the driver, which wasn't surprising. He slowly fished the keys out and was about to slide them into the driver's-side door when Scagnelli said, "The trunk."

Baby bin Laden waited without emotion while Goatbreeder opened the trunk. The laptop was lying there, along with a leather satchel bag.

"Here's what I don't understand," Scagnelli said. "You guys had orders to leak the information. But it wasn't leaked to me. I intercepted it fair and square. What I need to know is who you were trying to leak it to on purpose."

They looked at one another. A car started, probably the laughing couple's, and it backed out and exited the lot. The man with the cell phone was still in his car, not a big concern. The back door to the restaurant opened and a kid came out wheeling a gray trashcan, an orange dot marking the tip of his cigarette.

"We leak nothing," said Baby bin Laden, accent reverting toward his native tongue in his anxiety.

"Ah, crap, we didn't have to play it this way. But you're leaking one way or another."

When the restaurant worker banged open the Dumpster, Scagnelli squeezed the trigger twice. The agents slumped together for a moment before Goatbreeder slid against the side of the car and down to the cracked asphalt. Baby bin Laden flopped forward.

The restaurant worker wrestled with the garbage while Scagnelli flipped Goatbreeder into the small trunk. Baby bin Laden was a little less cooperative, still clinging to a faint pulse. There was no way to finesse a corpse into a trunk while out in public, so Scagnelli just shoved and rolled and folded, hoping he didn't get any bloodstains on his suit.

"Enjoy the ride," Scagnelli said, removing the laptop and satchel and slamming the trunk closed.

The man in the car with the cell phone must have heard the trunk's closing, because he turned but didn't pause in his conversation. Scagnelli ignored him, walking with purpose toward the restaurant as if he were a professor headed for a late martini. He continued down the sidewalk to his car parked along the street.

He was pleased to see in the glow of the streetlights that his suit was stain free. He popped a hit of speed in celebration. He felt like dancing, but on the sidewalks of the proud and free America, you didn't dare show any hint of joy. These days, happiness brought suspicion.

But at least you still own what happens in your head, right?

He walked faster.

At least for now.

CHAPTER TWENTY-SEVEN

Alexis had only been to Darrell Silver's lab once, when the hedonistic young chemist showed her his plan for refining Halcyon. He'd offered her a beer, which she declined, and he proceeded to pop one himself as he escorted her into the hidden recess where he'd installed his state-of-the-art equipment. Now, as she entered the former gas station, the greasy and musty aroma evoked memories of Sebastian Briggs's Monkey House.

"Darrell?" she called as she entered. The front door had been unlocked and she figured he would be waiting in the residential portion of the structure. She tried the light switch and the room stayed as dark as the falling dusk beyond it.

Alexis fished her keychain from her pocket and flicked on the attached penlight. She navigated the leather couch, the bowed shelves that were packed with vinyl records, and the strange alabaster sculpture that suggested a marine mammal. A gaping rectangle of darkness, oozing cool, metallic air, heralded the garage she remembered from her long-ago visit.

"Darrell?" she called again.

"Down here," he called from somewhere below.

A dim wedge of reddish light beckoned her. She knelt to see the narrow metal ladder that led down to Silver's workspace. The equipment was gone, but the stainless-steel fixtures remained, a few lighted candles on top of them. Silver sat in a swivel chair, holding a cigarette and smiling up at her. The candle flames bobbed as he waved.

"Been a while, huh?" he said.

"You're out of prison."

"I had a good lawyer."

"I shouldn't be here. If they see us together…"

Silver shrugged. He was wearing a button-up white shirt, a change from the rock band T-shirts he always wore. "You can leave any time. No biggie."

"You said you had something for me."

He snorted. "Yeah, some 'groceries.' Don't be so uptight. Come on down."

Alexis squinted into the darkness around her, wondering if anyone was hiding in it. She resisted the urge to flick the penlight around the garage. She'd have to trust Mark to watch her back, just like always.

Alexis went backward down the ladder, wondering if Silver was looking up her skirt. She turned off the penlight when she reached the concrete floor of the small chamber. The candles cast mesmerizing chimeras of yellow and black along the concrete walls.

"The place has changed," she said.

"The feds seized everything, Doc," he said. "You know how those fuckers are."

She rubbed her arms, feeling a little claustrophobic in the cramped lab. Despite a thorough cleaning and a paint job, the maintenance well still held the ghosts of all the vehicles that had been serviced from its depths. "So you finished the second batch?"

"No need to talk in code," he said. "We're among friends."

"Where's the Halcyon? I need it."

"Ah." Silver gave his goofy grin. "I didn't figure that stuff could be addictive. That puts a whole different spin on things. But I didn't tell you about the offshoot. You'll love this: tenocyclidine with extra fluorides."

"Fluorides."

"You know. Every chemical compound has a flip side, scramble the molecular structure, kinda like an echo. I played around with it and came up with a shit-kicking version."

"You extrapolated it?"

"Like a superduperfied version of angel dust." Silver spoke rapidly, excited about sharing his subject with someone who spoke the same language. "An analogue of PCP that blocks your glutamate receptors. PCP was a bitching pain blocker back in the good old days, but the side effects...whoa."

"Hallucinations, paranoia, schizophrenic delusions, rage. I know all about it."

"Heh. If I didn't know better, I'd say you've been getting wet yourself."

"Getting wet?"

"Yeah. They used to dribble the liquid on a cigarette. But you can snort it or carry it like a rock crystal. Versatile."

Alexis was uneasy, trying to comprehend what he was saying. "It's a dangerous dissociative drug."

He gave a casual wave of dismissal. "This new version would blow that shit out of the water. You're noodling around with neurotransmitters and they all run through the amygdala, right? I'm surprised you didn't see it yourself."

Alexis was, too. Briggs must have made the same extrapolation, linking the glutamate inhibitors with the role of serotonin and dopamine. She'd been so fixated on existing compounds that she hadn't made the leap into drugs that couldn't exist.

Darrell Silver, the scruffy, boyish savant who didn't even know the rules, much less play by them, was able to see without his vision being clouded by knowledge. That was a particular kind of genius Alexis would never possess.

But she sure as hell was going to possess Seethe.

"Did you produce any of it?" she asked, disguising her envy.

"I had some precursors lying around but they got seized. Give me a little time and I don't see any problem. Spinning off the fluorides might be a little tricky, though."

"We can go over the chemistry later," she said. "You've made a very valuable discovery."

Silver ignored her obvious impatience. "So I hear. No need to go baking up sheets of acid at two bucks a hit wholesale when I can auction Seethe to the highest bidder."

Goddamn. Somebody got to him. He knows what he has.

There wasn't time for negotiation. "You don't know what you're dealing with, Darrell. These guys are willing to kill."

Darrell gave a stoner laugh. "I used to hustle nickel bags in Needle Park. I know all about killing for a fix."

"I'll pay you double. But I need the Halcyon."

"Now we're getting somewhere." Silver fished around in his pants pocket as if looking for change. He came out with a tiny slip of rolled-up paper.

Alexis thought for a moment it might contain the revised chemical formula, but Silver jammed the paper into his mouth and leaned the tip toward a candle. He inhaled as the sweet, cloying odor of marijuana filled the maintenance well.

"I know you're in with them," Alexis told him. She didn't want to tip her hand, but she also didn't want to waste more time. Mark was running on fumes, and if she didn't get him some Halcyon soon, he might drift into a rage and kill them all.

"There are a lot of 'thems' running around, man," Silver said, taking another hit and holding it in his lungs a moment before blowing it toward Alexis with a flourish. She waved the smoke away, her eyes stinging.

"Well, you know you can't trust them, and you know I need you," she said. "I wasn't the one who turned you in."

"Here's the deal," he said. The marijuana must have been "superduperfied," too, because it had already relaxed him and he talked more languidly. "I got to have some cash. Lots of it. I'm heading for Canada. My lawyer thinks I can beat this rap, but I don't want to be locked in the loony bin for years while the wheels of justice are grinding."

"They didn't bust you for the drugs," Alexis said. "They busted you for Halcyon."

"That shit's not even on the books. I could patent it and sell it legit, but I don't want to hang around, if you know what I mean."

"This is bigger than you know."

"Tell me about it, Dr. Morgan. I've met some very interesting people lately. And I'm not talking about the nuts in the psycho ward. I'm talking about the nuts at the top of the tree."

Alexis wondered if Mark had entered the building and was listening from above. He'd dropped her off a block from the lab and promised he'd be watching. Of course, he was watching because he didn't trust her, not because he wanted to protect her.

She lowered her voice. "I can get you twenty thousand."

Silver giggled and took another hit of weed. "Doc, if I am going to be in exile, I want to live like one of these deposed dictators. I'm not going north to hunt caribou and sleep in an igloo."

She jangled her car keys. "My car, too."

"That's better. But somebody else made me an offer today. Six figures."

"CRO," she blurted out.

"Hey, I'm a dealer," he said, crushing out the joint on the tabletop. "No names. Sudden amnesia. I deliver and forget it."

"Do you have the new Halcyon here?"

He lifted his palms in supplication. "They picked the place clean. They didn't even leave a crumb for the mice. Not to mention the roaches."

"I can meet you here in an hour with the money."

"Whoa, whoa, whoa, Dr. Morgan. I know you gave me an A in neurochemistry, but I don't owe you any favors. I need to go with the high bidder here."

Alexis felt her own surge of anger and wondered if it was anything like what her husband experienced when the Seethe took control.

No. I'm in charge of my emotions. If the Monkey House trials proved anything, it's that I can survive.

Even if no one else does.

"All right," she said. "We'll have to do this the hard way." She raised her voice. "Mark!"

Silver let his eyelids droop and shook his head sadly. "Man, everybody's watched too many Coen Brothers movies."

"Mark!" Alexis shouted again, the name slapping off the concrete walls.

Mark's face appeared in the opening above the ladder. "Found a friend," he said.

He gave a grunt of effort and then Wallace Forsyth's wizened face emerged from the gloom.

"Hello, Alexis," Forsyth said. "I see we're both still engaged in the pursuit of happiness. But I think Mr. Silver there is happier than any of us."

"Dude, did you get busted?" Silver said to the older man.

Forsyth tried to smile but his face curdled as if he'd smelled something unpleasant. "I'm too old to play hide-and-seek."

Mark stuck his hand into the lighted space so that Silver could see the gun pointed at him. "Give Alexis what she wants."

Silver giggled. "Hey, Dr. Morgan, you have a well-trained husband there. A regular monkey on a leash."

"He's quite capable of murder," she said. Her coldness must have made an impression on the stoner, because his mouth fell open and he blinked rapidly.

"Okay, okay," he said. "That's the real bitch of the drug business these days. Used to be just people helping each other feel good, with a little spending money swapping hands. Now it's all guns and gangs and fucking conspiracy theories."

"Great," Mark said. "A hippie with a conscience. I thought you said this guy had a brilliant scientific mind. I think he's sampled a little too much of his product."

"Please, Darrell," Alexis said. "Your life is in danger."

Silver glanced at Mark's gun.

"Not just from him," Alexis added. "But from the people who put you in the hospital, the people who got you out of the hospital, and the people who don't trust either of those people. None of us are safe."

"Shit, Doc, you're higher than I am."

"Give me the Halcyon."

Silver looked up at the two men crouched on the garage floor above. Forsyth nodded at him and said, "Give them what they want."

Silver slid off the table and knelt over a tiny steel drain in the center of the maintenance well. The concrete was sloped so that liquids would flow to the lowest point and presumably be carried to the building's sewer pipes. Gallons of burnt motor oil, radiator fluid, and dirty water had probably swirled down the drain over the years.

Silver ran his fingers into the metal grid and twisted it. The drain fell open with a clunk. "Drug dogs couldn't smell it down here," Silver said. "Plus, they're not trained for this shit, whatever it is. They only do illegal drugs."

Silver ran his hand into the drain, digging and pushing until he was elbow-deep in the opening. After a moment, he pulled his arm back and held up an orange plastic vial.

"Every four hours or else," Alexis said.

"What's that?" Silver said, still kneeling on the floor.

Alexis took the vial and climbed the ladder. Mark moved Forsyth aside so she could join them on the garage floor.

"Hey, what about my money?" Silver shouted, his voice echoing up from the well.

"We'll mail you a check," Mark said.

"Seriously, what am I supposed to do?"

"I'd stick with Plan A and ride the Caribou Express," Alexis said. "After the heat dies down, I'll be in touch."

She left him as he fired up another joint, muttering to himself that nobody knew how to mellow out anymore. "Go easy on that Halcyon," he said. "It's my best work."

Outside, Mark said to Forsyth, "We've got a road trip planned, and since we can't leave you here, and I'm not ready to kill you yet, I suppose you'll have to come along."

"I understand," Forsyth said. "It's not like I had plans. Besides being vice president of the United States, that is."

"Give me your cell phone."

Forsyth fished inside his jacket and gave his BlackBerry to Mark. They walked up the street, keeping well off the pavement to avoid the passing headlights. Alexis hurried after them, wondering how she'd convince Mark to take one of the tablets.

The car was parked on a gravel service road outside an electrical substation. When they reached it, Mark waved Forsyth into the backseat. Then he flung the BlackBerry into the briars surrounding the substation fence.

"We can't have your pizza delivery boy using GPS to track us," Mark said as he slid into the seat beside Forsyth.

Alexis started the engine, turned on the headlights, and pulled onto the highway, heading west toward the Blue Ridge Mountains.

CHAPTER TWENTY-EIGHT

Roland had the dream again, the one in which he was running through a maze and the jagged metal sides of it were closing in. Something terrible was chasing him, and it wasn't a creature of bone and blood that might be fought and defeated.

No, this was a texture, a spongy, nameless dread, something that would overwhelm him and consume him in its gray depths.

Even as he fled, he suspected that whatever waited ahead wasn't so welcoming, either. But he could only flee in one direction, and he was about to turn that last terrible corner—

Roland awoke in a cold sweat, his heart pounding.

He stared up into the darkness for a moment, acclimating to the physical world and the cool spring night. Gradually, his senses settled and he was aware of the curtains shifting softly by the open window, the dim red glow of the alarm clock, the faint smell of mildew caused by the mountain humidity.

He listened for Wendy's breathing, still nearly paralyzed from the nightmare, his muscles quivering. The unease had accompanied him on his escape from his sleeping mind, and he half expected that odd spongy texture to drop from the cloaked ceiling and cover his face.

Roland reached out in the darkness to touch Wendy, but her side of the bed was empty. He rolled toward her until he came to the edge of the mattress. "Wendy?" he whispered.

He sat up, feeling for the night table. After retrieving the revolver, he stood with the sheet wrapped around him. They hadn't made love, so the sheet was dry and cool. But lately love had become something that wasn't just made, it was jammed together with a frenzied desperation.

"Wendy," he whispered again.

His mind raced down several avenues, all of them dead ends. She might have gone for a glass of water, but the bathroom was dark, no light showing in the crack beneath the door. No lights were on downstairs, either. If she were in the cabin, he'd easily be able to hear her.

That fucking liar.

He wasn't sure which liar he meant, Wendy or the agent who called himself "Gundersson." Roland hadn't completely bought the agent's story, but he figured the best approach was to play along while the truth revealed itself.

But the truth was a moving target.

And people could lie to themselves better than they could lie to others. Especially drunks like Roland.

There was another possibility, the one Gundersson had hinted at, of those "powerful elements" who might also be keeping an eye on them. Who might even abduct or kill them.

Unless Wendy is already on their side.

He crept down the dark stairs, the sheet trailing behind him. From below, he probably looked like a mad ghost, Hamlet's father made restless with betrayal.

The moon was high enough that it cast a blue glow over the couch, table, and refrigerator. Roland tiptoed to the door, ears straining for any sound. A porch board creaked outside.

He pointed the gun to the ceiling in a "ready" position and quietly opened the door. Easing it ajar, he put his face against the jamb to survey the porch.

Wendy stood in her bathrobe, painting by the light of the moon. The canvas he'd damaged earlier was now clotted with dark pocks of acrylic. She stabbed the brush against the canvas, dug the tip into the paint on her palette, and drove more color on with a wet slap.

Roland checked the perimeter of the yard. Moonlight illuminated skeins of silver mist that clung to the mountains. The world looked ancient, a faraway fantasy land where monstrous beasts might roll out of the fog and magic ruled the moment.

"Wendy?" he whispered.

"Shh," she said. "I almost remember the secret message."

"What secret message?"

"If I keep painting, I might uncover it."

Roland stepped onto the porch, wondering if Gundersson was watching from the concealment of the forest. The "powerful elements" might be watching as well. If he turned on the porch light, they would be exposed.

Wendy painted in a trance, dipping and jabbing, dipping and jabbing, a change from her usual broad, measured stroke. It almost looked like calligraphy, the small splashes arranging themselves around the perimeter of the canvas.

"That's not the monkey," Roland said, coming up behind her, attracted by her body heat. He hugged his sheet more tightly around his shoulders, keeping the gun concealed beneath his opposite armpit.

"It's the key to the Monkey House," she said, voice vacant.

"I thought you didn't remember the Monkey House." He checked the woods again for movement. If not for the strong scent of the acrylic paint and Wendy's body, he might have still been dreaming. Her flesh smelled raw and pungent, like a wild animal's. She hadn't smelled like that since...

Since the last time we made love.

"How long have you been out here?" he asked.

"How much of what you told Gundersson was true?" For the first time, she spoke with distinct clarity, as if finally aware of his presence.

"Most of it," he said.

"And about me and Sebastian Briggs?"

"Who the hell knows? Briggs scrambled our memories. But I've been piecing it back together as best I can."

She turned, her robe falling open. She was moist from more than the mist. Wendy occasionally painted in the nude, claiming that if models could strip for class, so could she. She swayed as if slow-dancing with her palette and brush.

"Briggs told me something," she said. "It's all I can remember from that night."

She hadn't been with Briggs long in the Monkey House, maybe fifteen minutes in the dark. He might have seduced her—*no,* Roland thought, *assaulted her, not seduced her*—in such a short time, but it's possible their relationship had been deeper eleven years ago, during the first Halcyon trials. She hadn't talked about it back then, and he was foolish enough and deeply enough in love not to press her on it.

"Briggs was going to kill us," Roland said. "We did what we had to in order to survive."

She shook her head. Her eyes were onyx, her pupils glinting amid her oval Asian face. "No, it was something to do with Seethe. He showed me."

"Showed you?" Roland found himself staring at the inner curves of her exposed breasts, where a discolored spot suggested a bruise. Someone had been playing rough.

Wendy pointed to the canvas. "Letters. Shapes. He arranged them in a diagram."

Roland strained against the dimness and now saw more of a pattern to her markings. A series of curls and short slashes were clotted against the canvas, covering the original form of the huddled figure, as if she were belatedly tattooing it.

It was difficult to discern the new markings, aside from their damp thickness, because the weak light blended the colors into browns and tans. But he made out what looked like a C and several crooked H marks.

"You're trying to spell something?" he said, recalling the "CRO" initials of the drug conglomerate that had been Briggs's financial backer. Those initials had been in the motel room where he'd awoken to find a corpse in the bathroom. He still didn't know who she was or who had really killed her. And he still wasn't fully convinced of his innocence.

"No." Again she shook her head, and the dangling cotton belt of her robe brushed gently against the porch. Besides the insects and the distant tinkle of the creek, the night was still. The mist around them seemed to thicken.

"You suddenly remember something from a year ago, but you don't remember what it is," he said, feeling his anger and mistrust rising.

"Something you told Gundersson jarred my memory," she said. "When you said Sebastian took me to his office."

He lowered his voice, unconsciously squeezing the barrel of the pistol. "Nothing happened in the office."

"Sebastian showed me a piece of paper. It had markings on it, letters. He took my hand and guided my fingers over them, again and again."

Roland didn't know what angered him more, her referring to him as "Sebastian" as if he were an old friend, or the image of the scientist's filthy hands on her flesh as he leaned over her. He took a couple of steps closer to the canvas. Now he could see another set of symbols.

"I thought he was…playing nasty…but he was teaching me," she said.

They were skewed and uneven, but the patterns appeared to be a set of linked hexagons. An F tilted to one side, and an S wound like a sick snake across the center of the painting.

"Did Briggs tell you what these were?" Roland asked.

Wendy stood back and studied the marks as if she had just painted over the ceiling of the Sistine Chapel. "It looks like graffiti," she said.

"But you were painting from memory." Roland understood how absurd that statement was. "Memory" no longer had any reliable meaning for the Monkey House survivors.

"The key," Wendy said. "That's what he kept saying."

The key.

A fine steam rose from her flesh, heat leaving her body and rising to merge with the mist. He went to her and closed her robe. The gun bumped against her hip.

"Maybe it's a code of some kind," Roland said. "All this secret-agent shit, I wouldn't be surprised."

"But why would he tell me?"

Because you were his little pet, his plaything, his lover.

But he couldn't think that way, because then he'd start raging, and the Seethe would rise from its slumber and own him. "He couldn't trust Alexis or Mark. David and Anita were already head cases. And he knew I hated his guts."

She turned her back to him and studied the painting. He pressed himself behind her, one arm wrapped around her stomach. The back of her neck smelled like the forest, wild and green and filthy with rot.

"The key," Roland said. "Whatever it is, we can't let Gundersson find out."

"I still don't know what it means."

That's when the pattern coalesced into something both familiar and frightening, as Roland recalled his rudimentary high school chemistry. The markings represented a diagram of a molecular structure, and the letters were the elements from the periodic chart.

Briggs had wanted to store the diagram in a safe place, in case he needed to recall it later. Maybe Wendy wasn't exactly safe, but she was a data storage unit that no one would suspect. Because she was the artist of the bunch, the least interested in nuts and bolts and how things fit together but the one most visually adept. And the only one Briggs could trust.

And now Wendy had unearthed a compound that half a dozen people had died to control. Wendy had drawn a secret chemical formula.

Wendy had drawn Seethe.

CHAPTER TWENTY-NINE

Scagnelli wasn't a hacker by profession, but he'd picked up enough skills to penetrate a firewall or two.

Not that he needed many skills. His level of respect for the CIA plummeted another few notches as he dug through the files on the stolen laptop. He'd previously hijacked their e-mails but he expected the case files to be secured. But Dr. Morgan's stolen collection of brain scans and her surveillance records were all stored on the desktop in plain sight.

Scagnelli initially suspected they were red herrings, because nothing important was ever hidden in plain sight. But he gradually accepted it was yet more incompetence by Goatbreeder and Baby bin Laden, agents with so little professionalism that they didn't even bother encrypting the files or using passwords.

When will the government learn that American pride can't be exported?

But something about the whole job still smelled funny.

The CIA had always been the wild card of the intelligence community, an independent agency that made presidents uneasy and kept generals in line. But the reorganization in 2004 punished the agency for the failure of the country's intelligence networks. The perception since then was that the CIA was more of a fringe watchdog group, useful in spying on everyone but not particularly reliable.

As such, it was the agency most likely to be exploited in a political bait-and-switch.

And from the information in the leather satchel he'd taken from the two dead agents, Senator Burchfield had triggered the investigation into Dr. Alexis Morgan, considering her research a matter of national security. That wasn't so unusual, since practically everything was a matter of national security these days, from the ingredients of ballpark hot dogs to the newest panelist on *American Idol*. Burchfield's primary influence was as chairman of the Senate health committee, but he also served on the defense subcommittee.

If Burchfield was applying pressure, he could have gone through one of the eight intelligence agencies in the Department of Defense. That meant he either didn't trust his own channels, or he wanted a smokescreen to keep anyone from tracing the footprints back to him.

But Scagnelli was already tracing the footprints straight to Burchfield's home in the Washington Park neighborhood of Winston-Salem, where million-dollar mansions covered the small rise where once Moravian settlers had hunted.

After returning to Darrell Silver's lab and finding the place abandoned, he'd called Burchfield and set up the meeting, making sure he could get past the Secret Service agents assigned to the presidential candidate. Scagnelli didn't mind adding another notch or two to his gun, but leaving blood on Burchfield's patio would be harder to erase than a couple of bumbling agents dumped in the trunk of a Honda Civic.

Now, as he pulled onto the bricked driveway leading to Burchfield's house, he mulled a plausible explanation for Forsyth's disappearance. Most importantly, he didn't want to be blamed for abandoning the stubborn old bastard. He was exiting his car when the obligatory Secret Service agent made a sudden appearance.

Jesus, these fuckers wear sunglasses even in the dark.

"Are you Scagnelli?" the agent said.

"No, I'm Peter Cottontail, hopping down the bunny trail."

The agent's face was stone under the porch light. It was nearly midnight, and he'd probably been on duty all day. The Secret Service wasn't known for smiles and giggles.

"You fit the description," the agent said, escorting Scagnelli to the door and even pressing the buzzer for him. "Right down to being a flaming asshole."

Burchfield was in a burgundy robe, although he wore a white T-shirt and sweatpants beneath it. Eyeglasses with thick plastic frames hung at the end of his nose, and his hair was casually raked to one side of his forehead. He looked like he'd been on duty all day as well, like a clown who'd just taken off his makeup but whose mind hadn't yet fully left the ring.

"Nothing on Forsyth?" Burchfield asked, not bothering with formalities.

"I tried his cell. No answer."

"He was meeting the Morgans, correct?"

"Yes, and they were having a little powwow over a drug called Halcyon. And from what I've found out, you and the Morgans have a history, too."

Burchfield bristled at Scagnelli's forwardness. "Why weren't you with him?"

Scagnelli held up the leather satchel. "He sent me on another job. So either he thought he could handle things on his own or he didn't want any witnesses for whatever he had planned."

Burchfield raised his voice. "I've known Wallace since my first Congressional run. And he's been both a mentor and one of my closest allies. Without his support, I'd still be a party delegate, not the next president of the United States. So if you're coming here to make accusations—"

Scagnelli gave a vehement wave to placate the senator. The man who looked so confident and handsome on television appeared slightly sunken and pale in real life. He reminded Scagnelli of a sad uncle who used to give him quarters for video games, as if vicarious pleasure was the only kind he could enjoy.

"Let me show you what I've found, and you can decide for yourself," Scagnelli said.

Burchfield tilted his head to invite Scagnelli deeper into the house. Two sets of stairs rose from the foyer, and the ceiling was fifteen feet high on the first floor. The walls were of dark wood, mahogany or some more exotic material that had probably dodged an import tax. An antique table bore a photo of Burchfield and his brainless-looking trophy wife, little wire baskets on each side filled with stinky potpourri.

Burchfield opened a door and ushered Scagnelli into a small office, shelves of books lining two sides. The room smelled of ink and furniture polish. An expensive collection of ceramic figurines lined the mantel of a gas-log hearth, representing notable historical figures such as Benjamin Franklin, Abraham Lincoln, and others that Scagnelli didn't recognize. They were hand painted and their eyes seemed to track Scagnelli's movements.

He wasted no time flopping the satchel onto a coffee table and spreading out the documents. In addition to the images of the brain scans, Scagnelli showed Burchfield copies of e-mails, decoded messages, and transcripts of intercepted phone calls. A few of the memos were cryptically coded "per Burchfield directive."

"I'm afraid you didn't do a very good job of covering your tracks, sir," Scagnelli concluded.

Burchfield, whose lips pursed increasingly tighter as Scagnelli presented the information, finally spoke. "None of this is mine," he said.

"The CIA's already been busted for running covert programs without telling Congress," Scagnelli said.

"Of course. That assassination program in the Bush era was a little embarrassing for us all. *Alleged* assassination program, I mean."

"This might be a rogue thing," Scagnelli said. "But if you're not the one who ordered the investigation into the Morgans, then somebody's setting you up."

Scagnelli didn't tell him about the e-mail messages he'd sent to Roland Doyle, routing them through a dummied-up CIA address. Those didn't have Burchfield's fingerprints on them, but an outside observer would probably lump them into the same ball of wax.

"Of course we were monitoring the Morgans, and everyone else connected to Sebastian Briggs," the senator said. "But it was a closed loop. Halcyon was buried by CRO, who wanted nothing to do with it anymore. And Seethe..."

"The rage drug," Scagnelli said, to let Burchfield know he was already in the loop.

Burchfield nodded. "It doesn't officially exist, either. Halcyon at least made it to clinical trials, but nobody knew about Seethe until last year."

"Nobody except the seven subjects in the original trial," Scagnelli said. "And only five are alive now."

"I have a personal stake in this," Burchfield said. "I feel responsible, and these drugs are a threat to national security."

The senator really meant they were a threat to his presidential bid, but Scagnelli kept quiet, knowing silence might elicit more information than agreement could.

"Wendy Leng has been in contact with Dr. Morgan," Scagnelli said. "They all could be getting back together, which means they're planning something, like maybe going public."

"That can't happen."

"I won't let it happen, if you like."

"And you tried Wallace's BlackBerry?"

"No answer."

"He wouldn't go dark on his own, not at a critical time like this."

"If I may be so bold, sir?"

Burchfield sat on the plush leather sofa. "Fire away. I can handle it. Hell, I've heard worse."

"There are a few options. One, Mr. Forsyth voluntarily went with the Morgans, wherever they are going."

"They could have kidnapped him and are going into hiding."

"It's a possibility, but Forsyth isn't good for anything except insurance. If they wanted value, they would have kidnapped the drug maker, Darrell Silver. After all, Silver is the one who cracked Briggs's Halcyon formula."

"So Silver's disappeared, too? Maybe the Morgans kidnapped them both."

Scagnelli pulled the miniature digital recorder from his pocket and placed it on the coffee table. "Audio proves that they left Silver there. No telling where he headed, but he was around at least half an hour after they took your friend, apparently uncovering stashes of drugs the feds missed."

"So Wallace expected Mark to kill his wife? I know Mark is a little...unhinged."

Scagnelli nodded. "From my understanding, Mark was the only one of the group who received his first Seethe exposure last year in the Monkey House. Besides, of course, you and Wallace Forsyth."

"Damn it. I can hold my liquor. I'm the Charlie Sheen of DC. I haven't noticed any ill effects."

No, I'm sure sociopathy is immune to the effects of personality-altering drugs, because there is no humanity left to destroy. "Oh, I'm sure of that, sir. You've behaved calmly and rationally through it all. The liberal bloggers can't lay a glove on you."

Burchfield gave a stately jerk of his shoulders, standing erect as if a camera and a flag were nearby. "I'll admit, Seethe can be quite effective, which is why it's so dangerous."

"And so useful," Scagnelli said. "I also discovered your plans to funnel Seethe to the Pakistan border. Enough crazy people killing themselves on both sides of the border, it will escalate pretty quickly, especially if some American troops go down as collateral damage. A hawk like you, already sitting pretty on the defense committee, would be very appealing to the voters."

"That's dangerous talk, Mr. Scagnelli."

Scagnelli was amused. Burchfield was just another cog in the machine, and even if he achieved the presidency, he'd be no more than a house servant for wealthy corporations and the finance sector. Much like Scagnelli was a slave to Burchfield and Forsyth. At least for the moment.

Power had a way of flip-flopping when one side possessed something the other side needed.

"You hired me for danger, Senator. And I'm not suggesting your plan is seditious. Hell, just between you and me, I like it. But it's not *you* I'm worried about."

"Wallace?"

Scagnelli gave a casual shrug. If Burchfield could play the role of world leader, why couldn't Scagnelli pull off the innocent bystander part as a supporting actor? "He's been going a little afield, sir. At first, I thought he had orders from you that he wasn't relaying to me. But he worried me a little with that Book of Revelations stuff."

"Wallace has always been fundamentalist. That's no secret. And I've found him to be a sincere man of faith."

Scagnelli tapped the documents on the coffee table. "But doesn't it make you wonder? It looks to me like the evidence puts him on the road to Halcyon and Seethe while pointing all the fingers at you."

"Wallace is loyal to me."

"A man of God will always choose the higher calling."

"No." Burchfield removed his glasses and tapped them against his thigh. "Wallace has always been a man of sound principle. And before you suggest it, he didn't suffer any lingering effects from Seethe, either."

"It might be cumulative. After all, Mark Morgan didn't turn into a rampaging, well-armed lunatic overnight. From what I've discovered, the others may have built a tolerance to Seethe, probably because the Halcyon suppressed it."

"Seethe is unpredictable. That's what makes it valuable."

And that's what makes it fun. Before this little adventure was over, Scagnelli planned on getting his hands on some Seethe. A guy never knew when dosing somebody into a murderous rage might be necessary, or at least entertaining.

"All I'm saying is Mr. Forsyth might not be his usual self," Scagnelli said. "If he's getting messages from God or whatever, then he's going to have a different set of motivations."

"Excuse me." Burchfield picked up his own BlackBerry and dialed, then ordered the person on the other end of the line to run a GPS search for Wallace's BlackBerry. "Call me when you know."

Turning back to Scagnelli, he said, "You mentioned other options?"

"Well, Mr. Forsyth had me kidnap Mark Morgan."

"Kidnap? I didn't order that!"

"I assumed it was to force Dr. Morgan to turn over the rest of her research records. But what if he wants to partner with them? Maybe even go public, too?"

Burchfield clenched his fist. "He'd never betray me like that. I am going to make him vice president."

"Why settle for number two in the U.S. when you can be number one in heaven?"

"No way. No fucking way." Burchfield stormed across the office. The windows were concealed by thick curtains, but Burchfield parted them to glance into the darkness. "Wallace, you son of a bitch."

Rage. That's an unhealthy emotion, Senator. Causes errors in judgment. Or maybe just allows us to give in to our true nature.

Scagnelli tossed some gasoline on the flames. "Of course, it's equally possible that he partnered with Darrell Silver. Who cares about the monkeys when you can own the banana tree?"

Burchfield growled deep in his chest, and Scagnelli was grateful the man was currently his boss and not his enemy. That could change tomorrow, and probably would, when Scagnelli ended up with the formulas for both Seethe and Halcyon and decided Senator Daniel Burchfield was no longer a necessary evil.

"Nobody stabs me in the back," Burchfield bellowed.

"Yes, sir."

"Nobody fucks with me."

"Yes, sir."

"Nobody takes away what's mine."

"Yes, sir."

Burchfield grabbed one of the figurines from the mantel, Thomas Jefferson if Scagnelli had to guess, and hurled it into the hearth. It cracked into a dozen pieces.

Let freedom ring.

Burchfield's BlackBerry buzzed and he immediately relaxed, his face going placid. Scagnelli wondered if Seethe had maybe dug a deeper hole in the senator than he realized.

"Yes?" Burchfield said into the phone, listening for fifteen seconds before clicking off. He spoke to Scagnelli without turning. "They found Wallace's phone in the weeds near Silver's laboratory."

Scagnelli decided to keep the kettle boiling. "He probably ditched it when he went with the Morgans. Didn't want to be tracked."

"And you said Wendy called Dr. Morgan?"

"My guess would be they're planning a little reunion."

"I don't pay you for guesses. I pay you for results."

Damn. You just about had my vote, but now you pull the plantation-owner crap. Oh well, I shouldn't expect too much. He's been snouting the trough for so long he can't smell his own stink.

"I can give you the results you want," Scagnelli promised. "Far more effectively than the CIA, the defense department, or the FBI." He thumped the stolen documents. "I don't leave paper trails or fingerprints, and I offer plausible deniability."

He wanted to add that he'd already taken care of one problem for Burchfield: Anita Molkesky. Instead, he just said, "It's possible they will be gathered in one place for the first time since the Monkey House."

Burchfield connected the dots. "The first and last times."

Scagnelli glanced around the room and mouthed, *Is it bugged?*

Burchfield spoke at his previous volume. "Everything stays here in this office."

"In that case, you're in luck. I'm having a half-off sale."

Burchfield ticked the names off with his fingers. "Alexis… Mark Morgan…Roland Doyle…Wendy Leng…Wallace…that makes five."

"'Five' rhymes with 'no longer alive.'"

"There's only one condition."

"Only one?"

"Wallace failed me, but you won't. Don't kill them until you have Seethe and Halcyon."

"You got it, Mr. President." Scagnelli flashed a cheesy grin before heading for the door.

Who knows? Maybe he'll choose me as his new running mate.

CHAPTER THIRTY

Mark's headache was getting worse.

Luckily, traffic thinned as they left the interstate and began the winding climb up into the mountains, but every sweep of oncoming headlights hit him like a sheet of battery acid laced with jalapeno. Closing his eyes didn't help, and he couldn't risk encasing his head in a jacket to muffle the external stimuli.

No, that's just what they would want me to do. I have to stay awake.

Alexis glanced from the driver's side once in a while, but Wallace Forsyth, who was in the passenger's seat, hadn't spoken in the past hour. In the seat behind them, Mark wondered if they'd devised some plot behind his back, perhaps to wait until he was asleep and take the gun away.

"You look bad, honey," Alexis said to his reflection in the rearview. She was calm, but the greenish dashboard lights revealed the strain in her eyes.

"I *am* bad," he said. "I thought that's what you wanted."

"Please take the Halcyon."

"Right. Like I'd trust something cooked up by your hippie sidekick?"

"No, it's not like that," she said, and her pleading tone disgusted him.

Amazing how you could live with someone, *sleep* with someone, for years and then one day realize you didn't know a thing about them. The stranger you loved was the strangest of all.

"What's it like, then, Lex? What's the latest reality you're trying to pitch?"

She glanced at Forsyth. It was just a glance, and though Mark could only see the back of her head and a faint flick of her eyes in the mirror, he knew.

"You haven't been the same since the Monkey House," she said. "The Seethe exposure has been eating away at you. The rage, the headaches, the paranoia. I know it's hard for you to see from the inside, but it's happening."

"Oh, yes. Nice sales pitch. Such sincerity. And you want me to see a shrink, right? Get help just like Anita did." He leaned forward, letting the barrel of his Glock rest on top of the front seat. "But we know what happened to Anita, right?"

"She was different."

Mark punched the gun against the seat, causing Forsyth to jerk a little. "Of course she was. Because she wasn't lucky enough to be under the care of Dr. Alexis Morgan. The only one besides the dear dead Sebastian Briggs who is an expert on Seethe and Halcyon."

"We've never had Seethe."

"Why should I believe you? You lied to me about hiding Halcyon, you never told me you developed it, and you lied to me about the CIA stealing your research."

Forsyth finally spoke. "She didn't know we were after it."

Mark laughed, and the air rushing up from his abdomen was sour and painful. "You've probably been working with her since the bioethics council. But it's all going to fall apart soon. The two of you have been planning this little reunion for quite a while, I'm sure. But I'm crashing the fucking party."

Alexis slowed the car, and Mark noticed they'd entered the rural foothills, the two-lane highway flanked by tall hardwoods, an occasional farmhouse dotting the side of the road. Mark had spent summer vacations in these mountains as a child, swimming on Watauga Lake, riding the Tweetsie Railroad steam train, and hiking on Grandfather Mountain. In the night, the destination took on a foreboding aspect, as if all the secrets of the Appalachian Mountains had grown deeper with no one looking.

"How much farther?" Mark asked.

"Maybe two hours. It's beside the Unegama National Wilderness Area."

So Roland and Wendy had found a hollow hidden deep in the land of legend. That made sense, considering they had played hide-and-seek in the Monkey House so well. And they would be waiting, because all of them had a hand in it. Sure, his wife was the one who'd been dosing him with Seethe, but they were all watching, waiting, eager for him to crack.

But I'm not going to crack. I'm the only one who remembers, and if I'm gone, they win, Burchfield wins, CRO wins, and Seethe wins. I can't let that happen.

Mark shoved Forsyth's shoulder. "So, what do you think of the doctor's theory? If Seethe is causing us to lose it, why are you so rational?"

"I draw my strength from the Lord," Forsyth said, evenly and quietly, barely audible over the hum of the tires on asphalt.

"If you've got a direct line to God, then tell me this: why would He turn Seethe loose on the world?"

"It was prophecy." Forsyth continued staring straight ahead, not giving in to the exhaustion that probably haunted his old bones. "'And I heard a great voice out of the temple saying to the seven angels, Go your ways, and pour out the vials of the wrath of God upon the earth.'"

"Falling back on the Bible. The coward's way out."

"I can't judge your soul, Mark. But that day is coming."

"So, what do you think, honey?" Mark said to Alexis. "Could Seethe be the cause of his religious delusions?"

"Seethe creates individualized responses, based on unique brain chemistry—"

"Shut up and give me the vial."

"Are you going to dump it?"

"After what happened in the Monkey House, I'd say you're the last person who should be dispensing little pills."

"What you said happened…it didn't happen."

"You killed him, Lex. You bashed his brains in with a hunk of metal. I saw it. Hell, I see it almost every time I close my eyes."

She shook her head. Forsyth reached across the front seat and touched her arm, a conspiratorial motion that caused rage to ripple up Mark's spine.

"Forgive him, for he knows not what he does," Forsyth said.

Mark put the tip of the barrel against the top of his wife's spine. "Give me the vial."

She slowed the car, fished it from her pocket, and held it up. He snatched it away and flicked on the dome light. He shook it once, like a maraca, and struggled with the lid.

"Goddamned childproof caps."

Finally, he popped it open. Forsyth had turned and was looking over the seat at him. Alexis kept glancing in the rearview.

Mark rolled a few pills into the palm of his hand. They were larger than the Briggs concoction, unmarked, with no hard coating. They were plain white and looked as if they would crumble if he squeezed them.

As a drug-company executive, he hadn't spent much time on the production end, but pills with such shoddy development were considered counterfeits. They were dangerous primarily because pills might cost only pennies to make, but drug companies claimed they need huge markups to offset the cost of research. Companies like CRO feared only one thing—cheap and plentiful drugs that did the job. Luckily, Congressional members like Burchfield were only too happy to adopt protectionist policies while slipping campaign contributions into their war chests.

But the politics of greed were far removed from this simple choice before him. Did he trust his wife, or did he believe what his admittedly confused mind was telling him?

He rolled down the window, and the moist rush of the mountain air filled the car. He could fling the pills into the ditch and be done with them, at least until Darrell Silver cooked up another batch.

But he'd already tried to push Halcyon out of his life. He seemed intricately bound to it, a junkie who even in abstinence was defined by his habit.

If Alexis had dosed him with Seethe, wasn't Halcyon the only alternative besides madness?

"I love you, Mark," Alexis said.

What's behind door number three?

As far as he could tell, he loved her in return.

And if he could think clearly, maybe he could rediscover what love meant.

And wasn't that worth a little risk?

He slipped one of the pills into his mouth.

CHAPTER THIRTY-ONE

Roland's first impulse was to destroy the painting.

But even if he doused it with kerosene and torched it, the inherent truth wouldn't go away. Somehow, Briggs had used Wendy as a living data bank, burying the molecular compound in her memory. If he destroyed this one, it might turn up on scratch paper, the dry-erase board on the fridge, or on a chalkboard somewhere.

The doc was smart. He knew computers weren't safe, not with all these federal agencies watching. Maybe he knew they'd eventually take it from him before he was ready. And, sick as it was, he wanted Seethe to live on.

But knowledge was power.

Gundersson had made a big deal out of protecting them, promising to spread false information that would move them off the radar. Maybe their chances were better if Roland handled the negotiations himself, played one side against the other, or maybe even took the drug public.

Roland didn't understand the symbols and structure of the diagram, but that didn't matter. It wasn't his job to mash molecules together. His job was to keep his wife safe and to secure their future. Apparently running to the remote Blue Ridge Mountains wasn't far enough. They might have to go overseas, maybe to Tibet.

You trade a painting for two tickets to anywhere. And they'll just let you fly off into the sunset. Right. You really ARE mindfucked.

Wendy had gone back to bed, but Roland was restless, sitting on the porch and nursing a cold cup of coffee. Dawn pinked the ridges on the eastern horizon, the first birds calling from deep in the woods. The revolver was on the table, but now it seemed ridiculous. Gundersson was right. He was a lousy shot.

An engine roared somewhere down in the distant valley, someone climbing the steep, winding grade. The road turned to gravel near the wilderness area, at which point traffic was limited to the occasional logging truck or maintenance crew.

They're coming.

Gundersson said bringing them together would give them a fighting chance, allow them to hone their cover stories and make it easier for him to provide protection. But it also made them easy targets for Gundersson's betrayal.

Roland pocketed his revolver. Gundersson wasn't the only possible chink in the armor. Alexis Morgan was a Briggs protégé, and Mark had been employed by the pharmaceutical company that funded the Monkey House trials. He couldn't fully trust either of them.

And that brought him to Wendy.

She might still harbor some sort of twisted loyalty to Briggs. After all, he'd entrusted her to carry the Seethe formula, even if she wasn't fully aware of what she'd done.

No. You love her. You went through hell for her. And if she turns out to be the devil, at least you made your choice with your heart instead of your head. Because you never COULD trust your head, could you?

He checked the bullets in the revolver. It held six .38 caliber rounds. If he went to his fallback plan, and his aim was accurate, he'd have two bullets left. The one destined for his temple probably wouldn't miss.

But before he cleaned Seethe and Halcyon from the face of the Earth and tore down the Monkey House once and for all, heads had to be counted. If anyone else knew about it, then their deaths would be wasted.

Roland gave a gruff laugh. David Underwood would survive. David, the most broken of them all, would carry the secret of Seethe's grim potential.

Kurr-rrrack-uhh.

The morning stillness was shattered by the reverberating gunshot, and its abruptness caused Roland to drop his pistol. He scrambled down to the rough pine boards of the porch, reaching under his chair for the weapon.

He found it and squatted, pointing it over the porch railing in the direction of the shot. After a minute, Gundersson came out of the woods, wearing a camo vest. A dark tuft dangled from his right hand to about the level of his knee.

Without a word of greeting, Gundersson kept walking until he reached the porch. He flipped the object onto Roland's chair. The foxtail still bled from the upper end where Gundersson had cut it off.

"Nice piece of tail," Gundersson said.

"Are you one for symbolism?" Roland said.

"Not unless it fits what I need to know."

"The fox is a creature of the afterlife, a sly messenger who guides people between worlds."

"So, I guess that means one of us is going to die?"

"We're all going to die. It's just a question of when."

The door swung open and Wendy came out in her bathrobe. She looked from Roland to Gundersson, as if searching them both for bloodshed. "I heard a shot."

"Roland missed, but I didn't," Gundersson said. She looked down at the foxtail lying between them. "Your chickens are safe now."

"Lex and Mark are coming up the road," Roland said to her, ignoring Gundersson. "You'd better get dressed."

She went back inside. Roland picked up his revolver and rested it in his lap. *Talk about your symbolism. Let's see who's got the biggest barrel.*

"Here's how we need to play this," Gundersson said.

"Wait a second. There's not going to be any 'play' here. Lex and Mark are our friends. We're fellow survivors."

Gundersson dropped his voice. "You know it doesn't work that way. If too many people know, then the information is worthless."

"Alexis knows more about Seethe and Halcyon than anyone alive."

"But Mark's a liability. According to my field director, he has too many suspicious connections. CRO Pharmaceuticals, Senator Daniel Burchfield, and a new cover story as a law-enforcement trainee."

Roland pondered letting Gundersson do the killing. And maybe while Gundersson was busy with Mark, Roland could put a bullet in the agent's back. Alexis wouldn't be too difficult to kill. All he had to do was picture her as the depraved savage in the Monkey House, holding a bloody tool as she stood over her victim.

"You'd better hide," Roland said. The car was nearer, barely a hundred yards away through the woods.

"I'll wait with Wendy."

Roland thought of the painting, with its graphic ladder of molecules, leaning against the wall. "It's too dangerous."

"They won't suspect anything."

"We've been exposed to Seethe." Roland let one side of his lips twitch. "We're suspicious all the time."

Before Gundersson could protest, the car came to a stop and its engine fell quiet, still out of sight and far from the yard.

"That's weird," Roland said. "The road gets a little rougher, but it's passable."

"It's not them," Gundersson said, drawing his firearm from a shoulder holster tucked inside his camo vest.

"But we're expecting—"

"Get inside."

"Hold on, cowboy, you're not my boss."

"I told you I'd protect you, but I can't do that if you're going to be a hardheaded jackass."

"If it's not them, who else would it—"

Gundersson leapt forward and shoved him just as an explosion ripped across the mountains. Splinters kicked up from the rail as Roland tumbled to the porch floor, pinching his fingers in the armrest of the chair. His revolver skated across the porch and his face was pressed against the foxtail, its pungent, primal mammal scent flooding his nostrils.

Another shot rang out, the report much louder than that from Gundersson's Glock, and one of the windows behind him shattered.

Wendy!

Moments ago, he'd been contemplating her death, followed by his own, but now that someone was taking the decision out of his hands, Roland was fueled by a savage desire to survive.

Gundersson crouched behind a support post, his pistol arm tracking the forest, looking for the source of the gunfire. "Rifle," he said under his breath. "Saw the reflection of the scope."

The door opened again and Wendy stood there, wearing jeans and a bra. She didn't speak, but her eyes were wide in surprise. Roland waved her back inside then rolled toward the door. Another shot plowed into the wood inches from his head, the bullet's passage causing his ears to ring.

He scrambled through the door and was about to kick it closed when Gundersson fired twice, duck-walking backward a few steps before rolling into a ball and taking a tumbling somersault through the door.

Wendy slammed it shut behind him and leaned against the wall, breathing rapidly. "Ro?"

"I need answers," Roland said to Gundersson.

"Do you need a scorecard?" Gundersson said. "Somebody found out, that's all."

The agent untangled his limbs on the floor. A red blotch had collected on the outside of his thigh, and Gundersson pressed against it with his palm. The effort didn't stanch the flow much.

Roland snaked along the wall to Wendy and put his arm around her. She appeared to be catatonic, helpless and vulnerable. *Just like in the Monkey House.* "I thought they wanted us alive," he said to Gundersson.

Gundersson rose, locking the door and limping to the nearest window. "I guess they changed their minds."

Wendy stuttered as if wanting to say something, but Roland put a finger to her lips. "Shh. It's going to be okay, baby."

He thought about sending her upstairs, but she might be visible through the windows as she climbed the steps. The walls of the cabin were made of thick beams of yellow pine, so she was safer staying where she was.

"How many are there?" he asked Gundersson.

"Hard to tell. The shots came from two different locations, but they could have a backup so they can cut off any escape."

Gundersson lifted away the curtain with the tip of his Glock, craning his neck to peer out.

"Pretty convenient, don't you think?" Roland asked.

"What?" Gundersson was barely listening.

"Staging an attack so we would trust you." Roland pointed his revolver at Gundersson, who didn't notice. "But you made a mistake. You should have waited until Alexis and Mark got here."

"Quit the goddamned crazy talk, Roland. They shot me in the fucking leg! My field director warned me that other agencies might be closing in. I just didn't think they'd be hostile."

"You guys are all on the same side to me. The *wrong* side."

Gundersson must have heard the menace in Roland's voice, because he finally turned. He might have said "Oh, shit" under his breath, or maybe he was wheezing in pain.

Wendy was moving behind him, but Roland didn't dare move his gaze from Gundersson. The revolver was his one chance to control the situation.

God, grant me the wisdom to know the difference...

"Just tell me one thing," Roland said. "Who is behind it?"

"We don't know. My field director was checking into it, and that must have raised some eyebrows. It wouldn't have been hard to track my location by satellite if you had the right gear." Gundersson was talking fast but calmly, and Roland almost believed him. But people lied to save their necks. Roland knew all about that.

"According to our information, a rogue element—"

"Well, I've got some new information," Roland said. "I have the formula for Seethe. The candy that everybody wants."

Gundersson checked outside the window once more. Roland had to admire the guy. Here he was with a pistol pointed at him from six feet away, and he was acting more worried about the guns out there a hundred feet away. Gundersson gave a little nod that Roland didn't understand, and then Roland's head exploded in violent flares of electric yellow and solar-flare red.

The dull *klung* filled his skull like a funeral bell, and as he slumped to the floor, his last image was of Wendy, standing there in her bra, a black cast-iron skillet in her hand.

CHAPTER THIRTY-TWO

"Wendy's not answering," Alexis said.

"Try again." Mark had grown more edgy and hostile the deeper they'd penetrated into the Blue Ridge Mountains, and in the first light of dawn, Alexis was horrified by her husband's appearance. He was unshaven and his hair was mussed, but it was his eyes that made him seem wild and dangerous. As she watched his face in the rearview, his eyes flitted from side to side, then to the back of Forsyth's head, and then to hers in the mirror.

They'd passed several recreational entrances to the wilderness area, and the houses had thinned out accordingly as the asphalt turned to gravel. Alexis was afraid they might be lost.

Finally she came upon the unmarked side road that was little more than two ruts running through the forest. There were only two mailboxes at the intersection, one of them dented and missing its flap. She pulled up alongside the mailboxes and on one of them, hand painted, were the words "Roby Snow Rd."

"This is it," she said.

"Try them again," Mark said.

She concentrated on punching the correct numbers, even though the reception was spotty and she only had half a bar of signal. Forsyth watched her with eyes like a vulture's.

"Did you hear that?" Mark said.

Alexis, who had been intent on the ringing of the phone, shook her head. "What?"

"A gun."

"Probably a hunter," Forsyth offered. "This looks like Daniel Boone country."

"Except hunting season ended four months ago."

Alexis lost the signal, but seven rings had failed to get an answer. She dropped the phone in her purse. She glanced at her husband, who was hunched in the backseat. The Halcyon had not seemed to ease his condition, and she was afraid to lure him into trying another dose. Maybe Darrell Silver's new formula wasn't as new and improved as he'd promised.

"Do you think Roland and Wendy set us up?" Mark asked.

"They wouldn't tell anyone," Alexis said. "They have as much to lose as we do."

"And as much to gain."

"What should I do?"

"Drive."

Alexis pulled forward, dodging the depressions and rocks in the road. The car jerked, slamming Forsyth against the door.

"Are you okay, Wallace?" Alexis asked him, slowing to about four miles per hour.

"'And the Lord instructed the angels to pour out the seven vials upon the Earth,'" the old man muttered.

"You can take that as a yes," Mark said. "He's never been better."

"I remember," Forsyth said. "I remember the Monkey House. That's when I had the vision."

A second gunshot sounded. "They're in trouble," Mark said. "Speed up."

The vegetation was thick on both sides of the road, waxy rhododendrons and laurels casting permanent shade. The trees were thick with green, and Alexis saw menace in their tangled branches, slowing the car to a hushed crawl.

She soon rounded a curve, swerving to avoid a large jagged stone, and ahead of them was a black SUV with tinted windows. It was pulled to the side of the logging road, two wheels in a ditch.

"Government license plate," Mark said. "Looks like the bad guys got here first, Forsyth."

Alexis braked to a stop. "Now what?"

Mark answered by racking a round into his Glock. "Now I go see what the hell's going on. You stay here and keep an eye on our friend."

"What if somebody comes?"

Mark passed the AR-15 over the seat, nearly bumping Forsyth's head with the muzzle. "The road looks pretty dead. But if anybody comes out of the woods carrying a gun, you want to make sure they're pretty dead, too."

She held the rifle as if it were a stiffened snake. Although Mark had shown her how to operate it before, she'd barely paid attention, because she'd been intimidated by it. "I can't."

Mark pointed to a small swivel knob. "Turn this safety. Pull trigger. Go *boom*."

"No, I mean I can't *fire* it."

"It's no harder than smashing a man's skull."

"What the hell is that supposed to mean?"

"What do you think it means?"

Something rippled in her gut like a greasy eel. "That never happened."

"You have thirty rounds. Just pull the trigger every time you want to shoot. The gun will do the rest."

"You don't want to play at this level, Mark," Forsyth said. "You thought things were bad in the Monkey House, but you're way out of your league here."

"Haven't you been listening to my wife? I'm a lunatic freaking out on a rage drug. I'd say this is the perfect league for me."

Mark opened the door as another shot sounded, apparently just over the hill. The echo of the gunfire drove an icy spear into Alexis's heart. She awkwardly cradled the AR-15, resting it against the steering wheel.

"If I'm not back in five minutes, turn around and head back to Chapel Hill," Mark said, stepping out of the car.

"I can't go back without you," Alexis responded.

"I'm feeling a little better." Mark twisted the vial open with his gun hand, slid out a couple more tablets, and closed it. "Maybe Silver got it right. And you might be the only one who can keep Halcyon safe."

He leaned over the seat and gave her a kiss on the cheek, dropping the vial beside her. She turned her head, acknowledging the trust he was placing in her, and kept turning until their lips met. After a moment, and another shot sounding in the woods, he broke contact and put the two tablets to his lips.

"I hope this works," he said, before popping them and crunching them between his teeth. "And if I forget who you are, it's nothing personal."

"I love you," she said.

"I know. And I'm sorry I gave you hell about sneaking the Halcyon. You were doing it to save me."

I was doing it to save both of us.

She squeezed his hand. "Protect Wendy and Roland. We need them."

He pulled away. "Doesn't it seem convenient? They invite us up here, and suddenly it's a survivalist showdown? But I think the feds jumped the gun. Right, Mr. Vice President?"

Forsyth remained silent, his head down and eyes closed as if he was praying. As Mark closed the door and headed for the woods, he jerked alert.

"You should do your husband a favor and kill him now, while his back is turned and he still trusts you," Forsyth said to her. His eyes were bright with secret, inner knowledge—or manic delusion.

"You're crazy."

"We all are. But I saw God in the Monkey House, Dr. Morgan. And I don't mean a presence, a feeling, a theory. I mean God. And He gave me a purpose."

"Come on, Wallace. You were dosed with Seethe. We all freaked out that night. It was a chemical reaction and nothing more."

She was only half listening, watching Mark through the front windshield. He waved from the edge of the woods and then slipped between the dark trees.

"Don't you believe in destiny and prophecy?" Forsyth said.

"I believe in science."

"Then here's some science for you."

Before she could stop him, Wallace grabbed the vial from the seat. "We knew Darrell Silver was refining Halcyon, but we didn't know where he'd hidden it. I apologize for using you as bait, but he wouldn't trust us. Especially when he started playing with Seethe."

"Seethe was destroyed."

"Silver is a genius. He was able to fill in the gaps and extrapolate it from Halcyon, just like Sebastian Briggs did. He claims he gave Seethe an upgrade, like he told you. But you didn't believe him." He held the vial up as if it were the sacramental chalice at a communion. "But I guess we'll find out soon enough."

His words finally dawned at her. "Wait. You're saying that's not Halcyon?"

He looked at the vial. "'And the fifth angel poured out his vial upon the seat of the beast; and his kingdom was full of darkness; and they gnawed their tongues for pain.'"

She struggled to keep the semi-automatic pointed away from Forsyth's face, because her finger begged to wrap around the trigger. "Mark just took three doses of Seethe?"

Wallace Forsyth grinned, and God wasn't behind those wicked, twisted lips. Only darkness.

CHAPTER THIRTY-THREE

Gundersson had been prepared for the unexpected.

It was part of his training, and Harding had warned him that he was walking on quicksand. Somebody wanted Wendy and Roland, and after Wendy had told him the Morgans were on their way, he figured the odds of all hell breaking loose had increased exponentially. But the preemptive strike caught him by surprise.

Just the way Wendy had the night before.

She stood over her husband, swinging the frying pan nonchalantly at her side as if she were on her way to cook some bacon. Her eyes were vacant and hollow, staring past the wall as if heeding some unspoken command.

Gundersson was familiar with that expression, because he'd seen it in the firelight as they'd coupled. She'd been ravenous, almost frightening in her passion, as if she wanted not just to seduce him but to consume him.

What in the holy hell did Briggs plant in your head?

"Did you kill him?" Gundersson asked her, glancing at the prone body before returning to his surveillance. He'd seen shadows in the underbrush, but he couldn't tell if the attackers were paramilitary or regular field agents of some kind.

"I just made him hurt," she said. "Like he hurt my painting."

Her gaze went to the chair, and Gundersson followed it. The painting was hidden behind the chair, leaning against the wall. He'd heard of people dying for their art, but *killing* for it?

"Keep your head down," he said. "These guys are pros."

"I thought you were a pro, too."

For all her sexual prowess, Gundersson found he didn't like her very much. She'd drained him dry and he still felt hollow, and the first twitch of guilt stirred in his gut. They had used each other, and now he was relieved he hadn't told her everything.

But you told her you'd help her. Those goddamned black, inscrutable eyes just pulled it right out of you.

Gundersson saw movement and he fired one round through the shattered window. He wasn't aiming to kill yet. He needed to know what he was up against. There was a possibility—a slim one—that these guys were on Gundersson's team.

Crouching, he hurried across the short expanse of the main room to check the rear of the cabin. The chickens squawked and clucked, unsettled by the noise.

If they're pros, they should have hit Roland on the porch. Something's not right here. Unless they just wanted to scare him, and it's me they really want out of the way.

Shifting his Glock to his left hand, he fished his Sectera from his pocket and hit the stored number for Harding's desk.

Harding answered on the second ring. "Gundy. I was just about to call you."

"I'm under fire, Chief."

"Damn. Are you hit?"

"Flesh wound. I'm okay but I'm pinned down."

"Secure?"

"Inside a cabin. There are at least two of them, maybe three. They have automatic weapons."

Harding didn't bother pointing out their range advantage over a handgun. "The closest backup is in Asheville. Two hours. Can you hold out?"

"Maybe. But I've got some civilians to babysit."

"That's what I was going to call you about. Roland Doyle's name came up in connection with a murder in Cincinnati. It was right around the time of that Monkey House business. He was on the suspect list at one point but for some reason he was cleared before he was ever questioned."

"Somebody's got a long reach."

"And it looks like they've reached you."

Wendy pulled the painting from behind the chair and was looking at it—*into* it—as if divining the future in its frantic swirls and zigzags. Gundersson's mind drifted to the tangling of their limbs by the fire, how she violently flung her body against his in disregard of her frail form.

"Gundy?" Harding's voice came as if across a vast gulf, but it was enough to remind Gundersson of his situation.

"Doyle's down. I don't have anyone to watch my back." Gundersson was relieved Wendy had put down the cast-iron pan before retrieving the painting. Roland's revolver lay on the carpet near the sofa, and Wendy hadn't even looked at it.

"This is what they want," Wendy said.

"What?"

"What's going on?" Harding demanded over the satcom link.

"Did you find out who's after these guys?" Gundersson said in response.

SCOTT NICHOLSON

"Best guess is it's an inside job."

"CIA? Fuck."

"I'm still backtracking. But don't forget, somebody put you there for a reason."

"Yeah," Gundersson said. "You did. To get my ass shot off."

"Maybe you didn't get the job done the way they wanted."

"You're all heart, Chief." Gundersson shifted to the side window, making sure the view was clear. Roland let out a low groan but didn't move.

"They wanted these drugs and thought you could get them the easy way, and then they could just intercept it. Now it looks like you're part of the problem, not the solution."

"What do you expect at my pay grade? I'm just goddamned dumb enough to do the right thing."

"Hang in there. Backup's on its way."

Gundersson wasn't sure he *wanted* backup. If the double cross was coming from within, then he wouldn't be able to trust anybody who arrived on the scene.

Including Harding.

But he didn't know anything definite, and he hadn't discovered the pills that were the supposed purpose of the mission. Harding was right: he hadn't done the job.

But it would have helped if he knew what the right thing *was*.

"You've got a warrior's heart," Wendy said, and he wasn't sure if she was talking to him, her husband, or the painting.

Gundersson bent low, blood splotching his thigh, his ankle screaming a reminder of its sprain. He scuttled across the floor until he retrieved Roland's fallen revolver. He thumbed open the chamber. No bullets.

The idiot was playing?

"Roland wanted to destroy it," Wendy said. "Sebastian wanted it to live."

Gundersson knew the feeling. But his gaze crawled to the canvas despite himself. The figure drawing was different from his last view of it yesterday. It was shot through with jagged lines and geometric shapes, and the whole aspect of it had changed. The huddled, shadowy figure was obscured by lighter gashes of color.

Shake out of it, Ace. So she's gone cubist or something. This isn't the Met Museum. This is a war zone.

He considered mounting the stairs for a more commanding view, but the loft was situated so he would only be able to watch two sides of the cabin. One of the attackers could have sprinted from the woods and even now be creeping along the foundation. The front door was locked but it wouldn't stand up to a couple of determined kicks, and a gunman also had the stealth option of breaking a window and firing inside.

And if there are three of them, and they all charge at once—

"Why would they want you dead?" Gundersson asked Wendy, bothered by the fact that it had been several minutes since the last round was fired. At least shooting would reveal their locations. Silence was even more stressful.

"What you told me last night," she said. "We have something somebody wants, and somebody else doesn't want that other somebody to have it."

Gundersson nodded. As screwy as it sounded, that was the simplest truth. And the "something" wasn't a pill, it was a secret carried inside them.

Gundersson glanced at the painting again. "What's that?"

"What Sebastian taught me. The key."

"The key to what?" Gundersson limped to the door, making a recon sweep of the yard through the tiny shattered window, but he only stayed long enough to make sure it was clear. The Glock held seventeen rounds, and he had another magazine in his vest, but he wasn't about to play Dirty Harry against marksmen with automatic rifles.

Even if he made a hobbled run for it and somehow reached the woods, his SUV was parked a mile away, on the far edge of the wilderness area. They could hunt him down easily even if he wasn't running on one leg.

Plus, despite his distaste for them, he felt compelled to protect Wendy and Roland and whatever secret they harbored. The fact that someone wanted them dead meant they knew something important, and the government had a right to any information that could threaten its interests. And Gundersson had sworn to uphold those interests.

Okay, Dudley Do-Right? Do you have the balls to back up what you believe? Even when your own government might be trying to kill you?

He was at the kitchen window, peeking through the curtains, when the meaning of the painting's symbols struck him. What he'd taken for abstract postmodernism was a formula of some kind, a cryptic code.

The key.

Roland stirred, letting out another moan. He wasn't bleeding, but a welt the size of a robin's egg rose above his left ear, rapidly becoming purple. Gundersson wondered if Wendy eventually turned on every man she slept with, a black widow in lovely skin.

A shot rang out, and it was of a different caliber and volume than the rifles.

Has one of them switched to small arms? That would be dumb, since they have the advantage.

A cluster of shots followed, the muffled rattle of automatic weaponry, followed by the louder gun. Somebody gave a high-pitched squeal that quickly trailed away. It was followed by a whoop of deranged and bloodthirsty triumph, like that of a boy taking down his first deer.

Either they're shooting each other, or the cavalry has arrived. But Harding said backup would take two hours. Who, then?

"Stay down," he barked at Wendy. She slouched from her sitting position on the sofa, still studying her painting. Smiling.

Someone shouted from the forest. "Roland! Wendy! Are you in there?"

Wendy looked up, snapping from her blissful stupor. "Mark."

Mark? The guy training to be a cop? Then his doctor wife couldn't be far behind.

So the Morgans had walked into Armageddon and had apparently managed to survive, at least to this point. Gundersson wondered how much they knew, and whether somebody wanted them dead as well.

CHAPTER THIRTY-FOUR

Mark had always wondered about that phrase "seeing red."

Red was the color of blood and passion and fire, the strongest impulses of the human mind, the devil's color. But this red that consumed him was beyond the mind, seeping from some hidden ancestral fountain. He felt simultaneously more and less human, a stack of stupid clay sparked to life by a lurid puppet master.

Slinking through the woods at dawn had stirred primal hunting instincts, and as he approached the gunfire, his anxiety and excitement grew. Common sense should be begging him to flee, but he knew sense had been burned out of him more than a year ago. He'd entered law-enforcement training partly out of a desire to protect Alexis from the unknown future, but the deeper truth was he craved the adrenaline high of that night in the Monkey House, the cat-and-mouse game of survival, and the simplest challenge of defeating pain, madness, and death itself.

Now the fucking monkey is locked and loaded.

The last gunshot had been a good hundred yards to the north, where lush oak trees dotted the ridge, so he felt relatively secure. But maybe the seeping, creeping redness had already clouded his judgment, because when he came around the moss-mottled stand of granite boulders to discover a man in a green jumpsuit, turned away and holding a blunt rifle, his first instinct wasn't to question the man, or yell "Police! Drop your weapon!" like that old bastard Frady Cat had taught him.

No, the red filled him up and *became* him, and the Glock was up and working, *pah pah pah*, just like he was shooting at a cardboard cutout on the range.

The man jerked in surprise, his sunglasses dropping away to reveal eyes turned up to heaven. Then he squealed and slumped to the ground, the rifle tumbling away into last winter's leaves.

The redness swelled until it burst from his lungs, and when he heard the triumphant roar echo off the rocks and trees, he mistook it for some rampaging wild animal. But the raw pain in his throat made him realize he'd been the one releasing that inhuman noise.

And just as suddenly, the red dimmed, and he was standing over the warm corpse, realizing he'd given away his position to the other gunmen.

And killed a man. Oh, yes, Mark, you certainly diddle-diddly-did. And don't even pretend you have any remorse. Because you loved it. This is how you were made, and the rest was just for show.

The cabin was below, and Roland's white Jeep was parked nearby, on the uneven, scruffy lawn. From this vantage point, the gunman could have picked off anyone running from the cabin to the Jeep. They were probably holed up inside, if they were lucky. Mark called to them while taking cover between two thick hardwoods.

There was no answer at first, and Mark knew he couldn't stay in one place. He didn't know how many gunmen there were, but the origins of the shots suggested at least two.

He backpedaled and checked the pockets of the dead man's jumpsuit, finding a two-way radio, a fancy cell phone of a brand he didn't recognize, and nothing else but a clip of bullets for the rifle. This guy had come outfitted for only one purpose.

The victim's face was white with the shock of death. Three glistening brownish-red dots pocked his rib cage, in the section where the center circle would be on a cardboard target. Frady would be pleased.

You don't know who this is or who he's with.

Mark laughed, like the chattering of some exotic, displaced bird. *And the same could be said of you, Officer Morgan.*

Mark glanced at the fallen rifle. It was an automatic weapon of the sort restricted to military and security agencies—or anybody working the wrong side of the street with decent connections and cash.

Mark was tempted by the MP5, but decided he'd be better off with the weapon he was trained to use. He scuttled across the leafy slope, working his way toward the opposite ridge where he'd heard the most recent shot.

Mark was glad he'd left Alexis in the car. Because, once in a while, a man just got in the mood to kill.

CHAPTER THIRTY-FIVE

Wallace Forsyth wasn't bothered by the rifle pointed at his face.

"Your heart ain't in it," Forsyth said.

"What?" She had her gun on him but was staring out the front window, straining forward as if anticipating the sound of the next shot.

"The gun. You wouldn't kill me."

Her face twisted as if annoyed at the distraction. "I'm quite capable, Mr. Forsyth."

"You killed a man in the Monkey House. But you're no murderer. That was Seethe working through you. The devil."

"My husband's out there with bullets flying around, and you're *preaching*? Don't push it."

"We've changed, Dr. Morgan. All of us. For some, it's been slow. But look at your husband. Did you see his face when he left the car? Something evil's took hold of him."

She shook her head, but Forsyth could see the doubt and concern weighing on her. Sweat glistened above her eyebrows, and her bright blue eyes were as gray as a troubled sea before a storm.

"He was happy," Forsyth continued. "Like a kid running down to the drugstore for a soda pop and a comic book."

"What are you talking about?"

"These pills." He shook the vial he'd been clutching since Mark had entered the woods. "All they do is release what's already inside us. They let us be who we really are. And we're all the devil's tool."

She lowered the rifle until it was resting on her knee. It must have been heavy. Forsyth probably could have snatched it from her, or at least grabbed the barrel and forced it in another direction, but he saw no need. He could defeat her with the truth.

The gospel according to Wallace Forsyth.

"I thought I could control it," Alexis said. "I could use it to help people."

"We will be judged by our works, and those not found in the Book of Life will be cast into the lake of fire."

"You said we've changed. But I haven't."

He could see the doubt in her eyes. But the Lord taught mercy. "None of them understand what all this is about. We can do this, Dr. Morgan. We can save the world."

"What about the senator?"

"Daniel was a good man. But in the past year, his heart's been eaten up with rot and war. He's become dangerous."

"Like you and your apocalyptic talk?"

Forsyth balanced the approaching lie against the higher purpose. "Daniel is seeking power for himself."

"And you serve a higher power, right?"

Forsyth smiled again. "I've changed, too."

Another shot rang out, this one more distant, and Alexis's fingers clenched on the rifle. She shifted in her seat, barely listening to him.

"We can do this," he repeated. "We have Seethe now. And you can develop it, refine it. The world doesn't need to know about Sebastian Briggs. Seethe can be all yours."

She was thinking about it, her tongue protruding slightly. Forsyth had guessed right. She had changed. The deep craving inside her was stronger than she realized, and her ambition owned her. She wasn't willing to admit she had killed, but she was capable of killing.

Oh, yes, she would kill for Seethe.

Forsyth twisted the lid from the vial. "We can produce millions of these," he said.

He shook one out and held his palm toward her. "Become more like yourself, Dr. Morgan. No need to hold back any longer. We're miles and miles from the world of morals and rules and civilization. Nobody to witness but God."

She leaned away from him, pressing against the driver's-side door as if he were pushing a serpent at her. He was patient, though.

"Seethe lets you be who you are running from," Forsyth said. He moved his palm to his mouth and partook of the fiery dragon. The devil worked in this world, but God's promise was one of ultimate victory, though the battles might be painful. "Become who you are."

As his teeth crunched into the pill and he swallowed the bitter chemicals, another shot rang out, closer, and Alexis spun, the barrel of the AR-15 knocking the vial to the floor and scattering pills across the carpet.

"Mark," she whispered, opening her door.

"We don't need him," Forsyth said, already feeling the self-righteous rage course through his spirit. All of God's warriors were justified in their actions, no matter how bloodthirsty.

"I do," she said. "And you can go to hell."

Alexis reached over the seat, grabbed her backpack, and jogged into the woods. After a moment, Forsyth stooped and began collecting the pills from the floorboard.

CHAPTER THIRTY-SIX

Roland's head felt like a lump of liver mush shot through with Louisiana hot sauce.

His cheek was pressed against sticky linoleum and his body was so heavy, he wondered if he'd ever move his limbs again. Voices came to him as if through a wall of water.

As he sucked for breath, he let his memory rewind, because he wasn't sure where he was, how he'd gotten here, or why his skull throbbed like a giant broken tooth.

Wendy's voice came to him first, and he made out the word "painting."

Roland opened his eyes, and the morning light hurled spears of electric torture deep inside him.

"Roland?" Wendy was closer now, talking softly, which was good, because the voices had been clanging his eardrums like a plumber beating a cast-iron sewer pipe.

He tried to speak but all he managed was an *urrrk*, which was just as well because he wasn't sure what he wanted to say.

"Sorry," she said as her shadow loomed over him. "You had a gun."

Another piece of the soggy jigsaw puzzle slid into place and Roland remembered the secret-agent guy who'd been hanging around. Whose side was he on? Whose side was *Wendy* on?

"No buh," he said, a strand of drool trailing out and linking his mouth to the floor.

"No bullets," said the man in the cabin. "The revolver's empty."

Of course it was. Roland didn't trust himself. He'd heard that crazy people never questioned the rightness of their bizarre beliefs, but he wasn't sure about that. And when he'd caught himself plotting to kill Mark, Alexis, and Wendy, he knew that was exactly the kind of thing Seethe would tell him to do.

The only way to prove Seethe didn't make you crazy is to not do crazy shit.

But the philosophical debate worsened his headache, and Wendy was gently stroking his hair, so he focused on her fingers and away from the hot, orange-red center of pain.

"One of them's down," the man said, and Roland remembered his name was Gundersson. Or at least that was his fake secret-agent cover story.

"Mark's here," Wendy said to him. "We're surrounded by men with rifles."

"Am I shot?" Aside from his sodden head, he actually felt okay.

"No, I…I hit you."

"Damn, honey. I thought we were past all that."

"I thought you were going to kill him, and we need him."

A sudden slew of bullets pierced the side window, shattering the glass and *thwacking* into the paneling above their heads. Wendy instinctively hunched over him.

"They're shooting wild," Gundersson said. "That means they're losing patience."

"Guess the floor is a good place to be," Roland said.

"I love you," Wendy whispered, squeezing his hand. "I'd do anything for you."

"Love leaves you brainless." He tried to smile but his face muscles were like barbed wire stitched into his skin.

"Listen, Roland," Gundersson said. "I've got backup on the way. But we need to hold out for two hours."

Gundersson made it sound like rescue would be a *good* thing. Which meant the backup could turn out to be the very people who'd started the whole hunt for Seethe and Halcyon. It wasn't a stretch to imagine Burchfield pulling the strings from a safe distance.

Someone shouted from the forest, and Roland recognized Mark's voice. He had to strain to make out the words: "You okay in there?"

"Don't answer," Gundersson said. "Let them keep guessing."

"But Mark's on our side," Wendy said. "He's trying to save us."

Gundersson hobbled up the stairs without speaking, and Roland heard his boots drum across the loft. He lifted one hand and motioned Wendy closer.

He whispered, "Gundersson wanted us all together. That's why he had you call the Morgans."

Wendy shook her head as if Roland was being a silly, silly boy. "We need to get our heads together on this. The four of us."

"Where's the painting?"

"Oh, so you're finally interested in my art?"

"Yeah, the deeper meaning."

"It's over there." She waved toward somewhere in the room.

Roland tried to turn in that direction but he was still too woozy. "Do you know what you've painted?"

"The Monkey House," she said. "The same thing I've been painting for the past year."

"You painted the formula for Seethe. If these bastards get that, they don't need us alive anymore. Did you show Gundersson?"

"He saw it but didn't make a big deal of it," she said. "I've not exactly had my shit together here for the last couple of days."

"Because Seethe is back. I don't think it ever left."

Wendy shook her head in denial. "No. They couldn't get us here. That's why we hid away, remember?"

"You can't hide from what's inside you."

Gundersson yelled from upstairs. "I don't see anything, but keep on eye on the back side of the cabin."

Wendy crawled across the floor to the kitchen window as Roland rolled onto his side. He groaned as a wash of fresh hurt rolled over him, and he felt for the lump above his ear.

If my skull cracked, maybe the Seethe poured out. And maybe I'm all better now.

In the Monkey House, Mark had taught him that pain trumped rage, that pain brought clarity, that pain was the most basic human condition. Pain ruled the kingdom of the mind.

"Keep that pretty head down, Wendy," he said, just before the glass erupted above her head and showered her with sparkling shards.

CHAPTER THIRTY-SEVEN

Scagnelli pulled up behind the car he recognized from the Morgans' driveway.

He'd made good time, thanks to the two dumbass agents who'd stored the cabin's address on the stolen laptop. He'd also learned a National Clandestine Service agent named Gundersson was monitoring the couple, but he didn't have a way to check out whether Gundersson was in the loop. He'd lost reception since entering the mountains, one of the pitfalls of cheap, prepaid cell phones.

So, while he expected the Morgans, he was not expecting the black SUV that was either official government or else trying damned hard to imitate it.

Fucking CIA is making their play.

Both vehicles were empty, and he had no idea how far the hike up the rutted road was. He debated pulling around and driving on to the cabin, but the first gunshot stopped him. He killed the engine and pulled the Heckler & Koch from the passenger seat. He'd intended to use the sawed-off 12-gauge shotgun, clearing the cabin with just a few rounds, but if a battle had already started, he couldn't count on close-range work.

Another shot came from the woods to the south, and he judged it to be from a couple hundred yards away, although the topography was tricky here, with ridges, rocky dells, and gullies pocked with thick undergrowth and high hardwood trees. He scanned the treetops just in case someone had the road under surveillance, and then checked the two vehicles. The front doors to the Morgans' car were open, but he didn't see anything of value and he didn't have time to search.

The black SUV was locked, and its interior was empty except for some rolls of vinyl that could have been tents or body bags.

Someone was planning ahead.

Scagnelli smiled. Maybe the mess would take care of itself, or at least he could let someone do half the dirty work before he moved in to mop up.

But a flurry of shots inspired him to head for cover in the forest. Someone was using automatic weaponry, which meant professionals were taking care of business.

Getting the job done. I like that.

He stuck near the granite ledges that protruded from the ancient soil, choosing safety over speed, and nearly stumbled over the old man, who was sitting huddled in a gray, moss-covered cleft.

"Mr. Forsyth," Scagnelli said. "Sorry about what happened in Chapel Hill. I guess I'm not the only one who underestimated Mark Morgan."

Forsyth's eyes glistened and he looked past Scagnelli to the gaps in the forest canopy. "Babylon has fallen, Mr. Scagnelli, and there's an angel sitting on the sun. Do you see him?"

The white-haired man's hands shook, and the tremors radiated throughout his body. One of the hands was clenched into a tight fist.

"Whatcha got there?" Scagnelli asked.

Another shot sounded, this one farther away. The battle was spread out, which meant its scope was larger than he would be able to handle with a submachine gun.

Forsyth didn't react, so Scagnelli bent down and pried open the man's fist.

Pills.

The vial was about a third full, but it was impossible to know how many pills it had originally contained. "What is it?" Scagnelli asked. "Doesn't look like the speed you've been giving me."

"It's the seventh vial."

"We're not in church or in front of the cameras. Talk to me straight."

The old man's eyelids twitched spasmodically. "Satan owns the world, Scagnelli, and he won't be vanquished in this season. Not while Seethe lives."

"How many of these did you take?"

"It is done," he rasped.

Forsyth slumped forward and Scagnelli caught him, gently pressing two fingers against the carotid artery in his neck. The man's pulse was weak, firing out of rhythm before galloping toward the next lull of heartbeats.

"So this is Seethe, huh?"

Forsyth didn't answer, foam appearing around his lips.

"Damn, I'm tempted to try one myself, but you don't make such a good advertisement for it," Scagnelli said. He was turning away to head up the slope when the old man's fingers wrapped talon-like around his wrist, nearly pulling him to the ground.

"Those...are...*mine*," Forsyth wheezed. "We have a... purpose."

Scagnelli didn't want to waste a round and give away his position. Forsyth's circulatory system couldn't handle such a strain for much longer, anyway. This particular job was taking care of itself. Scagnelli bent back one of the wrinkled fingers until it snapped, and the vice-presidential candidate and former Congressman whimpered in pain but didn't scream.

"Burchfield said to tell you you're off the team," Scagnelli said.

The old man's eyes clarified and burned with such pure hatred that Scagnelli fought a surge of alarm. He had to break two more fingers before Forsyth let go, and then Scagnelli slunk away, expecting the crazed old man to scream or curse or damn his soul to the everlasting fire.

Scagnelli wasn't worried about the next life, because there would be dirty work waiting on the other side, too. People like him always had a job to do.

And this job was shaping up nicely, because he had Seethe, and it looked like Forsyth had taken himself out of the running.

I could book it with this shit and make my fortune, but, hey, I promised the senator five pelts. One down, four to go.

Another burst of shots sounded, and he headed for the rocky ridge slightly north of them so he could look down on the valley and sort things out.

Sweet. Maybe the CIA will finish the job for me.

CHAPTER THIRTY-EIGHT

The automatic-weapons fire should have changed Mark's tactics.

In basic training, they'd mostly drilled in one-on-one confrontation, and the instruction was geared toward safety and restraint instead of killing.

But Mark didn't give a damn about training, or Frady, or the little happy rule book. And he sure as shit had no use for restraint. The sickness surged through him, but it was also *joy*, the best high he'd ever felt. If this was what Alexis had been trying to bring into the world, he didn't understand why he'd tried to stop her.

The world needed Seethe. Or Halcyon. Or whatever the hell it was.

Or maybe the two drugs were twins, the yin-yang of psychopathic biology, the Alice-down-the-rabbit-hole of the soul. One side makes you crazy and one side makes you stupid.

He wanted to climb one of the protruding boulders and scream his rage and pleasure across the mountains. He'd never felt so alive, and if all he had was one moment of it, he'd take that. Gladly. No matter the price.

But one face swam up from the sea of red, one beacon of purpose in the turbulent storm of sick self-indulgence.

Alexis.

She needs me. She needs Wendy and Roland. The original monkeys, together again.

A burst of gunfire rippled across the hills. Soon the cops—the real cops—would be responding to reports of multiple gunshots. The area was remote, but the roads were passable enough.

We need to get them and get out of here.

Sweat painted his skin, even though the air was cool and dry. The base of his skull tingled as if someone were striking a small flint and hoping to spark a fire.

He heard a gurgling and moved toward it, then saw a creek tumbling away across a sheet of rocks. He used the white noise to disguise his descent as he skidded in the moss and mud. His senses were heightened and time seemed suspended, and he was able to focus on each detail around him, his predator's instinct sharpened to a keen edge.

Mark spied the second black jumpsuit about a hundred feet from the cabin, the man wriggling on his belly under a dense stand of laurels. Mark's impulse was to empty his clip in the man's general direction, screaming as he did so, but the deeper predator instinct overruled.

Mark waited until a shot sounded—this one emanating from the cabin—and hurried forward to level his pistol grip in the twisted crook of a limb. The man in the jumpsuit was blond, youngish, a guy who would have looked more at home on a soccer field than in paramilitary gear.

These idiots have even less training than I do. Or maybe they're killing for a reason, while the best killers need no reason at all.

Killers like me.

Mark waited while the man flipped the bipod legs of his gun, apparently planning to set up and spray the cabin, which Mark could only barely see through the thick leaves.

Shooting a man in the back was cowardly.

But bravery was an abstract moral concept, lumped in with the honor-duty-courage triumvirate that the powerful had always used to manipulate fools.

Mark didn't need a goddamned reason.

From eighty feet away, he fired three times in rapid succession. If the man had been moving, Mark probably would have missed all three, but at least one of them hit the target. The man's head flopped forward without a sound.

The clap of a single shot issued from the cabin, the bullet whistling through leaves overhead.

Roland, you crazy bastard. I'm here to help you.

But Roland was likely just firing in the direction of the shots. In Roland's position, Mark would attempt to keep the attackers away from the cabin, because if they all rushed it at once—depending upon how many there were—Roland wouldn't be able to cover all the windows.

The SUV couldn't have held more than six passengers, and with two down, the odds were a little better. From the location of the shots, though, Mark believed there were only three attackers.

So the job was nearly finished. If only Roland didn't kill him before he had a chance to finish it.

Mark didn't bother checking his latest victim's pockets. Instead, he worked his way to his right, through a section of old pines and maples where the creek cut through the rotted stumps and ancient black dirt.

A stone bounced free behind him and he spun, Glock leveled, and if it wasn't for the soft, feminine whimper, he would have cut loose with half a dozen rounds.

She stood there between the scabbed trunks of two white pines, the AR-15 limp in her hands, dirt streaked across her face, blonde hair stringy with sweat. A long red weal, moist with blood, ran up her forearm where she'd been scratched, and her bare knees were muddy.

"Lex. I told you to stay in the goddamned car."

"You're Seething, Mark. Darrell Silver was working on Halcyon but—"

"Keep your voice down. The woods are full of killers."

"Don't you understand? You're not yourself."

"When have I *ever* been myself?"

Her eyes were heavy and sad and her tears sickened him. "I can help you."

"Yeah, you and Briggs and CRO. Let's all just hold hands and follow the Yellow Brick Road."

"I…" She shucked her backpack from her shoulder while Mark glanced around the perimeter. "I have something."

"Where's Forsyth?"

She waved the barrel of the rifle vaguely behind her. "Back there."

Another burst of gunfire sounded from the ridge opposite them, and a couple of shots responded from the cabin. Mark glanced around, waving his wife into the protection of the pines.

"Mark, you're sick," she said. "That wasn't Halcyon in the vial. It was Seethe."

Her words hit him like a mag clip. "The fuck you talking about?"

"Forsyth set us up."

She leaned her rifle against a tree trunk, knelt in the mud, and unzipped the backpack. She brought out a bottle of water.

Mark laughed and waved the gun at the rushing creek. "I'm not thirsty."

"It's Halcyon."

"No one has Halcyon."

"No one has Seethe, either. But how do you *feel*, Mark?"

He felt pretty damned good. He had a warm Glock and a full clip and some people to kill. Life couldn't be better.

She moved closer. "Like in the Monkey House, right?"

She was saying "Monkey House" like it was a bad thing. She didn't understand.

"I've been treating you with this," his wife said.

"Treating me?"

"You're losing it, Mark. You've been slowly falling apart since the Monkey House."

"Shut up about the Monkey House. I'm fine."

She thrust out the plastic bottle. "You need it."

"You never had Halcyon."

She looked away, but then stepped forward and gazed into his eyes, filling him up, leaving him no place to escape. "I lied. I had to do something to save you."

"Lied?" Mark fought the wash of red that threatened to sweep over him like the water sluiced over the rocks. He didn't want to kill her.

But he had to. Seethe demanded it.

Sometimes a guy just got in a killing mood. And now he even had a reason.

"No, Mark," she shouted, backpedaling and tripping on vines that grew in tangles along the creek bank. She dropped the bottle and it bounced off a stone, tumbling to Mark's feet. He picked it up.

"You did this for me?" he said.

"Yes," she hissed. "I love you, you bastard."

She's a liar, but she's the only one I can trust. Love is crazier than Seethe and Halcyon put together.

And his choice was to trust her or kill her.

He twisted the cap from the bottle and was about to put it to his lips when he heard a voice yell, "Don't move or I'll give you a third nostril."

CHAPTER THIRTY-NINE

Killers without and killers within.

If Harding's background digging had any merit, then the two people in the cabin with Gundersson were unstable and sociopathic. He had personal proof of Wendy's traitorous nature, as her scent still clung to him and her whispered passion and sweet lies still swirled inside his head. But her response had seemed simultaneously robotic and disturbed, as if she were following a compulsion she didn't quite embrace.

And Roland had displayed his homicidal bent several times, snapping from dutiful and even dull husband to a ranting, destructive force. Harding's research had revealed Roland's troubles with alcohol, but Gundersson hadn't seen so much as a drop in the cabin. No, this anger made its own sauce.

Whatever had happened inside the Monkey House, three people had died there, and Roland and Wendy survived.

Through whatever means.

So he was afraid to turn his back on them, which made it difficult to keep from getting his ass shot off by the mysterious gunmen.

But he couldn't watch all the windows, and the bursts of automatic weapons had grown more desperate, spraying the cabin until the windows held only the most stubborn shards of glass.

So his choices boiled down to making a deal with the devil, or just trusting the devil to help him out simply because he already owned Gundersson's soul and didn't much care one way or another.

"Roland, where are the bullets for your revolver?" he shouted from the south window.

The couple was huddled on the floor by the couch, Wendy clutching her rolled canvas to her chest as if it were a rare and precious artifact. Roland said, "I dumped them outside because I didn't want to kill anybody."

Just my luck. I get the world's first psychopathic killer with a conscience.

Like many agents, Gundersson carried a backup weapon, a SIG-Sauer P232 that was a popular conceal-carry weapon. He fished it from the inner pocket of his vest, hammer-dropped the safety off, and held it behind him without breaking his surveillance of the window.

"Seven shots, just pull the trigger," he said.

The forest had been quiet for a couple of minutes, and he wondered if Mark Morgan had taken out a couple of the black jumpsuits. Harding had told him about Morgan's cop training, but it was hard to imagine a trainee tackling guys who were by all appearances professionals.

If Morgan's on Seethe, then maybe the rules don't apply. No wonder so many people are willing to kill for this stuff.

He felt the fingers on his wrist and the SIG pulled away. Wendy whispered, "Your gun's cold and short."

Bet you say that to every man except your husband.

"Just go to that window across the room and fire a round every couple of minutes," he said. "Try not to be too predictable or they'll know you're a decoy."

"I'll do it," Roland said, although he still sounded groggy.

"Do you want to risk your wife banging you in the head again?"

A staccato burst peppered the side of the cabin, a couple of rounds flying through the window above their heads. Wendy scrambled away on her hands and knees and Gundersson couldn't help looking at her undulating rear.

These people are going to get me dead, one way or another.

"Roland, can you yell something to Mark?" Gundersson said. "Let him know you're still alive in here?"

"He won't be able to yell back. It would give away his position."

"Have you considered the possibility that Mark is on *their* side?"

"Yeah. And I've also considered the possibility you'd pull that trick to make me paranoid. *You* might be on their side, too."

"Yeah, like I'd fake playing a firing-range dummy? Or give a loaded pistol to Wendy? We're beyond that, Roland. We're just going to have to trust each other."

Roland sat rubbing his head. Across the room, Wendy had reached the window and crouched beneath the ledge. She said, "Should I shoot now?"

"Yeah," Gundersson said. "Just squeeze the trigger once."

Wendy fired and the interior of the cabin thundered. Sheet rock dust snowed from the ceiling.

"Uh...I think he meant for you to point it outside," Roland said.

"Call Mark now," Gundersson said. "Tell him Wendy's shot and you're alone."

Gundersson stood and peered around the edge of the window. A shadow darted between the trees, but he didn't fire. He couldn't risk hitting Mark or any other innocent bystander.

Though at this point, he didn't think anybody was truly innocent.

Gundersson glanced at Roland, who had unrolled Wendy's painting. He recognized the basic form of the figure she'd been working on the day before, but it was shot through with connected lines and letters. The new graffiti was smeared a little, as if the acrylic paint hadn't completely dried before the canvas was rolled.

The images clicked into place, pulling him back to high school chemistry, the periodic chart, and Mrs. Stallworth's chalkboard.

A chemical compound.

The one people were dying over.

Hidden right in front of his eyes.

This was the secret she'd whispered of, the reason she'd seduced him in exchange for his help.

He glanced at Wendy, and saw that she knew he'd put it together. A cold smile crossed her face, a ghost of the expression she'd worn the night before. It was a reptilian face, shaped by survival and the Monkey House experiments.

"It's like a living thing," Wendy said. "An organism. Seethe wants to survive, and it will do whatever it needs to do. Kill whoever it needs to kill."

Gundersson had never gone in for Good versus Evil debates. He'd accepted his work for the government as Good, because the United States had a moral role as leader of the free world. And his work helped the country remain free.

At least, that's what he'd always told himself. Or it could have been the Captain America comic books he'd read as a kid, the wearing of the red, white, and blue as a badge of honor.

But was saving Seethe really in the country's best interests? Was his idealism blinding him to the terrible damage the substance was already inflicting?

And what if it fell into terrorist hands? What if it crept across the globe, and the madness and mayhem proliferated a billionfold?

"Shut up, Wendy," Roland said, reaching the window beside her.

"Once it's in you, it never gets out," Wendy said.

"Shut up," Roland repeated.

"You can water it down with Halcyon, but—"

Roland covered her mouth with his palm, and she struggled to break free. *"I told you to shut the hell up!"*

Gundersson was so fixated on the sick drama before him that the nearby burst of automatic weaponry seemed a normal part of the mad tapestry, the perfect syncopated soundtrack for the end of sanity. The reverberation deafened him, bullets spraying across the interior of the cabin as the walls erupted in pocks and scars. A framed painting above the mantel fell from its perch, and an oil lantern shattered.

Then the shooter filled the frame of the window, sweeping machine-gun fire and stitching the walls, but he'd sprayed too high. Gundersson reacted, lifting his Glock and squeezing off five rounds. The face disappeared in a gout of blood and the corpse flopped backward.

The man must have rushed the window while Gundersson wasn't watching, perhaps growing desperate when he realized his comrades were being picked off from behind.

Which meant this wasn't a mission designed to capture.

It was all or nothing.

He'd told Harding most of what he knew. And if his own government was willing to kill all involved to suppress Seethe, then Gundersson's idealism was shot to shit.

Freedom, like Seethe, would destroy you in a heartbeat and never mourn your loss.

CHAPTER FORTY

My wife's fault. If not for her, I'd have heard Scagnelli sneak up on us.

Scagnelli lowered the binoculars after the last round of gunshots.

"I believe that was the last one," he said. "Right, Mark?"

Mark and Alexis sat side by side on a sunlit boulder, a little away from the creek and perched on a ledge so the cabin was visible in the valley below. Scagnelli had taken their weapons, and Mark's restlessness caused him to twitch. Memories of the Monkey House danced in his head like primitives around a bonfire. He wanted to leap from the boulder and run screaming through the trees, raging at the intense awareness of sunlight and breath and the rushing water and the crisp, naked rocks.

But that final shred of self, the vestige of his ego, hung like a spark in the darkness, the lone, distant star in a rapidly dimming universe.

Alexis.

He forced his hands to quit shaking, gripping the slack fabric of his pants.

"Only three," Mark said, the words feeling strange on his tongue, as if language were a lost thing. "There were only three gunmen."

"He needs the Halcyon," Alexis said to Scagnelli. "Please."

Scagnelli pointed the AR-15 at her. "Did your husband really expect you to use this? Looks to me like Seethe turns you into a goddamned idiot. But that's good news for me. People pay dearly to turn themselves into idiots."

"You have both the Seethe and the Halcyon now," Alexis pleaded. "Just give him a few sips of the Halcyon, and then go."

"Yes, I have both. I'm not sure what the hell I have, except two tickets to paradise. Or hell. But why should I help your husband?"

Mark wanted to tell her to shut up, but language was lost in the Seething storm of his skull.

"Because," she said. "Seethe and Halcyon are useless without us. We're the test subjects. We're what happens."

"Plenty more where you come from."

"Sure, if you want to wait a decade. A lot of people want those drugs. Powerful people. If you stay with Daniel Burchfield, you're going to lose a lot of money."

Scagnelli chuckled, turned for a quick squint through the binoculars, and said, "Who says I'm working for Burchfield?"

"He's had a taste. He's motivated. And he's infected enough to crave the power it will give him."

"So, what's the problem? Burchfield's going to be president. I'd say being on his team is a good thing."

Mark gauged the distance between him and Scagnelli. Twenty feet. Semiautomatic rifle. He'd get hit, for sure, probably four times.

He raked his knuckles across the rough skin of the boulder. The pain felt good, an echo of the Monkey House where it had saved his life.

Pain is your friend.

And, in the deepest truth of existence, pain was the dominant story. It was the core truth, maybe even the entire point, of life.

Suffering.

When people invented God, they invented suffering. And God was the relief from suffering.

Death was deliverance.

But on this Earth, God was pain.

Or pain was God.

Scagnelli's bullets wouldn't hurt him. They would just be part of what already *was*, the story of Mark Morgan's pain.

His wife's words came to him as if through a fog on a hidden lake full of slithering leviathans.

"You can do better," she said, and Mark wasn't sure if the words were meant for him.

"I've considered it," Scagnelli said. "But the way I look at it, six people know what this stuff is. Two of you are here, Wendy and Roland will probably be coming out of the cabin any minute now, and Darrell Silver is probably on the run to New York or San Francisco or wherever else the drug culture will give him a home."

"You forgot Wallace Forsyth," Alexis said.

Scagnelli took the vial from a pocket of his cargo pants and held it to the light. He gave it a little shake, and the rattle reverberated in Mark's head like a stone bounced down an elevator shaft. Mark ground his fist against the boulder, drawing blood until the sound went away.

"Your fundamentalist friend took the express elevator," Scagnelli said. "Guess he couldn't wait to get his wings and harp. But I'll bet God has a special floor for former politicians, don't you?"

"That vial was nearly full," Alexis said.

"Yeah, and I can't waste another pill. And I can't waste one drop of Halcyon. So your dear, sweet husband will just have to ride it out."

Scagnelli was talking as if there would be a future, and Alexis was playing along. No way could Scagnelli let them live.

No way *Burchfield* would let them live.

Mark scraped his knuckles back and forth, rasping his flesh open, and the pain was like fire, but it was also ice. He narrowed his focus to the expanding pain and allowed it to fill his skull.

The monkey brain says, "Ease the pain."

He took it up like a chant, his own personal mantra as he danced around the bonfire of war, the bonfire of harvest, the bonfire of the kill. His muscles coiled as he soaked in its macabre heat.

The monkey brain says ease the pain, the monkey brain says ease the pain, the monkey brain says ease the pain…

Voices came from the cabin door below, calling his name, and when Scagnelli turned toward them, Mark exploded off the rock.

He was half-right.

Scagnelli hit him with only two rounds.

CHAPTER FORTY-ONE

Alexis froze when Mark leaped at Scagnelli, but the shots from the AR-15 broke her daze before the chill had a chance to settle deep.

Mark grunted in pain, and the groan rolled up into a roar of animalistic ferocity as he slammed into Scagnelli, knocking him down the embankment. The AR-15 flew away and skittered across the leafy ground before thumping into a gnarled root.

Scagnelli cursed, fishing into his cargo pants for his pistol, but Mark was on him, clawing, wallowing, and snarling.

Mark fought with desperation, but Scagnelli was ruthless and experienced, punching Mark twice in the neck and causing his head to snap to one side. Alexis resisted the urge to join the battle, knowing she'd be no good in close combat anyway.

Get the gun.

She slipped on the damp leaves, tumbling into the ferns and low tangles of doghobble and Virginia creeper vines. She dragged herself forward, clawing in the dark mud, the flesh of the ancient mountain giving way beneath her fingers.

Kill or be killed.

The Monkey House flashed in her mind, only a moment— *the bloody metal tool in my hand*—and then she reached the rifle.

Mark said it contained thirty rounds, which meant it had plenty more to go.

She heaved the thing to her shoulder but couldn't get a clean shot. The barrel swayed back and forth before her as she wilted from exhaustion and anxiety.

"Shoot!" Mark bellowed, a plaintive note in his cracked voice.

That was when she saw the two crimson blossoms on his back, spreading fast through his tan shirt.

Scagnelli bucked and kicked, nearly throwing Mark from atop him, but Mark curled his fingers like claws and jammed them into the killer's collarbone, sinking in to grip the man's meat.

Mark moved his face near Scagnelli's, and Alexis aimed at the man's torso. Mark drove his mouth forward and sank his teeth into Scagnelli's cheek, ripping away a chunk of flesh.

Mark turned toward Alexis, eyes gleaming and crazed, a strip of pale gristle linking him to Scagnelli, who screamed and stopped fighting long enough to reach for the wound.

"Shoot!" Mark shouted again, and this time it wasn't a request, it was a decree from hell, issuing from that bloody, grinning mouth that had kissed her so often.

Oh, my God, he's ENJOYING it.

And this was Seethe, condensed to its purest essence.

The thing she'd fought to preserve.

The secret she wanted to possess.

From the bottom of Pandora's blackest, bitchingest box.

"Do it," Mark snarled, and she wondered if she meant *him*, if he was begging for an end to his suffering.

Scagnelli's hand made it into a side pocket and she saw the metal target guide of his pistol.

"Druh-drop it," Alexis said, but she didn't even convince herself.

Mark thrust an elbow into Scagnelli's kidney, slowing the draw, but more of the gun slid into view. Then she saw the bulge of the barrel tilting up in his pants, and then came a muffled explosion.

Mark rolled away at the sound. The bullet had struck a tree three feet to the right of her, head high, and Scagnelli could shoot plenty more.

If she didn't shoot first.

She wasn't sure if she kept her eyes open or not, but she remembered Mark's words—*squeeze once for every shot*—and before she stopped, her finger was numb.

Scagnelli lay on the ground, moaning, his limp fingers still dug into his pocket, although they'd gone slack around the gun's grip. She didn't know how many bullets he'd taken, but the one that mattered most was just below his heart, the stain on his green T-shirt growing larger with every weakening surge of his pulse.

"Finish him," Mark wheezed, and now she could see the two wet blotches in his own abdominal cavity, creases of meat below his ribs.

"No," she said. "That's murder."

"You can do it. Just like in the Monkey House."

"I didn't kill anybody in the Monkey House, goddamn it." Her rage shifted from Scagnelli to her husband.

Even in his pale, depleted state, a vicious sneer twisted Mark's lips. "Do you want Seethe or not? If he lives, then it's Burchfield's. Sooner or later, it's Burchfield's."

Scagnelli's eyelids fluttered, and he seemed to come around long enough to focus on her face. He smiled, and it was the arrogant benevolence of Sebastian Briggs, the populist solicitude of Senator Daniel Burchfield, the false piety of Wallace Forsyth.

All mirrors, all the things that she'd become.

Seethe had made her just like them.

Mark was right.

Not only could she kill Scagnelli, but she would love it.

The next best thing to suicide.

The only question was whether her husband should be next.

She staggered to Scagnelli and stood over him, his blood seeping down to feed the organisms in the soil. His arm gave one final spasm as he tried to make it operate the pistol, but he finally sagged in acceptance.

"Just doing my...job," he wheezed, causing the wound in his chest to gurgle.

"Me, too," she said, pointing at his head and squeezing the trigger four times in rapid succession.

Alexis heard Mark laughing behind her, and the triumphant sound mutated into a moist, ragged cough. She ignored him, bending to fish through Scagnelli's pockets until she found the vial of pills.

Mark wouldn't keep her from them this time.

She smiled.

Seethe is mine. As it was meant to be.

To do it right and make it look good, she'd need to use Scagnelli's pistol to kill her husband. Someone was going to reconstruct the scene using advanced forensic techniques, and lying would only tell half the story.

Facts are troublesome things. But they're the currency of knowledge.

And knowledge is the price we pay to ease the pain of ignorance.

"Lex!" Wendy said, stepping from the shadow of the forest, with Roland and a strange man standing beside her. Both were armed.

Alexis fought the rage that wanted to claim her face, that screamed at her to raise the AR-15 and empty the rest of the clip, that owned her deepest and most intimate core.

Instead, she smiled as if glad to see her old friend. "Wendy!"

Roland rushed to Mark's side, while the strange man in the camouflage vest looked from Alexis to Scagnelli's corpse, trying to connect the two. His pistol was pointed skyward, but at a crisp angle that suggested he could lower and fire in the blink of an eye. Alexis let the rifle drop and the man relaxed a little.

"Mark's been shot," Alexis said, giving Wendy a quick but desperate hug, already building the lie in her head.

As they gathered over her husband's unconscious form, Alexis slipped the vial into her hip pocket.

Mine.

CHAPTER FORTY-TWO

"Gundy, where the hell are you?"

Harding's voice sounded tinny coming from the Selecta's tiny speaker, or perhaps it was the vast sky and towering trees that made the CIA field director seem diminished and far away.

Gundersson sat on a rock, peering down on the cabin, wondering how many rounds had stuck in the rounded pine logs. "Why didn't you send choppers, Chief?"

Harding fell silent, and then cleared his throat. "You know that would draw attention. They have press, even out in hillbilly country. Send helicopters overhead and every phone in the county starts ringing."

"You could have had agents here in twenty minutes."

"We have protocol and chain of command, Gundy. We can't just—"

"Chain of command. And who is pulling *your* end of the chain?"

"Just stay on the scene. Federal agents are less than an hour away, and we have a damage-control team in place, too. Don't worry, this will get a creative cover story, and your career is well on its way. Couldn't happen to a more qualified officer, if you ask me."

Gundersson watched Alexis tending her husband's wounds. Roland had volunteered his shirt for bandaging and was busy ripping it into cotton strips. Wendy knelt over Mark as well, applying a cool compress to his forehead.

"These agents who are coming," Gundersson asked. "Are they ours?"

"Of course. You know the CIA doesn't play well with others."

"Neither do I."

Gundersson terminated the call and limped to the creek, electric streaks of pain shooting from his wounds. The water rushed away in a thundering, constant volley, a sheer drop of thirty feet between two massive towers of granite worn slick with time. The pool at the bottom was skimmed with violent froth, and the water beneath it was black with the promise of sunken secrets.

He dropped the Selecta into it, and any sound it might have made was lost in the rush of a current hell-bent for the sea.

Joining the others, he said, "My SUV is a mile away. It's parked on a logging road."

"We're parked on the driveway," Alexis said, packing cotton swathes around Mark's two abdominal wounds. The man was deathly white, and he occasionally groaned in pain.

"We can't risk it," Gundersson said. "We've got company coming."

Roland gave a rough laugh. "If *these* were the good guys, I can hardly wait."

"We need blankets, to keep him warm," Gundersson said. "They're flesh wounds, but if he goes into shock, he won't last long."

"How do we carry him a mile through this terrain?" Roland said. "Roll him up like a burrito and play 'pack mule'?"

"Something like that. One thing's for sure, you don't want to wait for medivac. You guys got targets on your backs."

"We'll tell them everything," Wendy said.

"Shut up!" Alexis's outburst was brittle in the peaceful woods, silencing the birds.

Roland touched his wife's hand, and Wendy looked at Gundersson. *Our little secret.*

"I'll go to the cabin and get blankets," Gundersson said, not giving anyone a chance to question his leadership. "Then we're heading out."

Alexis fished a bottle of water from her backpack and put it to her husband's lips. "Drink this, honey. It'll help ease the pain."

"What's that shit?" Roland said.

"Water."

Gundersson navigated the animal path back down the mountain, limping on his wounded leg. He wondered if the chicken-thieving fox had used this route on its nightly excursions.

He'd heard a legend that if you killed an animal, you took on its aspects and traits. The predator became its prey.

Wendy hadn't mentioned her painting, and he sure as hell wasn't going to carry it back.

Some people said art was timeless, and all art was worthy and had a place in the world.

But Gundersson didn't believe that.

Some forms of human expression didn't deserve an audience.

No, some just plain needed burning. And he had a lighter in his pocket. What was one more campfire?

Somewhere out there, Senator Daniel Burchfield was smiling at a camera or shaking hands with a geriatric widow in a wheelchair, promising a secure future built on a strong America.

All while standing on bones and bloody lies and a mountain of ruthless ambition.

Gundersson would go back to the CIA when this was over, when the spin cycle had rinsed away every corpse and every stray bullet, when Burchfield's mourning for Forsyth ended in primetime melodrama and the selection of a running mate just as ruthless. Gundersson would be there in the shadows, gathering information and keeping a watchful eye.

Maybe he was still an idealist, but he believed in freedom, even if he had deep doubts about his country and its kings.

If Seethe and Halcyon had taught him anything, it was that you had to stand guard most faithfully against the enemy within.

The path opened before him, and he became a fox on the prowl.

CHAPTER FORTY-THREE

"How much does he know?" Alexis asked.

"Some," Roland said.

"Do you guys trust him?"

Roland shrugged and Wendy looked off in the distance with the vacant expression she'd worn in the Monkey House when Sebastian Briggs had lulled her into surrender.

"Wallace Forsyth is dead," Alexis said. "Seethe and Halcyon dies with him. Okay?"

"That's bullshit, Lex," Wendy said, suddenly present. "It lives inside us. There's only one way out."

"We're not going out like Anita did." Alexis nodded toward Scagnelli's cooling corpse. "I'll bet that scumbag did her in."

Roland put his arm around Wendy, brushed a sweaty, stringy strand of hair behind her ear, and kissed the side of her filthy face. "We're sticking together this time, honey," he said. "All of us."

He broke away and did an awkward, pained dance, breaking into a variation on the old television theme song, "Hey, hey, we're the Monkees."

That drew a smile from Wendy, and even Alexis felt a surge of hope. She squeezed Mark's hand. He'd stabilized and his pulse was steady, if a bit sluggish.

"You hear that?" Roland yelled up to the trees and to God. "We're getting the band back together, man."

"Save your strength," Alexis said. "You've got a human burrito to haul."

"It lives inside us, but it ends with *us*," Wendy said, covering Alexis's and Mark's hands with her own. "Deal?"

Roland came over and bent to put his own palm on the pledge pile. "Deal."

"Deal," Alexis lied.

They fell silent, lost in themselves, or as close to themselves as they were able.

Soon Gundersson returned and they began their trek across the ridge, each contemplating the full weight of suffering and wondering if they'd be strong enough for whatever the future held.

For whatever Seethe demanded of them.

And none of them—none—would be allowed to forget this time. Not the past, not the promise, not the monsters they all carried inside them.

Alexis would make sure of that.

ABOUT THE AUTHOR

Scott Nicholson is author of more than a dozen novels and seventy short stories, as well as six screenplays, four children's books, and three comic book series. His novel *The Red Church* was a finalist for the Bram Stoker Award and an alternate selection of the Mystery Guild. He also has collaborated with bestselling author J.R. Rain on several paranormal novels. He has served with the Mystery Writers of America, the Horror Writers Association, and International Thriller Writers. A former journalist, radio broadcaster, and musician, Nicholson won three North Carolina Press Association awards. To learn more about him, check out his website at www.hauntedcomputer.com.